THE

DEVIL
YOU
KNOW

QUENTIN SECURITY SERIES
BOOK ONE

MORGAN JAMES

THE
DEVIL
YOU
KNOW

PROLOGUE

Bekah

"Bekah, look! There's Andy Williams." Before I could even glance over my shoulder, Leah's elbow landed in my ribs. "No, don't look!"

"You know, you shouldn't tell someone to look if you don't want them to actually look." I rolled my eyes and turned back to the wall of DVDs, running my fingers over the title of the new horror movie that had just been released. My parents would flip if they knew we were even considering watching the gory, R-rated film. Hopefully they would never find out. Since I was staying at Leah's house tonight, I prayed the Wilsons wouldn't tell them at church tomorrow.

Leah and I both loved scary movies. Our parents, though? Not so much. Our families were both dedicated to the church and, while a good cause, I had to admit that it was sometimes exhausting. For supposed Christians, they could be awfully judgmental sometimes. I had nothing against the institute of religion; I just didn't like people who took it upon themselves to be God's judge, jury, and executioner. Dropping my hand from the DVD case, I moved on down the row.

"Oh, my gosh, he's so cute!" Leah's voice squealed in my

ear as she grabbed my arm.

Ignoring her enthusiasm for a boy who was notorious for being a player, I gestured to the movies. "What are you feeling tonight?"

Leah spared me the slightest glance before grabbing the horror flick. "This one."

"Are you sure? Your mom and dad freaked out last time when they caught us watching The Hills Have Eyes. They'll kill you if we get this one."

One shoulder lifted in an indifferent shrug and she tossed her mane of long blonde hair behind her. "Whatever. We'll be going to college next year. We're old enough to make decisions for ourselves."

Leah had always been the defiant one, pushing boundaries that I abided without question. She'd lost her virginity at fifteen to one of the school's bad boys and rebelled at every turn, from stealing merchandise to smoking pot. Leah was often in trouble, but her parents always smoothed the way, keeping any infractions off her permanent record. I'd wondered on more than one occasion if Leah was crying out for attention from her parents, but I never said anything to her.

I'd always been the shy one, self-conscious of my petite, curvy figure and mousy brown hair. Leah was popular, outgoing, always comfortable in her own skin, and she exuded confidence to the point of arrogance sometimes. The Wilsons were wealthy, Leah's father being the third-generation owner of a very successful local plastic manufacturer, so her self-importance came honestly. Yeah, Leah was kind of a mean girl, but I loved her anyway. We'd been friends forever, and I knew that behind the blonde exterior lay a smart, sweet person, even if Leah didn't let her out nearly as often as she used to. Since we'd been in high school, Leah had lorded her superiority over others, and I sometimes wondered if she kept me around to make herself look better.

Leah spun on her heel and strode toward the rental counter, DVD in hand. With a resigned sigh, I made my way to the front of the store where Leah was already flirting shamelessly with the cashier, a boy she'd fooled around with a couple of times. Leah had told me how incredible sex was, but I hadn't met anyone yet that made me want to take that next step. Maybe once I got to college, I'd find a nice guy who did it for me. Until then, I was happy enough to just listen to Leah talk of her exploits and learn from the best.

The hair on the back of my neck prickled with awareness, and a quick glance over my shoulder revealed Andy Williams. I discreetly bumped Leah's shoulder to get her attention. She threw a flirtatious smile Andy's way, and I drifted away to peruse the DVDs at the end of the aisles. Leah's too-loud laugh drew my attention and I decided to save her from herself.

I laced my arm through hers. "Got the movie?"

"Right here." She held it up and smiled at Andy.

"Cool. See you later, Andy." I dragged her toward the exit, and the doors opened with a *whoosh* as we stepped into the warm summer night.

She leaned into me as we rounded the corner of the building. "I wonder if he's going to Angie's party next weekend."

A figure in the shadows caught us both off guard, and Leah let out a high-pitched squeak of surprise. A man stood on the sidewalk, lit from above by the yellow glow of the four-foot-tall Blockbuster sign on the side of the building. My heart jumped into my throat as my eyes swept over him. Somewhere in his early twenties, his eyes were black as midnight behind his thick glasses, and his sandy blond hair was parted to one side, giving him a serious, bookish demeanor. The most outstanding feature, though, was the abnormal cleft in his upper lip.

Swallowing down my initial fear, I nodded in silent greeting and skirted him as I pulled Leah toward my car.

"Oh, my God!" she exclaimed. "What a creep."

I lightly elbowed her in the side. "Stop it, he can hear you!"

The man lifted a hand our way, and I offered a small smile even as Leah yanked on my arm.

"Um…" His voice stopped me in my tracks just as I grabbed the handle to open the driver's side door. The man's gaze dropped to the pavement as he shifted from foot to foot. "I hate to ask, but um… do you think you could give me a ride?"

"We're busy, sorry," Leah's unrepentant voice cut in before I could even open my mouth. Shooting me a hard look over the roof of the car, Leah made a face before sliding into the passenger seat.

I studied the man. "How did you get here?"

He shrugged uncomfortably, his eyes reluctantly meeting mine. "My friends." He pointed to a car peeling out at the red light on the main road. "They decided to play a joke on me and left me here."

They kind of sounded like assholes, to be honest. "I have a cell phone. Can you call one of them?"

"Thanks, but I don't have their numbers memorized." He dropped his gaze to the ground and shoved his hands in his pockets. "It's no big deal, I can walk. Maybe someone at the truck stop will help me out."

The truck stop was all the way out by the freeway, several miles away, and it was already dark out. Sympathy tugged at my heart. How often did this happen to him? How often did people treat him badly just because of the way he looked?

"Where do you live?"

He glanced up, hope and wariness mingling in his eyes. "Just out of town, near Cherry Ridge."

Cherry Ridge was a fairly upscale rural area, the homes large and placed far apart, surrounded by dense woods flanking the river. He didn't really look like he fit in with the Cherry Ridge crowd, but I tried not to be judgmental. His clothes were cheaply made but clean, a sign that he took care of himself.

The trailer park. Rolling Meadows was out that way, too, a rundown grouping of doublewides spread over a few dozen acres. My heart went out to him. He probably couldn't afford a car, let alone a cell phone. Guilt assailed me.

"Well..." I bit my lip, carefully considering the dilemma. I'd been raised to help people, and he seemed harmless enough. "I guess we can take you."

"Bekah!" Leah screeched from the passenger seat. "Are you crazy?"

"Hold on one second." I held up a finger to the man and leaned into the car. "He's stranded, Leah. We should help him."

She shook her head. "No way is he getting in this car!"

"Leah." Was she serious right now? "He needs help."

"Not from us!"

It was rare that I ever stood up to Leah, but... I shot the guy a look again. Standing with his shoulders slumped forward dejectedly, he made for a pathetic sight.

"What's your name?"

His gaze darted to mine. "Marcus. My friends call me Marc."

"Hop in, Marc."

"Really?" Hope lit his features, and I smiled.

"Yep, come on."

"Thanks!"

I slid into the driver's seat and shot a look at Leah who glared back at me, arms crossed over her chest.

"This is a terrible idea," she tossed over her shoulder as Marc climbed into the backseat and closed the door with a *thunk*. "I can't believe we're doing this."

I glanced in the rearview mirror and caught Marc's grim expression. Having been on the receiving end of Leah's sharp tongue before, I knew exactly how he felt. I quickly changed the subject.

"Cherry Ridge, right?"

He met my gaze in the mirror. "Yep. Head that way."

Something in his tone made my insides twist. The way he phrased it made me think that my initial assumption was correct. He'd have us drive toward Cherry Ridge, then let him out before we got to the trailer park. Probably a good thing, too. Rolling Meadows wasn't exactly known for its upstanding citizens.

Putting the car into gear, I backed out of the parking spot and pulled into traffic on the main road, then headed toward the truck stop. Passing the ramps for the freeway, I gestured at the road. "How much farther?"

"Just a few miles. There's a road up here to the right. I'll let you know where to turn."

With a nod, I turned my attention back to the road. Streetlights became fewer and farther between, and traffic was almost non-existent at this time of night. Out here in the country, most everyone was probably already bedded down for the night, ready to greet an early dawn and work the land.

"Right up here."

A road came into sight and I flipped on the blinker. Dust clouded the rearview mirror in the red glow of the taillights as the car churned down the bumpy road. Trees flanked us on both sides, blocking the light from the moon, and I glanced around. I hadn't seen any houses out this way yet, not even a light of any sort indicating anyone lived out here. Unease crept into my stomach, sending up a flurry of butterflies.

"How much farther?"

"Not long now."

I took a deep breath and pressed the brake. "I'm sorry, this is all the farther we can go. We're running late, and we really need to get home."

"This is close enough." Marc's voice was suddenly at my shoulder as he leaned forward between the front seats.

"What are you—?" Before I could even blink his hand whipped out, and I froze as the blade of a knife pressed against my throat.

Leah sucked in a gasp as Marc stretched his free arm toward her, shoelaces dangling from his fingers. "Tie her hands to the wheel."

Leah hesitated, and the blade dug deeper into my skin. I cried out in pain and tears welled in my eyes, clouding my vision. "Oh, God, just do what he says, Leah."

Leah's hands trembled as she reluctantly took the shoestrings and secured my right hand, then the left to the steering wheel. Marc deftly slipped the keys from the ignition, and I heard the soft jangle as they hit the floor somewhere in the back.

In the passenger seat, Leah whimpered. I tested the bonds around my hands, but they were too tight. I didn't have a chance—but Leah did. "Leah, run!"

With one last beseeching glance at me, Leah pushed open the door and sprinted from the car. Marc let out a low curse and slid out behind her, then took off into the darkness. Fueled by terror, I pulled at the bindings. The more I struggled the tighter they became, rubbing my skin raw. Tears coursed down my cheeks as I fought to get free, to no avail.

Oh, God. The silence outside was deafening, and I prayed that Leah had managed to evade him. I had to get the hell out of here before he came back. I did everything I could think of to get someone's attention—screamed at the top of my lungs, pressed my head against the horn. The night air remained quiet and still, devoid of life. My heart rate increased with each minute that ticked by. How long had it been now? Where was he? And was Leah safe?

A loud thump on the window made me scream, and I jumped as Marc threw the door open. The deadly, metallic glint of a knife suspended the breath in my lungs as he slashed at the shoestrings binding me to the steering wheel.

"Come on." He jerked me roughly out of the car, and I stumbled as the rocks slid precariously under her flip flops.

"Where's Leah?"

His grip tightened on my arms, fingers digging into the tender flesh. "Don't worry about her."

His words sent a ripple of terror racing down my spine. I had to find Leah and get away from here. I could barely make out his face, even from just a few inches away, but I could feel his cold gaze on me. A breeze whipped through the trees, parting the branches overhead and allowing the bright light of the moon to spill over us. His face looked demented in the dim light as his deformed mouth curled into a menacing sneer.

My mind spun frantically as I followed beside him, tripping over branches littering the uneven forest floor. Finally he clicked on a flashlight and the ground in front of us glowed yellow in the bright beam of light. The leaves on the forest floor looked disrupted, and my blood ran cold as my gaze fell over a scrap of fabric. The material was ragged and marred with dark brown stains. I stepped closer to inspect it and froze, my heart tripping in my chest as a logo jumped out at me. Leah had been wearing a shirt with that same distinct alligator logo tonight.

Reluctantly, my gaze followed the trail to a large, pale lump on the ground twenty feet away. A familiar shoe stuck up from the leaves and I stared uncomprehending at Leah, her body twisted at an unnatural angle, the same brown stains marring her skin. My eyes fell to the wide, dark gash that split her throat, stretching from ear to ear.

No, no, no...

Bile rose up, burning the back of my throat. Dropping to my knees in the crumbling leaves, I retched until there was nothing left in my stomach. A rough hand bit into the flesh of my arm again, and I pulled against his grasp.

"Get up." Marc dug his fingers in and yanked me to my feet.

Feeling lightheaded and swaying unsteadily, I wiped my mouth with the back of my hand and regarded Marc. Rage welled up inside me. Pulling my arm back, I threw as much force into the punch as I could. His hands flew up to cover his nose, and I placed a well-aimed kick between his thighs. With a muffled shriek of pain followed by a string of curses, he dropped to his knees.

Not wasting a second, I broke free and ran. My feet slid over the uneven ground, and my lungs burned with exhaustion as I searched the darkness for some sign of life—a house, a road, anything. The reflection of moonlight glinting off of metal came from up ahead as a bridge came into sight, and my heart leaped in my chest. With a burst of energy, I pumped my arms faster, pushing myself to keep going despite the urge to break down and cry. I would *not* think of Leah right now.

Obscured by darkness, I didn't notice the railroad ties until it was too late. My foot caught on the rail and my teeth gnashed together, sending a frisson of pain through my entire body as I sprawled face-first onto the tracks. Shaking off the pain, I scrambled to my feet and dashed forward as the sound of footsteps reached my ears.

Just as I reached the middle of the bridge, a hand closed around my hair and I was yanked back roughly. The motion brought me to a jarring halt, and I fell to my knees with a sharp cry as pain exploded over my scalp.

One hand still fisted in the long strands, Marc dragged me to my feet. "It didn't have to be this way."

Those fathomless black eyes bored into mine, and ice streamed through my veins. I'd invited this monster into the car with us—and now I was going to die at his hands.

Slowly backing me toward the railing of the bridge, he continued to speak. "You want to know about your friend?"

Tears clouded my vision, and I shook my head violently. I wanted to remember Leah vibrantly alive and happy, not cowering in fear before she died.

Despite my denial, Marc leaned in close and continued. "The whore couldn't even make it good. She tried to fight back, scratched my face until I broke her fingers, one by one. It would have been so good with you."

He rubbed his nose along my jaw and I let out a strangled sob. "Please don't do this, please just let me go!"

He shook his head. "I can't do that."

"Please, I..."

"I'm sorry it has to be this way."

He lifted the knife to my throat, the tip of the blade pressing into the soft flesh. His eyes glowed black in the moonlight, and I forced myself to meet his gaze through the blood-spattered lenses of his glasses. *Leah's blood.* My pulse raced and instinct took over as my knee jerked up and connected with his groin. A scream stuck in my throat as he thrust me away from him. The back of my legs hit the railing, and I teetered there for a moment before I lost the battle to stay upright. Suddenly I felt nothing below me but air. I didn't have time to cry out, didn't see anything flash before my eyes as I plummeted toward the black water of the river below.

CHAPTER ONE

Blake

The hot midday sun beat down, the heat scorching in its intensity, and a trickle of sweat beaded at the nape of my neck before slithering down my spine and into the waistband of my cargo pants. Shielding my eyes, my gaze swept over the decrepit storefront before returning to my one-time Lieutenant and friend.

"Jesus, Con, couldn't you have found something a little nicer?" A few streets away from the heart of industrial Dallas, the building was situated amongst factories and warehouses, a decaying pile of wood and steel.

I could feel Connor Quentin's black eyes bore into mine even through the dark lenses of his Oakleys. He gave a nonchalant shrug. "Got it cheap after the hurricane wiped everything out down here. Needs some refurbishing, but it has good bones."

I grimaced. If by 'bones' Con meant the structure needed to be placed six feet under, then I was inclined to agree. It would take nothing short of a miracle to salvage this place.

"Besides, we need to be close enough to the center of things to be reputable, but far enough away that no one reads too much into it."

Well, I couldn't argue with that. No one in their right mind would come near this place. I tipped my head in agreement and resumed studying the building. "Is it safe to go in?"

"We'll find out." Con pulled the key from his pocket and pushed open the heavy steel door—or, rather, tried to. It was either blocked or swollen from the humidity and refused to budge more than a couple inches. Con put his shoulder against the door and threw his considerably bulky weight into it, but even though it groaned with effort, the door refused to move.

Stepping forward, I added my own weight and together we shoved the door open, inch by excruciating inch. A mixture of foul smells greeted us—mildew and rot, followed closely by the smell of roadkill and feces. Clearly, more than one animal had made its way in and expired, the smell permeating the warm, stale air. Having been stationed all over the globe, we'd experienced worse in some of the third world countries we'd been in. But at least no one was living here—not of the human variety anyway. I hoped.

"Great," I remarked, sarcasm saturating my tone, and Con smirked. Debris littered the floor of the warehouse, a collection of things left over from a time when the building was operational, as well as shit—literal and figurative—washed in by the recent hurricane. I imagined that the building had been vacant prior to the flooding, otherwise the owners would have taken care of it. Dampness hung in the air, except where it had managed to escape through several broken windows.

"Please tell me you've hired someone to clear this shit out." So help me, if I had to wade through four feet of garbage to refurbish this damn building, I was going to choke the life out of Con.

A smile flitted at the corners of his mouth. "I should've made you chip in, grunt. But yes, they'll be in here next week, so we should be ready to go within the next month if all goes well."

"Sounds good."

To be honest, it sounded like a miracle, but I wasn't going to look a gift horse in the mouth. I'd been looking for something to do since being discharged almost two months ago, but civilian life hadn't appealed to me in the least. There was no way I could go from holding a rifle in the sandy, rocky mountains in the armpit of the world to sitting behind a desk eight hours a day. I didn't have the patience or people skills for that.

Con had reached out to me one day, asking if I'd be interested in working personal security. Over the next several months, Quentin Security Group had been formed via Face-Time and several hundred emails—one of which was precisely how Con had ended up with this Godforsaken building. Halfway across the world at the time, a realtor had sent—I now realized—extremely doctored photos of the building we were now standing in. In an inch and a half of water, shit and God only knew what else. Fucking fantastic.

Still, the prospect was better than anything I could have dug up on my own, and I was grateful for that. We had another handful of guys on the way, too, due stateside within the next couple of months. Con had connections all over the place; some were guys he'd grown up with, others were soldiers, paratroopers, or snipers he'd met and worked with over the years. The goal was to land a government contract, but in the meantime, we'd start with small jobs, working security for high-end functions or as bodyguards to some of Dallas's elite. We'd take whatever we could to get our name out there, but Con had a ten-year plan and a vision of putting QSG offices on each side of the country.

"Reception will go right over here"—Con pointed to an open area immediately to their right—"conference rooms down this hallway. The gym will go upstairs so we can hold self-defense courses on site."

"We're going to have a receptionist?"

Con nodded. "Abby's gonna take the calls, decide which scenario is best for which agent. She'll consult with me in the beginning, of course, but ideally she'll be able to take over that aspect of it so we won't have to bother with the mundane every day shit."

I nodded. Paperwork sucked. Better to let Con's little sister take care of that. I loved Abby like a sister, but damn, the woman could talk a man to death. She and Con had been in constant communication while he'd been overseas and the tiny spitfire had an opinion on everything. I liked a smart woman who knew her own mind, but Abby took things to a whole other level. I couldn't wait to meet the man who would one day take on the challenge.

"Why is the gym going upstairs and not in the basement or on the ground floor?"

Con shook his head. "Not enough space on the first floor, and no basement. City won't give us a permit to go so far underground in an existing building, and the previous owners didn't want or need one." I raised a brow and Con shrugged. "Something about excavating the terrain. All the limestone makes it too costly."

That sounded like a whole bunch of bullshit to me, but what the hell did I know? I'd grown up in Wisconsin, which was about as far the fuck away and as different from Texas that it may as well have been the moon.

My vision blurred as a bead of sweat slithered down my forehead and into my right eye. Whipping off my sunglasses, I used my sleeve to ease the burning sensation. Christ, it was fucking hotter than Hades here.

Sliding my glasses back into place, I canted my head toward Con. "Remind me again why the hell you chose Texas? Other than the fact that we're surrounded by God-loving Republicans willing to grease the wheels to give you anything you want?"

Con grinned. "That's about it, my friend. Plus, it's home."

I shook my head. "All that ass kissing and you can't get someone to sign a damn permit to dig a basement?"

Con's expression turned serious. "I tried, believe me. But it's actually better this way. All common areas and meeting rooms will be on the first floor so we won't have the added expense of needing to install an elevator for any visitors with disabilities."

Made sense. "So, what's the plan for reconstruction?"

"Company's coming in next week to clean up all the debris, then the construction workers will be here the week after to take a look around see what's salvageable. We'll need to move walls around anyway, so I anticipate that it'll just be easier to gut the place and start fresh." Con shrugged. "They could be here for two weeks or two months depending on what all needs to be done, but I'm hoping to be ready by the end of next month."

"Solid. What do you need from me?"

"Get our name out there. Talk to your friends, I'll talk to mine. Pick up any gigs you can find and get in touch with Abby." Con whipped out his phone and tapped it a few times. Seconds later, my phone lit up with a message. "I just sent you her contact info. Call that number and she can put it on the books. She'll work remotely for now, until we're ready to move her in here."

"And if we get any interest until the building's ready?"

"Get their info, put them on the books with Abby, and do what you can to spread the word. I don't figure we'll get anything major in the beginning, but if it sounds like a good gig, take it. I've ordered us some polo shirts, and I'll get cards made up soon so we can start marketing ourselves."

"When are the other guys landing?"

"Xander and Clay are still out of country, but both should be ready to take jobs in the next couple of months. Jason and Vince are stateside, but I gave them a couple of weeks to tie up some loose ends."

I dipped my chin in acknowledgment. "I'll see what I can dig up. Ready to get out of this shit hole?"

Con lifted one black brow. "Too much of a pussy to handle a little shit and some dead rodents?"

I lifted my foot out of the water and examined my now stained boot. "Doesn't this constitute hazard pay?"

Con snorted. "Get the fuck outta here."

I grinned. "Hey, it was worth a shot."

CHAPTER TWO

Victoria

I glanced up from my computer as my eleven o'clock appointment strode into my office and sank onto the couch with an insolent sigh. Pasting on a polite smile, I swiveled my chair toward him. "Hello, Greg."

"Hi, Victoria, how have you been?"

I tipped my head toward the man. "It's Dr. Carr, but fine so far, thank you. How about you?"

Greg Andrews was known for taking liberties, and he was both pompous and overbearing. He was far too familiar sometimes, and it grated on my nerves. He'd first come to counseling about eight months ago when his mother had passed away after a long, difficult battle with cancer. He'd recently taken it upon himself to start calling me by my first name, which irked the hell out of me. I insisted on keeping a professional distance from my patients, and I didn't encourage his familiarity. Still, he persisted.

He let out another beleaguered sigh and allowed his head to drop back on the couch. "Exhausting. I have to drive down to San Antonio tomorrow, and I won't be back until the beginning of next week."

"What are you working on this time?"

"I have a project for a new client." His mouth kicked up in a haughty smirk. "He said my designs are the best in the state."

"That's fantastic. Work seems to be going well—what about everything else?" I bit back a sigh. He was the most self-important man I'd ever known, and I'd foist him off on someone else in a heartbeat if I could. Unfortunately, the weekly appointments paid well and put food in my fridge.

Nearly an hour later, Greg leaned forward and lowered his voice. "So, I ran into *Ashley* on my way in." He emphasized her name with no little amount of distaste. "What a mess. How's the transition coming?"

Despite the tension in my shoulders, I kept my face impassive as I responded. "You know I can't talk about other patients, Greg."

He rolled his eyes. "Oh, come on. Aren't we past that?"

I merely blinked at him, unwilling to rise to the bait. "Is there anything else you'd like to discuss before we wrap up for today?"

Greg studied me for a moment, his eyes raking over me from head to toe, and a shudder of revulsion threatened to overtake me at his intense perusal. "You know, Victoria, you've really helped me these last few months."

"That's wonderful, Greg. I'm glad to know our sessions have been productive."

"How about you let me thank you?" A sinking feeling gathered in her gut as he continued. "Let me take you to dinner tonight."

"I appreciate the offer, but I don't date patients."

"What if I stop seeing you professionally? Would you go out with me then?"

Not in this lifetime. "I'm sorry, Greg. I just wouldn't feel right about it."

His face fell into a mulish expression, and I smiled as gently as I could. "I really am flattered, though. You're smart and successful, Greg, and you'll find a woman who's perfect for you."

His lips tipped up in a tight smile and he stood to leave. "See you next week, Victoria."

"Can't wait," I mouthed silently as Greg strode from the room. I let out a little sigh as I jotted down a few final notes from our session to enter into the computer later. My mind whirled as my pen scratched against the old-fashioned notebook I used during sessions. Something about putting pen to paper was oddly cathartic, and it helped to seal details in my mind better than tapping letters on a screen.

I really had no idea why Greg kept coming back, except obviously to bother me. I hated to judge my patients, but he didn't speak of anything of substance during our sessions. He'd initially opened up to talk about his relationship with his mother, but it seemed that her battle with cancer and subsequent death didn't compare to his constant need to speak about himself—his job, his success, his wealth. Greg had basically spent the last few months bragging to me once a week.

I cringed at the direction of my thoughts. He paid well, and I really shouldn't judge. He just made it so damn hard.

A faint stirring in the lobby caught my attention and I followed the litany of raised voices. My receptionist, Phyllis, stood between Greg and my next patient, Rachel Dawes.

"Good afternoon, Rachel," I said warmly. "Is there something I can help with?"

Rachel turned a pained look my way. "This jerk"—she pointed a finger wildly at Greg—"needs to mind his own business."

A cocky smile flitted across his lips as he held up his hands in a show of mock surrender. "I was just trying to be helpful."

"You know nothing about my life," Rachel shot back. "So feel free to keep your questions and 'advice' to yourself." She glanced back at me. "He's antagonizing me."

I turned my gaze to Phyllis. "Did you happen to hear anything?"

My receptionist nodded. "Mr. Andrews here"—she narrowed her eyes at the man, who in response just rolled his own—"was asking Ms. Dawes *personal* questions."

The way Phyllis stressed the word sent a niggle of worry down my spine. "Mr. Andrews, may I please see you in my office for a moment?"

With a smirk at the two other women, he preceded me into my office. Trying to give him the benefit of the doubt, I tipped my head at him. "I'd like to hear your side of things, please."

He lifted his hands in a shrugging motion. "I was merely offering some advice."

"Such as?"

He clasped his hands behind his back. "Rachel's a bit high-strung, don't you think? I mean…" He began to walk a circle around her office. "Don't you ever think that she just keeps coming here for the attention? Do you really think she's depressed?"

"I don't believe that's any concern of yours," I bit out. "I am your doctor as well, Mr. Andrews, though one could argue that you need me as little as you seem to believe Ms. Dawes does."

His eyes jumped to mine. "Maybe I keep coming back because I want to see you."

Unease caused the hairs on the back of my neck to lift, and I stiffened. "Mr. Andrews, I believe I've been quite clear on the matter. I cannot in good conscience date patients, either present or former. Regarding other patients," I ground out, "you may not interrogate them or pry into their lives."

"I merely suggested she take a chill pill," he laughed. "A Valium, actually. I think it might help mellow her out a little."

At his flippant statement, a red haze filled my vision. "You are in no position to counsel my patients on any matter. In fact"—I strode to my desk and riffled in the top drawer for a moment before extracting a card and holding it out to him—"I believe you will find Dr. Martin more helpful than myself."

His mouth dropped open in shock. "You're… dismissing me?"

"I'm recommending you to a colleague. In lieu of today's events, I believe it's best if someone else were to treat you."

His face flushed with anger, and he ripped the card from my hand, knocking it to the floor. He took a step toward me, his gaze dark and menacing.

Despite my heart racing in my chest, I squared my shoulders and stared up at him. "I strongly advise you step away before you do something you'll regret."

"You can't do this." His eyes burned into mine and I almost shivered at the hostility lurking in their depths.

"Please, Greg, take my advice and speak to Dr. Martin."

He stared at me for another moment before spinning abruptly on his heel and striding for the door. "You'll be the one who regrets this, Victoria."

With those final parting words, he swept from the room and seconds later I heard the outer door slam, punctuating his dramatic exit. With a shaky breath, I sank into one of the plush armchairs and dropped my head into my hands. A soft touch to my shoulder made me jump.

Phyllis stared down at me, concern etched into her features. "You okay?"

I patted her hand where it rested on my shoulder. "I'm fine, thank you. Just a bit shaken up."

"Do you want me to have Ms. Dawes reschedule?"

I shook my head. "No. She probably needs to speak with someone now more than ever. Can you please just give me a minute before sending her in?"

"Of course." The receptionist offered a soft smile and retreated soundlessly from the room.

I closed my eyes, allowing the warmth of the sunlight filtering through the window to wash over me and thaw the ice streaming through my veins. I'd dealt with disgruntled patients before, but for some reason, Greg Andrews had gotten to me on a more personal level. There was something about him that made me uneasy, reminding me of someone long ago. Looking around the room I contemplated my present—and my past. This was a far cry from the place I'd come from, and I was no longer the naïve young girl who trusted too easily. I had to wonder sometimes, did people like

Greg even want help? Or was he here for something else?

Pushing the thought from my mind, I rose from the chair and walked to the doorway just in time to meet Rachel.

I shot her an apologetic smile. "I'm so sorry about that."

The young woman made her way over to one of the chairs and sat gingerly. "It's fine. He just... put me on edge."

I closed the door then settled into the seat next to her. "I know, and I truly apologize. Just so you know," I continued as Rachel opened her mouth to speak, "Mr. Andrews will not be back. What he did goes against our ethics here, so I've recommended him to a colleague of mine."

A watery smile lifted her lips. "Thank you. You have no idea how much you've helped me, you know?"

I smiled. Rachel had struggled with depression for several years, even trying a variety of medications at the urging of her family and friends. She hadn't liked the way the drugs had made her feel, though, and she'd opted for a different solution. The barb coming from Greg this morning must have stung, making Rachel feel insecure and incompetent. Since coming to me nearly six months ago, Rachel had been making significant strides.

"So tell me, Rachel. How have you been?"

"Great." She smiled. "I took your advice and joined a gym. I think the exercise has really been helping my mood. There's, um..." She glanced away for a moment and bit her lip. "There's this guy there."

"Oh?" It was good and bad news, in my opinion. While getting out and meeting new people could be good, I wasn't quite sure that Rachel was ready to get involved romantically.

"Yeah. I haven't... we haven't gone out or anything. But he seems really nice."

I nodded. "Well, just don't forget what we talked about."

"I know." Rachel smiled. "For the first time in a while, I feel really good like everything's exactly the way it should be."

"That's wonderful." I smiled at her. "You've come a long way, Rachel. I'm really proud of you."

"Thanks. Me, too." She smiled and a lightness filled my heart. All thoughts of Greg Andrews were pushed from my head as I focused on the good part of my job—the part where I made a difference, just like I was helping Rachel.

CHAPTER THREE

The man shifted where he sat behind the house, ensconced in the trees, and he watched as the navy sedan turned into the driveway and parked beside the small house. The woman stepped out of the car and walked to the mailbox. Her blonde hair floated behind her, glimmering in the light of the setting sun as it fell halfway down her back. She reminded him of his first, all those years ago. It'd been almost a year now since he'd allowed himself to hunt, and the urges were getting harder and harder to ignore.

Would this get the doctor's attention? He'd been trying to get her to notice him, doing everything he could think of to put himself in her path. And she was a psychologist now, of all things. He smirked at the irony of it. He wondered what she'd say when he finally revealed himself to her. She'd run so far, tried so hard to escape her past, but he'd been right under her nose.

It had taken a little while to track her down, of course, since she'd changed her name. Her records had been sealed, and for a long time, he'd despaired of ever finding her. But things had changed a couple of years ago when he'd gotten his first lead. A different person himself now, he'd gone back to Ohio and kept his ears low to the ground. Although the tragedy had died down over the years, people still remembered it like it was yesterday. With a few well-placed questions, he finally heard that she'd moved to Texas her senior year.

He applauded her choice of name when she reinvented

herself. Her new surname was Carr, which in many cultures meant survivor. And Victoria for obvious reasons. She believed she'd been the victor of their little game, escaping her fate that day. But he'd come a long way, too. No longer ruled by his impulsive urges, he was more efficient, infinitely more sophisticated. He was an exceptional hunter, always well-prepared, researching for days or weeks before making his move. He prided himself on his perfect execution, and he never rushed into anything. People who hurried made mistakes—and he never made mistakes.

A feral smile broke across his face as he watched the young nurse stride back up the driveway, head bent as she flipped through the collection of bills and junk mail. Darkness crept over the evening sky, turning it from orange to pink, then finally a dark lapis as daylight bled away completely. Lights flickered to life inside and he watched her shadow move around the small house as she settled in for the night. He'd watched her for more than a week now, and he closed his eyes, mentally tracking her movements from room to room. First, she would head into the kitchen to make dinner—typically a frozen TV dinner, judging from the containers he'd found in the trash can. Afterward, she would move across the house to the bathroom where she'd shower and brush her teeth, then finally to the single bedroom. Alone. Her routine was entirely too predictable. But that was good for him.

Opening his eyes again, he watched her shadow as she carried her dinner to the couch and turned on the TV. Last night she'd watched that horrendous show about spoiled housewives. What would it be tonight? Forty minutes later the glow of the TV was extinguished, immediately followed by the small lamp on the end table, bathing the room in darkness. The kitchen light came on as she discarded the remains of her dinner, then flicked off again as she made her way down the hall to the bathroom.

Not long now. Another hour and she'd be asleep, but he'd wait a little longer. People were unpredictable. Never knew when one of the neighbors might step outside for a late-night smoke or let an animal out before going to bed. The house two doors down had some little ankle biter that yapped at everything. It had almost ruined his recon two nights ago, tearing across the yard toward him before being jerked back by the jolt of the electric fence buried in the ground. He'd retreated then, making his way back into the trees and waiting until the owner had called for the dog to get inside. Tonight, it was quiet—so far. He continued to watch, waiting with barely restrained anticipation as night settled fully over the quiet street.

A little after one o'clock he crept from the trees and approached the house, hunkering down to blend in with the shrubs that separated her lawn from her neighbor to the left. Cutting across the narrow strip of yard, he bent down to the basement window that he'd left unlocked several days prior. He'd checked routinely to make sure that it was still open, but apparently the room was seldom-used since she hadn't yet noticed it was unlocked.

Swinging the pane inward, he crouched down on the soft, dewy grass and slid feet-first through the narrow rectangle. Dropping swiftly to the floor, he kept one hand on the window to keep it from slamming closed behind him. He quietly lowered it into place and stood stock still as his eyes adjusted to the dark, listening for any sounds of awareness in the house. Only the soft hum of the appliances answered him, and he moved toward the stairs.

This part was trickier. The house was old, and the wooden stairs groaned and creaked with each step. He placed his left foot on the first step all the way to the left. Slowly transferring his weight, he stepped dead in the middle on the second tread. Methodically he climbed the stairs, moving from the memory of having done it dozens of times one day while she was at work.

Finally reaching the door, he turned the handle and inched it open a crack. Eyes and ears on alert he scanned the area, but all was quiet. He crept through the kitchen then down the narrow hallway to her room. The door stood open, and he watched her a moment before stepping silently up to the side of her bed.

The woman lay curled on her side facing away from him, and he stroked a finger down the length of her arm. She shivered at the feather-light touch and rolled toward him, her lashes flickering several times before opening. He could see the wheels turning as she gradually came awake and his presence registered. "Hello, Monique."

Her lips parted on a silent scream but he covered her mouth and nose with a gloved hand, one knee pressing into the soft cavity of her stomach. She thrashed beneath him, eyes rolling in terror, and he climbed atop her, using his weight to pin her to the mattress. Incoherent sounds came from low in her throat as she tried to scream, call for help, plead for her life.

Pulling a roll of duct tape from the pocket of his sweat-shirt, he glared down at her. "I'm going to move my hand now. Scream and I'll kill you. Nod if you understand."

Her head moved briskly up and down, and he lifted his hand. Her words came out on a whisper. "Who are you?"

Ignoring her question, he tore a strip of tape from the roll. "Lift your hands."

She did as he asked, and he looped the strip around her hands.

"Why are you doing this?" Her voice shook, and he pressed his lips into a firm line as he wove the tape in a figure eight around her wrists.

"Do you know what happens to cheaters, Monique?"

She blinked up at him, her entire body shaking with fear. "Wh-what?"

"You're a dirty slut. Aren't you?"

"No!" She shook her head furiously. "No, I—"

He made a tsk-tsk sound low in his throat as he pulled another strip of tape from the roll. "Come now, Monique. I've been watching you." Her eyes widened, and a grim smile cut across his face. "Oh, yes, I've seen you with both of them."

"N-no, I..." He placed the duct tape over her mouth. A

gamut of emotions flashed in her eyes: fear that he would kill her, despair that she wouldn't see another day, hope that he would let her go. His free hand lifted the fabric of his ski mask so she could see his face, and recognition dawned across her beautiful features.

"Yes, Monique." A cold smile curled his lips. "It's me."

Reaching into his black boot, he retrieved the knife and held it up, the long blade glinting in the moonlight. Her eyes widened, and she fought in earnest, swinging her bound hands like a club. The blade slashed against her forearm and blood trickled from the wound as a thin red line appeared. Her voice was muffled as she tried to scream, hampered by the tape. She yanked her arms away and he shoved them over her head, digging the blade into the fleshy part of her upper arm before slicing into the soft skin. A strangled cry came from beneath the duct tape and he smiled.

"You've been a bad girl, Monique." He smiled before pulling the ski mask down once more and raising the knife, dousing that last vestige of hope she harbored in those wide green eyes. "You must be punished for what you've done."

Nearly two hours later, he picked up the woman's phone sitting on the nightstand and used her lifeless hand to bring up the main screen. Tapping in the number he knew by heart, he placed the woman's hand at her side on the bed waited for the call to connect.

His heart leaped in his chest when she answered, her voice husky with sleep, but still his favorite sound in the whole world.

"This is Dr. Carr. How can I help you?"

A slow smile spread over his face. "Hello, Bekah."

CHAPTER FOUR

Victoria

The ringing of the phone jarred me from a sound sleep. Bleary red numbers on the digital clock relayed that it was just shy of four a.m., and I rubbed the sleep from my eyes with the heel of my hand. Propping myself on an elbow, I disconnected my phone from where it lay plugged in on the nightstand. An unfamiliar number flashed across the screen as the phone pealed its third ring. Biting back a yawn, I swiped my thumb across the screen and held it to my ear.

"This is Dr. Carr." Deep, raspy breaths filtered through the phone and I waited a beat, but the caller remained silent. Fatigue pulled at me, and frustration rose to the surface. Keeping my voice as even as possible, I tried again. "How can I help you?"

The man's voice was low and dangerous, and I had to strain to make out his words. "Hello, Bekah."

Oh, God… That voice. My blood ran cold. "How… how did you find me?"

A cruel laugh crackled over the phone line, raising the hairs on the back of my neck. "Still so naïve, aren't you?"

"What do you want?"

I heard him draw in a deep breath before exhaling. "I want you."

"I don't—"

"1143 Woodard Drive. Monique needs your help, Bekah."

"What did you do?" My voice was little more than a whisper as I gripped the phone.

"It's almost time."

"Wait, I don't—"

I pulled the phone away from my ear and stared at the blank screen. Shivers racked my body and my hands shook as I dialed the police.

"911, what's your emergency?"

"M-my name is Dr. Victoria Carr." I swallowed hard and tried to modulate my voice. "I just received a phone call from someone asking for help. 1143 Woodard Drive. I... I think she might be hurt."   •

"Ma'am—"

"Just send help!"

I hung up before the dispatcher could say another word. Springing from the bed, heart racing, I yanked on the closest pair of jeans and a sweatshirt to ward off the chill that snaked through my body. Grabbing up my phone, I ran down the steps, taking only a moment to gather my hair into a ponytail and check my reflection in the mirror that hung in the hallway. Snatching up my keys and purse from the side table, I threw the front door open then quickly relocked it before sprinting toward the driveway.

Heart still racing, I backed down the driveway and sped toward the exit of the allotment. I braked as I passed the guard station, suddenly realizing I had no idea where I was going. Digging my phone from my bag, I spoke into the microphone. "Find directions: 1143 Woodard Drive."

The stilted voice in the phone called out directions and I cut across a back road to a small suburb of Dallas. Blue and red lights pierced the dark sky, and dread congealed in my stomach as I pulled up in front of the small house. The men and woman on scene moved slowly, milling around the lawn, and my heart dropped to my toes. I was too late.

✳

"What exactly did the caller say?"

I wrapped my hands around the Styrofoam cup, trying to absorb what little warmth filtered through the thick material. "He called me Bekah, told me that the woman—Monique—needed help. I... I was still half asleep, but I remembered the address. I called you guys as soon as I hung up."

"You said that a male called you, not Ms. Henderson herself?" Detective Sanchez propped a hip on the table and crossed his arms over his wide chest as he inspected me.

"Yes. He had a deep voice and the way he said it, to send help soon, I had a feeling something bad had happened. He seemed... familiar."

"Because he called you Bekah?"

"Yes." I gave a jerky nod. "But there was something else. I can't describe it, but... I feel like it's him."

Detective Sanchez studied me. "You believe this is the same man who killed Leah Wilson?"

"He sounds older, more mature... but there was something about his voice. The tone, maybe. Just the sound of it..."

A shiver raced down my spine at the memory of his words grating over the phone line, and the coffee sloshed precariously in the cup. I leaned forward and set it on the table before lacing my fingers together and pressing them between my thighs, a gesture that always made an appearance when I was nervous.

"The only person who knows about my past is my friend Kate—Dr. Winfield. We've known each other since college, but I haven't told anyone else. I moved in with my grandparents in Snyder before my senior year of high school and changed my name. No one here has ever known me by anything other than Victoria."

"I see." Sanchez dipped his chin. "Ms. Henderson was a nurse at St. Mary's Hospital. Were you ever in contact with her?"

I shook my head. "No. I'm not a licensed physician, so I don't have to make rounds. I've never met her that I'm aware of."

"Did the caller say anything else?"

"No, not that I can remember." I wrung my hands together. "Oh—he did say something like 'it's almost time.'"

"In reference to Ms. Henderson?"

"I don't know." I lifted one shoulder. "He hung up before I could ask."

The detective nodded as he pulled a card from his pocket and handed it over to me. "Thanks for calling it in and for answering our questions. I assume you'll be around if we need anything?" At my nod, he continued. "Let me know if anything else comes to mind."

"Thank you." I accepted the card and stood. "I appreciate your help."

Detective Sanchez held the door for me as I left the small interrogation room. Over the past few hours, the sun had risen fully in the sky and its bright light streamed through the glass doors. I walked outside, shielding my eyes, debating what to do. Still shaken from the call this morning, I debated canceling today's appointments but quickly nixed the idea. It would give me something to do—something to keep my mind off the woman's murder.

Shortly after I arrived at Monique's house, reporters had flocked to the scene in droves, the information apparently leaked by a neighbor or someone working the case. I'd spoken with the patrolmen as well as the coroner but it seemed they'd never had a chance to save Monique.

The killer must have spent several hours with her, judging from the damage inflicted on her body. The deceased woman had several defensive wounds, as well as the deep laceration that stretched from ear to ear and ultimately ended her life. *Just like Leah*.

I shivered at the thought. I'd tried for so long not to think about that night, but it always loomed in the back of my mind. I recalled each detail as if it were yesterday instead of almost ten years ago now. Leah had put up a good fight, but her killer had overpowered her, taken advantage of her before killing her with a vicious slice across the throat. And now he was back.

Looking left and right, examining my surroundings, I strode quickly through the parking lot and climbed into my car. As soon as the door closed, I locked it. Even the oppressive heat couldn't dispel the chill that had seeped into my bones, and I ran my hands briskly over my arms. Starting the car, I headed toward my office building and made my way to the top floor.

Phyllis met me in the lobby. "Good Lord, girl, what in the name of all things holy happened this morning?" Dogging my steps the entire way back to her office, she continued, "I turned on the news this morning and there you were. I couldn't believe my eyes."

I scrunched up my nose. "They already ran the story?"

Phyllis shook her head. "They only showed a little clip this morning. Said they'd have the 'full story' at six."

I rolled my eyes. "Vultures."

"So?" She stood next to the desk, hands propped on her generous hips. "What happened?"

Sinking into my chair, I leaned back and rubbed my temples. "I got a call this morning from the killer. He said a woman needed help and gave me her address, so I called it in to the police and drove to her house. I'm sure the police would have stopped by to check things out, but I needed to see for myself."

"Why in the blue blazes did he call you?"

I bit her tongue. I'd never told Phyllis of my past and I didn't intend to now. No use worrying the poor woman until the police were able to find more information. Little spooked Phyllis, though; the woman would probably take it upon herself to be my personal protector.

"I'm not sure. The police are trying to figure that out."

Concern settled over her face. "Are you sure you don't want to go home and relax?"

I shook my head. "No, I need something to take my mind off it all."

Phyllis nodded sagely. "Well, if you change your mind or

if you need anything, you just let me know."

I shot her an appreciative smile. "Thank you. I'm sure I'll be fine."

Shutting off thoughts of Monique's murder, I turned my attention to the computer, determined to lose myself in work. Four sessions and several hours later, I walked though the front door and dropped my purse and keys on the console table in the foyer. Exhaustion pulled at me, my mind and body tired from having been roused from bed so early. Too tired to cook, I poured myself a bowl of cereal and carried it to the living room.

Curling up in a corner of the couch, I flipped on the TV. Immediately, my face filled the screen and a female reporter spoke in the background. "... local doctor was called to the scene early this morning. Monique Henderson, a resident of a quaint community just outside of Dallas was the victim of a brutal..."

I flipped channels until I landed on a home and garden show. I couldn't believe the news had spread so quickly. And why did they have to involve me? It was bad enough that a woman had been brutally murdered, but now everyone would think I was somehow involved. We hadn't attended college together, nor were we even passing acquaintances. I'd told the cops the same thing this morning, but the reporters didn't know that. Hopefully, no one leaked any details of my past. I'd reserved that information until speaking with Detective Sanchez, and he seemed intent on keeping it secret as it wasn't yet relative to the case. If they found new evidence though, they might have to dig further into my background. I had no desire to dredge that up again.

I'd spent months after Leah's death working with the local police, appealing to the community, trying to find the killer. It seemed he'd just vanished into thin air. No one had seen him, no one had recognized him or come forward. But now I knew—he'd always been there watching, waiting for the right time.

I carried my bowl to the kitchen and rinsed it in the sink

before climbing the stairs to my room. After a quick shower, I slid into bed, the events of the day replaying in my mind, and finally fell into a fitful sleep, Leah's face haunting my dreams.

CHAPTER FIVE

Victoria

"Dr. Carr is busy, you can't just—"

Dr. Johnathan Martin strode through the door of my office and stood at the corner of her desk. "Victoria, thank God you're all right."

I flicked a glance at him over my computer as I entered notes from the previous session. "Hello, Johnathan."

From the doorway, Phyllis huffed. "Dr. Carr, your three o'clock is here. I tried to tell Dr. Martin that you were busy, but—"

Johnathan spoke over her, waving a hand dismissively at Phyllis. "Please excuse us for a moment."

Pink bloomed over Phyllis's dark brown cheeks, and I decided to intervene. Swiveling my chair toward them, I stood. "Give us two minutes and then please send Mr. Pruitt in. Thank you, Phyllis."

"You're interfering with my business," I chastised Johnathan. "It's nice of you to stop in, but I do have another session starting"—I checked her watch—"three minutes ago."

Johnathan heaved a sigh. "I know, I just wanted to make sure you were okay. I saw you on the news last night, you know."

"Poor girl." I barely repressed a shudder. "It was just brutal."

His brow furrowed. "How did you get involved?"

I actively avoided his gaze. "After he killed her, he... called me from her phone."

"*He called you*?" His voice was sharp, and my eyes flicked to his. "Good God, why?"

"You know how it is, Johnathan. Killers occasionally reach out. They either want to be stopped or they want to be recognized, taunting the authorities for not being able to catch them." I shrugged. "I told the police everything I know, but it's up to them to decide how to proceed."

His face turned pensive. "Did he say anything specific?"

I froze, remembering the way he'd called me by name— *my real name*. "Nothing of significance," I lied. "I'm not entirely certain why he would call me specifically. Monique wasn't a patient of mine, and I can't recall ever meeting her."

"And what about the killer? Is it possible it's someone you know?"

"Of course it's a possibility, but the likelihood of that is slim. The only person with whom I've had an issue recently is Mr. Andrews—the man I referred to you."

"I never did hear anything from him. What if it's him?"

I thought about the way we'd parted after his last appointment. Greg had been furious, but would he have killed a woman out of spite?

"I don't know, Johnathan. I just don't think it fits. That's awfully fast to find and kill a victim, unless he either knew Monique or happened, by some miracle, to meet her that very same day or insinuate himself in her house."

"But—"

I waved away his response. "I'm sure the police are looking into all the different leads. Something will turn up eventually."

I truly hoped he would get the hint and drop it. The whole situation made me uneasy, and I was sick to death of talking about it. I'd never met Monique and according to the police, the woman didn't appear to have any enemies. It really made no sense, but then, murder was often emotional and messy, lacking any rational thought.

His eyes bored into mine and I once again glanced away, pretending to absorb myself in my files. "You know, the offer to join practices still stands."

Air rushed from my lungs on a soft sigh. "We've talked about this."

He held up a hand. "Just think about it. Have dinner with me."

"Johnathan…"

"Okay, we don't have to go out. I'll stop over later and bring some takeout. Italian?" Before I could respond, he was already striding toward the door. "See you at seven."

I flopped back in my chair, rubbing my temples in a calming circular motion. He meant well, but sometimes Johnathan could be so… overwhelming. He'd been a good friend during the past two years since we'd met, but the way he looked at me sometimes hinted that he was interested in far more than just friendship or a business partnership.

Phyllis appeared in the doorway, a grim frown on her face, and I knew I'd have to make up for Johnathan's rudeness. Short and stocky, Mr. Pruitt followed just behind looking very uncomfortable for his first session. Smoothing out my facial expression, I greeted him with a serene smile.

"Good afternoon, Mr. Pruitt. Please, make yourself at home." With a grateful look at Phyllis, I settled into a plush armchair.

Turning my mind away from the murder, away from Johnathan and my disgruntled receptionist, I focused on Mr. Pruitt and spent the next hour delving into his concerns over his sexuality.

After Mr. Pruitt left, I drummed my fingers on the desk, considering Johnathan's words. Maybe he was right. I'd been on edge the last couple of days since the murder, and a little extra security would go a long way to making me feel safer, at least at work. My community was gated, so I didn't worry too much about someone gaining access to my house. Here, though, I felt exposed.

Picking up the phone, I dialed the building manager's number.

"Ramirez."

"Hi, Benny, it's Dr. Carr. How are you?"

"Just fine, Doctor, how about you?"

"Great, thanks." Formalities out of the way, I dove right in. "Benny, you may have heard about my recent involvement in a woman's murder."

"I sure did. Sorry to hear about that. Is there something I can help with?"

"Actually"—I rubbed my damp palm briskly on the material of my dress slacks—"I was wondering what kind of security this building has."

"Well, now." His voice was tentative and a bit defensive. "We don't usually have too much trouble here. We just call the police if anything happens. Why do you ask?"

I sighed. "I've had a little trouble with an ex-patient of mine and I was just wondering if there's any chance we could get some extra security around here for a while. I'd feel safer if someone was here in case anything happened. I don't want to jeopardize my staff or my patients. Just until things blow over," I added.

"I suppose I can ask, Doctor. Don't know what the owner will say, though. Security can get awful expensive."

My hackles rose at his dismissive tone. I wasn't above playing hardball. "Well, Mr. Ramirez, many medical facilities have full-time security guards. I'm sure the owner wouldn't want anything to happen in his building. I'm certain he values the safety of the people here and will justify the cost. It would be just awful if something were to happen to affect business, and I imagine he'd rather be proactive since the safety of his building and the people here is paramount..." I trailed off, allowing him to draw any conclusion he liked. I really had no other avenues to pursue if he turned me down, but Benny didn't need to know that. In truth, nothing bad had ever really happened here that I knew of, and I was asking quite a lot for the owner to provide additional security for what may possibly have been a fluke.

"Of course." The building manager's voice was stiff. "I'll see what I can do."

"Thank you, Benny. I really appreciate it."

"My pleasure, miss. I'll be in touch."

I hung up with a grim smile. I wasn't completely confident that Benny had taken me seriously or that the owner would even consider my request without laughing at me, but at least I'd tried.

CHAPTER SIX

Blake

I tapped the screen of the tablet, pausing the video taken Tuesday morning just before dawn. "What do we know so far?"

"Jack shit." Con shook his head. "Dr. Carr claims to have never met the victim. According to the police reports, there was no sign of forced entry."

"Boyfriend?"

"No one serious that any of her friends or colleagues are aware of. The police don't have any leads yet, or, if they do, they're not sharing that information."

I frowned. It was a gruesome murder, but they'd always look first at people closest to the victim. How the hell was Dr. Carr tied into this? "Why the hell call her?"

He shrugged. "She's a psychologist. Maybe a former patient or a boyfriend trying to get her attention?"

I turned my gaze back to the beautiful woman on the screen. Her long dark hair was pulled back into a ponytail and she looked exhausted. "So, what are they requesting?"

"Basic security at the healthplex on the south side. Her practice is on the fifth floor." He lifted a shoulder. "You'll make rounds through the building, put any precautions into place that you feel necessary. You're just hired muscle to make sure she's safe."

I lifted a brow. "Isn't that a little much after only one incident?"

"Better to take the preventative measure than risk something happening to her."

"I just can't believe the landlord's going to foot the bill for that without any evidence. At this point, isn't it all conjecture anyway?"

Con settled back in his chair. "I've known the owner for several years. Ben Kingsley dabbles in real estate and owns several businesses around town. He's a good guy. He saw the news and decided to grant her request on a temporary basis."

"How long?"

"Four weeks. He's given the go-ahead to install additional cameras around the property, so I've put in an order."

I nodded. Maybe the phone call was a fluke, but maybe it was more. Probably wasn't a bad idea to make sure some stalker wasn't after her. She'd at least be safe at work and, if nothing else, it would give the office the added benefit of tighter security for their patients.

Con studied me. "I'm supposed to head to D.C. soon. I can either take this once I get back or you can head this one up. How soon you looking to start?"

I turned my gaze back to the screen. Under her grim composure, the woman looked... scared. I wasn't sure why, exactly, but something in her expression called to me. "I'll handle it."

CHAPTER SEVEN

Victoria

I entered the lobby of the healthplex and stopped dead in my tracks, arrested by the sight in front of me. Benny caught my eye and waved me over, and I found my feet carrying me closer against my will. Next to the building manager stood a golden-haired man, tall and broad-shouldered. Despite the constrictive suit he wore, the man's build spoke of power and raw masculinity, his muscular arms and legs straining against the material.

My gaze slid over his chest and up to his angular face. His hair was military short, with just enough on top to run my fingers through the silky strands. Hazel eyes sat over high cheekbones, and a neatly trimmed beard covered the lower half of his jaw. I typically opted for the men I dated to be clean-shaven, but the facial hair on this man seemed appropriate, as if it enhanced his features rather than detracting from them. He was too rugged to be considered traditionally handsome, but the man was gorgeous in a rough sort of way. He looked as if he could bench press me with one arm, and my blood ran hot at the thought of his hands all over me.

I had little experience with men of his caliber—okay, none—but I knew instinctively that he would know exactly how to treat a woman. He exuded confidence, an arrogance I imagined most men of his stature exhibited, and I wondered what it would feel like to have that rapt attention focused on me. The thought simultaneously thrilled me and irked me, because a man like him would sure have a girlfriend who was just as beautiful. A twinge of jealousy curdled in my gut and I clenched my teeth, pushing the useless emotion away and replacing it instead with cool aloofness.

As I approached the duo, the man flashed me a smile, his teeth perfectly straight and white against his deeply tanned cheeks. The action made me self-conscious of my own slightly crooked incisors, and I pressed my lips into a tight line. Irritation flared again at the sight of the insolent grin twisting his lips. It was a smile designed to draw women in and make them lose all sense as they flung themselves at him. Oh, yes. This man was used to getting whatever—and whomever—he wanted.

I gritted my teeth. I couldn't believe I'd allowed him to get under my skin and undermine my confidence without so much as a word. He meant nothing; he was probably just being interviewed for the security position. Once he left, I'd tell Benny that the man wouldn't be a good fit. Then I wouldn't have to worry about seeing him ever again.

Benny spoke up as I came within a couple feet of them. "Dr. Carr, this is Blake Lawson with Quentin Security Group."

The man held out a hand. "Nice to meet you, ma'am."

I bristled, narrowing my eyes at him as I offered a brief handshake. "*Doctor* Carr."

After almost ten years in the South, I still wasn't used to the precipitous use of the word ma'am. I knew it was supposed to be a sign of respect, but the man's tone had an almost mocking quality to it. If the faint smile tugging at the corners of his mouth was any indication, he clearly found my indignation humorous. I didn't normally think so highly of myself, but he had me on guard. Better to distance myself now and put him in his place. I steeled my spine and stared him down. His eyes twinkled with mirth but his face remained impassive, stoking my ire. Good thing he wouldn't be around long, otherwise we were bound to butt heads.

Benny interrupted her thoughts. "Mr. Lawson will resume duties beginning Monday."

I startled, and my mouth dropped open a fraction. "I'm sorry?"

The building manager nodded. "I'll get him a set of keys, so you can lock up like normal when you leave for the evening. We've been discussing the option of installing cameras at each entrance, as well as in the elevator and on each floor."

Blake opened his mouth, but I cut in and spoke over him. "Clearly, Mr. Lawson, you are aware of the sensitive nature of my work. It would be an infringement of my patient's rights to track them all over the building." Again, his mouth opened to speak, but I continued. "They need to feel comfortable here, not like prisoners."

I turned to Benny. "I will not consent to cameras. Besides, they seem to be a completely unnecessary expense if Mr. Lawson here"—I gestured to the man to my right—"is truly as competent as he says he is."

I felt more than saw his look of disdain, and I kept my gaze firmly on Benny as Blake spoke up. "I assure you, *ma'am*, I am completely capable of securing a single building." There was no mistaking the derision in his voice this time, and I cut a glare at him as he continued. "However, in my expertise, it is better to have too many precautions in place rather than too few. I was led to believe that a call was made to you from a recent crime scene. Is that correct?"

His hazel eyes burned into mine, and I crossed my arms over my chest. "Yes, but—"

"Then it would appear," he cut in, "that you could potentially be in danger. I don't know the how or why of it, *Doctor* Carr, but I am here to prevent anyone from harming you."

I notched my chin up a degree. "And what qualifications do you have, exactly?"

Condescension flickered in the hazel depths of his eyes as he regarded me. "I've been trained in a range of weapons as well as hand-to-hand combat."

"That's—"

"In addition to that," he barreled over me, "I also completed four tours as a US Marine where I served in the Special Forces. I've been to thirty-two countries and am equipped to navigate any terrain and survive in any condition so, yes, I believe I am. *Ma'am*."

Infuriating man. I bit my tongue and clenched my hands into tight fists as he tacked on that last parting shot. I refused to let the man rile me. Since Benny had obviously already offered Blake the position, I would just have to suck it up and avoid him at all costs. I lifted my chin and stared at him.

"Fine. I expect you to leave my office alone during business hours unless you are expressly requested to intervene. I will accede to cameras in the elevator and main access points, but none on my floor, nor in my office. Will that be a problem for you, Mr. Lawson?"

His only response was a curt shake of his head, his eyes cold and hard.

"Have a nice day." Without another word, I strode across the lobby, opting to take the stairs instead of the elevator. Stomping up the five flights of stairs, I willed my anger to abate. Instead, it only grew. I briefly considered calling Benny this afternoon and having him replace Mr. Lawson, but that would appear too suspicious. Better to wait a few days, make a complaint about his behavior or work ethic, then have Blake's company send a new guard in his stead.

Decision made, I reached the top of the stairs and pushed open the heavy steel door before stepping into the hallway. The door to my office was just to my left, and the soft, calming notes of lavender and vanilla greeted me as I unlocked the door and stepped into the lobby. It was a technique I'd employed shortly after opening my own practice. The subtle scent made patients feel welcome and relaxed before they even stepped foot into my office. For first timers, it was incredibly important for them to feel comfortable. In addition, I wore a light vanilla fragrance to blend harmoniously with the atmosphere. I wanted the office to feel homey, so we replaced the fragrance each week to keep it fresh. I'd also opted for comfy, overstuffed couches and chairs rather than standard, office-issue furniture. Abstract paintings in jewel tones hung on the walls, and the large picture window highlighted the beautiful cityscape of downtown Dallas.

I unlocked the staff door as I passed, then made my way to the end of the hall to my own office. Located in the corner of the building, there were windows on two walls, allowing the bright morning light to filter in. The room itself was a large square, with my desk situated directly across from the door. A couch took up most of the right wall and two large armchairs sat to the left of the desk in a cozy nook, flanking the other window. Bookshelves covered every inch of free wall space, books and journals stacked two-deep in some places. I typically loved coming in here, but even the sight of my perfect little space couldn't raise my spirits after that altercation in the lobby.

Striding to the desk, I sank into the chair and fired up my computer, tilting the monitor away from the glare of sunlight streaming through the window behind me. Today's schedule was pretty light, thank goodness, with only two appointments this morning and one this afternoon. After almost two years in my own practice, I was finally getting to the point where I could take cases on a selective basis. My clientele had grown steadily over the past couple of years and through word of mouth, I'd been able to steadily develop my patient list.

Out of college, I'd interned with a local group but had ultimately decided to move on. I learned a lot during my time with the Wellness Group, but I had principles and ideals that I preferred to focus on. I'd begun scouting the outlying areas of Dallas close to the suburbs where real estate was less expensive when I'd found this little gem. A friend of mine, Dr. Kate Winfield, had an office in the same building. Kate and I had met in our second year at the University of Texas, where we shared several of the same classes. We'd become fast friends and, although Kate had ultimately decided on family medicine, we remained close. As soon as one of the offices had opened up in her building, Kate had called and told me to come check it out.

It was love at first sight. The five-story white stucco building was perfect, and the small office on the top floor was the icing on the cake. The space was small since the fifth story was divided into two areas, the other reserved for some use dictated by the owner. It was the perfect size to venture out on my own, and I'd signed the lease less than a week later.

The first six months had been difficult. A handful of patients had followed me, but like most who attended counseling, several stayed for only a few sessions before moving on or giving up. I'd spent the first few months trying to drum up business while running the office alone. I was almost at the end of my rope when I hired Phyllis. A cast off from the building, Phyllis had been let go after fifteen years of service to Dr. William Harbaugh, one of the most pretentious, supercilious men to ever walk the earth. I'd learned of his reputation within days of moving into the building, and I avoided the old curmudgeon at all costs.

I'd met Phyllis only a handful of times before that fateful day when we'd shared the elevator down to the lobby of the building. The older woman had a box of knickknacks tucked under one arm and a small potted palm in the other. Tear tracks marked her cheeks, and I'd offered to buy her lunch at a nearby cafe. Two hours later, I had a new receptionist and the right hand I never knew I was missing. Phyllis ran a tight ship and kept everything running smoothly. She also wasn't afraid to tell me exactly what she thought, offering her opinions freely and without restraint.

A soft click of the door in the lobby heralded said receptionist's arrival. I waited patiently for the woman to make her way back and give a rundown of her morning. It didn't take long.

Phyllis breezed into my office moments later and collapsed on the couch to my left, fanning her face dramatically. "Lordy be, girl, did you see that slice of Heaven disguised as a man downstairs?"

I rolled my eyes, not even bothering to look away from

the email I'd opened. "I assume you're referring to the arrogant jerk the security company sent over this morning?"

"He seemed nice enough to me." Phyllis lifted a pencil-thin brow my way. "Did you have a run-in with Mr. Sex on a Stick already?"

A flush of embarrassment crept over my skin. "No, he just seems like the type."

In truth, I really had no idea why Blake Lawson irked me so much. There was no one thing in particular that bothered me; it was just... him. He seemed arrogant, self-assured, and he was definitely more handsome than any man had a right to be—and he knew it. But that wasn't a crime. The more I thought about it, the more I began to think I was just being extra sensitive. The guy would be here for a few weeks until the cops figured out who had murdered the girl downtown, then he would be on his way. Until then, I would just ignore him... and all of the unwelcome feelings he stirred within me.

CHAPTER EIGHT

Blake

"I'm telling you, she hates my guts."

Con laughed. "What the hell did you do to her?"

I threw one hand in the air. "Why the hell do you assume it's my fault? She literally walked through the door, sized me up, and then ripped me apart. She asked for my credentials, Con. Who the fuck is this woman?"

He took a swig of beer and tipped his head. "Well, she did get a call from a killer just a few days ago. Maybe she's still on edge, wants to make sure you're legit. Can't blame her for that."

I nodded reluctantly. It was true, although personally, I still thought the woman's reaction was uncalled for. It was literally the last thing I'd expected.

As soon as she'd walked into the lobby, something had shifted. It was cheesy as hell, but the sight of Victoria had been like a sucker punch to the gut. I'd recognized her immediately from the clip I'd watched the other night, only then she'd been in jeans and a hooded sweatshirt. In person she was even more gorgeous, even in the ill-fitting suit meant to downplay what were surely mouth-watering curves beneath the bulky material.

She'd stopped in her tracks, and I was sure she'd felt it too—whatever the hell it was. Lust, definitely. Something else, though, too. Her steel-gray eyes were devoid of makeup and I'd felt her gaze brush over my skin as surely as if she'd touched me. But before I'd really even had a chance to introduce myself, she'd lit into me with a vengeance. And now I was stuck working with her every day.

Not that it would be a problem. The woman really wasn't even my type. Beautiful, yes, but too buttoned up. She hid behind drab, dark clothes that hung shapelessly from her body and hair that'd been pulled ruthlessly away from her face in a style that reminded me of a nun—a very sexy nun, but the kind who rapped knuckles for the pure enjoyment of it. Maybe that was half the appeal, though.

God, what I wouldn't give to strip her out of those dreary clothes and see what really lay beneath. The woman was naturally beautiful with her coffee-colored hair and sharp gray eyes that sliced through me, missing nothing. For some reason, though, she was dead set against me. I'd just have to put her out of my mind and treat her like the job she was. Four weeks and I'd be free of the Ice Queen.

I set my beer on the bar. "Pretty sure I felt my balls shrivel up out of self-preservation."

He scoffed. "How bad can she be? I saw her on the news after the murder. She seemed okay, and she's nice enough to look at."

"Just don't be surprised if you get complaint from her. To say we got off on the wrong foot is an understatement."

Con sighed as he rolled the beer bottle between his hands. "If it's that bad, I'll try to find someone else. I want our first jobs to go as smoothly as possible, so it's best if we can avoid any altercations. Xander will be stateside soon, but he has some shit to settle before he can come down here. I leave for D.C. on Monday, but I should be back by Thursday, Friday at the latest. If you can make it through this week without killing each other, I'll take over when I get back. I'll try to drum up another job for you in the meantime."

I dipped my chin. "Appreciate it."

It was probably better that way, even if I already regretted not being able to see her. Didn't matter that she seemed to hate me, the little spitfire turned me on something fierce. I couldn't help the overwhelming desire to fuck the anger and condescension right out of her until she melted into my arms, pliable and sated.

"The workers installed the carpet today, so the furniture is scheduled to be delivered next week. Wanna stop by on your way home, pick out your office?"

Con's words snapped me back to reality. "You giving me preferential treatment?"

He snorted. "I shouldn't since I have to take over for you, watching some hot little piece of ass."

Something akin to jealousy snaked through me. "Just wait 'til she tears you a new asshole."

He laughed. "Maybe she just needs a real man to settle her down a bit."

"Come on." Irrational anger surged to the surface and I dropped my feet to the floor. "Let's go check out my new office."

Throwing an extra couple bucks down on the bar, I nodded to the bartender dressed in a too-tight shirt and cut-off shorts, her long, lean legs enhanced by the fringed cowboy boots she wore. The woman winked, and I shot her a lazy smile. Worst case, looked like the pretty little bartender would be more than happy to share my bed. Why, then, couldn't I stop thinking about the prickly little doctor?

Maybe because she was the first woman in a long time—maybe ever, honestly—who hadn't fallen into my arms. I wasn't vain by a long shot, but I was a decent looking guy. If nothing else, women loved a man in uniform, and I'd enjoyed a fair share of the bunnies who'd hung out in the bars around base. But Dr. Carr was the furthest thing from a groupie. She was obviously smart and driven, and she didn't put up with shit—especially from a man she didn't know from Adam.

We headed out of the bar and turned east toward the industrial section of town. Con's voice cut through the silence. "So, what's the real story?"

I knew exactly what he was asking, but I played dumb. "What story?"

"With the broad. I've seen you with women, so what's different about this one?"

"I told you, she hates me."

"I'm calling bullshit. Why do you want out so bad?"

"She bit my head off before I even introduced myself. She's sexy, but..." I shrugged. "Guess it's not in the cards."

"You give her that stupid smile?"

I lifted a brow his way. "What smile?"

"That same asinine smile you just gave the bartender. The one that has woman falling over themselves to get to you."

Was it that obvious? Con took my silence as agreement, and he shook his head. "I'm going to guess that's a yes. She's smart, right?" He didn't give me a chance to respond. "She's probably used to fighting her way to the top, and there's nothing worse than being undermined by some guy who thinks he's hot shit."

I opened my mouth to protest, but he held up a hand. "You have sisters, don't you?" At my nod, he continued. "Just like with Abby—I want the best for her, someone who will always be around when she needs him."

"I'm putting down some roots here. Not like we'll be overseas anymore." My words came out terse, more combative than I'd originally intended, but I couldn't stem the need to defend myself.

"No," he agreed, "but we'll always follow the job, whenever and wherever we're needed. It's what we do. Dr. Carr strikes me as the type of woman who needs stability. Do us both a favor and cut her loose before anyone gets hurt."

Easier said than done. There was something about her that drew me in. Despite our encounter yesterday, she intrigued the hell out of me. Maybe he had a point. Did I want a relationship? I'd spent the past dozen years chasing the newest adrenaline rush, not bothering to form any kind of real attachment. I did my own thing, came and went as I pleased. But now it all seemed a little... shallow.

I thought of my parents, now going on their thirty-eighth wedding anniversary. Things hadn't been perfect growing up, but I'd always admired them. They'd made it through plenty of tough times with me and my two sisters, and they were probably more in love with each other now than they were thirty years ago. Someday I wanted to do the same—find a nice girl to settle down with, someone who could put up with my crazy family.

Con slipped the key into the lock and pushed open the door. Instead of mildew, the scent of fresh paint and new carpet assaulted my nose.

I glanced around the newly renovated lobby. "Which office is yours?"

He pointed down the hallway. "Last one on the left."

I peered into each office as I passed before pausing at the end. "Mind if I take the one across the hall?" I flipped on the light and strode toward the center of the room. A single office chair sat to one side, a cardboard box propped on the seat.

He smirked. "I guessed well." He gestured to the box. "Cards for you and new shirts."

I lifted an eyebrow. "Shirts?"

"Marketing."

I pulled the polo from the box and studied the thick color-blocking stripe across the chest and shoulders. "There's no fucking way I'm wearing this."

He rolled his eyes. "What the hell's wrong with it? Our colors are blue and black."

"That is fucking purple. And I'm not wearing it."

"You will if I say you will."

I glared at him. "I really hate you sometimes. You know that, right?"

A grin spread over Con's face. "Yep. Just once or twice, that's all I ask. You can go back to your regular suits or TDUs or whatever the rest of the time."

"Am I the only one who gets this kind of preferential

treatment, or will the other guys have the same pleasure?"

He shrugged and smiled. "I prefer to think of it as hazing."

I shook my head with a resigned sigh and slung the offensive article over my shoulder as I strode toward the door. "Asshole."

Con grinned. "Takes one to know one."

CHAPTER NINE

Victoria

I glanced again at the clock in the corner of my computer screen. Worry and something else prickled at the back of my neck. It was now almost two o'clock and Rachel hadn't shown up, hadn't even called to cancel or reschedule. I picked up the phone and dialed the number again. It was my third attempt today, and it rolled over to voicemail unanswered, just like each previous call. It wasn't like her to just not show up. Any time she'd been sick or unable to make it, she'd called to let me know.

We'd developed a strong bond over the last several months, and I saw a bit of myself in the young woman sometimes. Rachel had been subjected to sexual abuse at the hands of her stepfather for years before finally gaining the courage to press charges against him and put the man behind bars. She'd struggled with depression off and on and had started therapy almost three years ago after her attorney suggested it. After the incident in high school, I'd developed serious trust issues, wondering if I'd ever feel normal again. I thanked God every day Marc hadn't raped me that night, and I couldn't begin to imagine what Rachel had endured for all those years. When I'd stumbled into a psychology course as an elective my freshman year, I'd immediately fallen in love. It had helped me to understand some of my deep-rooted fears and I wanted to help others like Rachel.

I wasn't perfect, I knew that, but I'd come a long way in the last ten years. While I'd dated in college, I never quite found anyone who made me feel… more. Both of my boyfriends had been extremely staid, but I hadn't been able to open up to either of them. Without a foundation of trust, the relationships had quickly fizzled out. After college, I'd been too busy first with clinicals, then opening my practice. With everything going on in my life, dating had fallen by the wayside. Sometimes I felt like the last single virgin in Texas. Most of my friends were married, and many had already started families or had babies on the way. I didn't want to settle, but I wasn't quite sure I was ready for more, either.

The phone vibrated in my hand, jolting me from my thoughts, and relief washed over me as I glanced at the screen.

"Rachel, thank goodness."

A shaky breath exhaled on the other end. "Dr. Carr?"

I tensed. The voice was most decidedly *not* Rachel's. "This is she."

The woman faltered. "I… I'm sorry it took so long to return your call."

"It's no problem at all," I assured her. "What can I help with?"

"It's about Rachel. We would have called sooner, but there were so many things…"

That prickly sensation on the back of my neck magnified, and goosebumps raced down my arms. I didn't recognize the strangled voice coming from my mouth. "Did something happen?"

A choked sob came from the other end of the phone. "I'm sorry, Doctor. Rachel's… gone."

"Gone?" My mind whirled with possibilities, and a sense of foreboding had my stomach clenching into a tight knot. "I don't understand…"

The woman on the other end let out a shaky breath. "Rachel took her life last week."

*

My fingers tightened on the wheel as I pulled into my driveway and parked next to Johnathan's shiny red Porsche. He glanced my way through the window then stepped out of the sports car and shot me a sympathetic smile over the roof.

Start to finish, today had just been crappy all around, and the only thing I wanted to do was go inside, take a long, hot bath, and drink a glass of wine... or maybe the whole bottle. Entertaining really hadn't been on my agenda, and I couldn't help the trace of annoyance tingeing my voice. "What can I do for you, Johnathan?"

"I know it's been a bad day for you, but I thought you might be hungry." He held up a brown paper sack with a sweet smile, and I groaned inwardly. It was hard to stay mad at him when he went out of his way to be nice, but sometimes it was all just a little too much.

I'd been in shock when I hung up the phone this afternoon. Rachel's sister Elizabeth had haltingly relayed the details of Rachel's overdose last week. Though they weren't sure exactly what had transpired, Rachel's mother had called her on Tuesday afternoon but hadn't been able to reach her. They'd found her later that evening, but by then it had been too late.

Elizabeth had apologized again for not calling sooner and invited me to both calling hours this evening and the service tomorrow afternoon. After thanking Elizabeth and hanging up, I'd sat frozen until Phyllis had come in. I vaguely remembered stumbling over the explanation, and Phyllis had immediately taken charge, rescheduling the rest of today's appointments as well as those lined up for tomorrow. I left in a daze, then drove home to prepare for calling hours. I'd spent the last three hours at a funeral home on the outskirts of town, speaking with Rachel's family and friends. The last thing I wanted to do tonight was put on a happy face and pretend everything was okay.

With a soft sigh, I locked the car then made my way past Johnathan and up the stairs of the porch, leaving him to follow. I unlocked the door and stepped inside, tossing my keys and purse on the table and kicking off my shoes by the door. I plodded toward the living room where I curled up in the corner of the couch and closed my eyes. I heard Johnathan come in and close the door behind him. His soft footsteps approached the couch, and the paper bag rustled as he set it on the coffee table.

"I'll grab us plates. I'll be right back."

As soon as his footsteps moved away again, I dropped my head back against the couch and rubbed my temples. My mind felt like it was full of white noise, a constant buzzing that wouldn't go away. I still couldn't quite believe she was gone. What had caused the sudden change in attitude? Could I have stopped it? My heart twisted with regret. God, I wished Rachel had given me some sort of indication that something was wrong.

I opened my eyes just as Johnathan strode through the large archway separating the living room from the main hallway, his arms full. He set down the plates, forks, and wine glasses, then pulled the bottle of wine from where it was tucked under his arm. Digging a corkscrew from his back pocket, he efficiently uncorked the bottle and filled my glass. With a grateful nod, I swiped it off the table and took a long swallow.

The cushion beside me dipped as Johnathan's weight settled into it. His hand landed on my knee, and I fought the urge to squirm under his touch. I appreciated everything Johnathan had done—really, I did—but right now, I just needed some time and space to myself.

"How are you feeling?"

Like crap. Clearing my throat, I sat up and discreetly shifted away from him. "I'm... I don't know, honestly. Her death was a shock. We had a good session last week, and I still can't believe she's gone. I really thought she was improving. I guess it just wasn't enough."

Already emotionally exhausted, I had no desire to deal with him tonight. I didn't want to vocalize my thoughts and feelings, even with Johnathan. I knew I would need to deal with my errant emotions eventually. But not yet.

"It happens, Victoria. It's not your fault."

I sighed. "Her poor family. I just feel so bad."

"Maybe she should have stayed on her medication. We could have switched it up, found something that worked for her so it would have been better controlled." As he spoke, he opened the paper bag and began to extract small white boxes, the flavorful aromas permeating the air.

Bristling at his comment, I leveled an irritated glare at his back. "She tried several if you remember. She said she hated the way they made her feel."

"We can't fix it tonight," he said softly as he passed her a plate full of General Tso's chicken. "Have some of this. You need to eat."

Half-heartedly, I obediently scooped up a bite of food. Despite the delicious smell, it tasted like cardboard and what little appetite I'd had fled. I set the plate on the coffee table and picked up the wine glass.

Johnathan studied me from the corners of his eyes as he ate, methodically cutting the chicken into precise pieces. "Rachel's death today got me thinking about something."

I closed my eyes, wishing I could tune out whatever he was about to say. I was sure it would be some variation of the argument we'd had many times before. I had no intention of joining practices with him—ever. I opened my mouth to stop him, but his next words surprised me into silence.

"I think you should go on a date."

My mouth dropped open as I swung around to look at him. Was he serious? He didn't know the extent of my past, but he certainly knew enough. I'd spoken with him once about trust issues, but I couldn't bring myself to fully open up to Johnathan, either. It was like there was an entire part of me that I refused to let people see, and I didn't want to let anyone in. I hated to admit it, but I still struggled with the idea of intimacy.

Except... The moment I'd laid eyes on the security guard, he'd turned me inside out, warming my blood and sending a frisson of awareness slithering along my nerve endings all the way to the tips of my fingers and toes. Never before had a man affected me that way.

My thoughts from earlier bubbled to the surface. I did eventually want to find a man and fall in love. Kate had suggested online dating or going to singles functions, but I'd always waved it off. I knew she only wanted the best for me, just like Johnathan. Maybe it was time to put myself out there and at least try to make a connection with someone.

I regarded Johnathan warily. "Why?"

He took off his glasses and polished one lens with the hem of his shirt. "You said that Rachel had been moving on with her life."

"She was. And?"

"What have you done to address your own fears?"

I immediately bristled. Even though I'd been thinking the same thing just a few seconds ago, hearing the words from him hit a little too close to home. "I'm just fine."

"Are you?" His chocolate brown eyes stared into mine as if probing my soul, and I snatched my gaze away, pinning it instead to the wall across from me.

"I dated in college. I just never found anyone I was really interested in. And now I'm just too busy." I took a sip of wine, feeling his intense gaze on me all the while.

"Maybe you could try again. Many successful marriages and partnerships start with friendship."

I stiffened at the implication. Though he'd never said as much, I'd wondered from time to time if he wanted to ask me out. The way he looked at me sometimes hinted at more than friendship and as much as I liked him as a person, I had no interest in dating him. To avoid answering his question I tipped the glass upward again, then realized it was empty. I reached for the wine bottle but Johnathan beat me to it.

"What about you?" I asked as he filled my glass. "Are you

still dating… whoever that was?"

Had he ever told me the woman's name? I didn't think so.

Something flashed across Johnathan's face as he recorked the bottle. "No, that's over. And we were speaking of you, not me."

He shot me a look, and I rolled my eyes. "I just don't think this is a good time."

He stared at me for a moment before responding. "Well, just think about it."

I offered him a small smile and picked up my fork. "I will."

We spent the next several minutes eating in silence. Once I'd forced a few more bites down, I scooped up the dishes and carried them to the kitchen.

Johnathan brought in the leftovers and placed the cartons in the fridge. "Are you working tomorrow?"

I turned to face him. "No, I had Phyllis cancel my appointments. I'm going to Rachel's service tomorrow afternoon."

He nodded. "Would you like some company?"

I considered it briefly, then shook my head. "No, thanks, I'll be fine. Besides, it's something I need to do by myself."

"All right. If you change your mind, just give me a call."

I feigned a yawn. "Sorry, it's been a long day."

His lips curved into a tight-lipped smile, clearly interpreting my evasion tactic for what it was. "I'd better head out, then."

We headed to the front door in silence and Johnathan hesitated, his hand on the knob. "Why do you park out front?"

I studied him. "What do you mean?"

"Why don't you park in the garage?"

I lifted one shoulder. "I do, sometimes. But if it's nice out, it's just easier to come in the front."

His lips turned down in a disapproving frown. "With everything going on, it might be safer to park inside."

I waved off his concern. "Crime here is non-existent.

Besides, everyone has to stop at the security gate before coming in."

I'd added Johnathan to my list about six months ago, a decision I'd recently begun to regret. With that single invitation, I now realized I'd given him the impression that I might one day entertain the idea of a relationship with him.

"I worry about you." His eyes searched mine as he spoke, and my heart softened, touched by his show of concern.

"I know you do. But really, everything will be fine. I promise." I pasted on what I hoped was a convincing smile and, after a moment, he relented.

"Fine. But if anything happens, please let me know. I hate having to read about you online or see you on TV before I hear it from you."

I blushed, suitably chastised. "I'm sorry. Next time I promise to keep you in the loop."

He smiled and brushed a hand down my arm. "That's all I ask. Good night, Victoria."

"Night."

Johnathan stepped outside and closed the door behind him with one last smile, and I immediately flipped the lock into place. I tapped the code into the security system and trudged up the stairs to the bathroom, turning the water on as hot as it would go. Stripping off my clothes, I stood under the spray and allowed the water to beat down on my back and shoulders, the knife-like pricks pelting my skin no match for the tumultuous emotions roiling inside me.

I hadn't cried yet, but that would come later. Grief was a funny thing. Until you really acknowledged it, allowed it to take over, you could push it down, pretend it wasn't there. Failure, however, wasn't. It hung heavy around my neck and I touched my chest, the action dredging up the memory of a necklace that had once hung there years ago. It was a replica of one that Leah had owned, the one that had been stolen from her the night of her murder. My locket lay in the bottom of my jewelry box, broken but not forgotten. I knew where I'd gone wrong that night with Leah and the stranger, but what about Rachel?

Heart heavy, I climbed out of the shower and toweled off. Not bothering to dry my hair, I pulled on an old pair of sweats and a t-shirt, then curled up in bed, thoughts of Rachel and Leah parading past my mind's eye. The darkness outside turned almost to dawn before I fell asleep.

Somehow, I made it through the morning, dressing and heading to the church for Rachel's service. Elizabeth and Rachel's mother, Joanne, were welcoming and kind, and both expressed their thanks for helping Rachel over the past few months. I wanted to refute their statements, protest that I could have—should have—done more for Rachel. What had I missed?

Fueled by the need for answers, I drove to the healthplex and took the stairs in lieu of the elevators, hoping to avoid any stragglers. As soon as I reached my office, I locked the door behind me. Finally alone, I leaned my head against the cool glass of the door and drew in a shuddering breath. A riptide of emotions rolled through me and I wished that, just once, I had someone to lean on—someone to hold me and promise me that everything would be okay.

Shaking off the thought, I pushed off the door and made my way through the dark room. Satisfied that I wouldn't be interrupted, I gathered Rachel's files from the cabinet. Hugging them tightly to my chest like it would contain the emotions within, I leaned against the wall. The reality of Rachel's death finally hit me with brutal force, and I slid to the floor. Hot tears slipped down my cheeks as I cracked open the first folder and began to read.

CHAPTER TEN

Blake

I pushed open the door of the stairwell and stepped into the darkened hallway, the corridor lit only by the faint red glow of the emergency exit sign hanging overhead. I stepped up to the frosted glass door of the office to my left—*her* office. For some undefinable reason, the hair on the back of my neck stood at attention, anticipation and apprehension snaking through me. I shook my head and shoved the feeling aside. I couldn't put a finger on it, but something was bothering me. Probably just the thought of Dr. Carr herself. The woman grated on my nerves something fierce, and every inch of this space reminded me of her.

The healthplex was small and I'd spent the past two days acquainting myself with the layout, searching out each small alcove and closet that could pose a threat. The building housed several private practices, all medical, but vastly different fields. The bottom floor of the building belonged to a group of dermatologists, including two elderly men I was fairly certain should be taking medical advice rather than giving it. A married couple, Dr. Steven Gerber and Dr. Kate Winfield, occupied the second floor with their family medical practice. I had met Dr. Harbaugh on the third floor, a self-absorbed man who considered himself a god of maxillofacial surgery, as well as Dr. Sosa, a neurologist on the fourth floor.

Since Dr. Carr had barred me from her office during business hours, I usually roamed the lower portion of the healthplex and hung out with Benny in the security office until it was time to make my final rounds. I'd walked all four floors this afternoon long after everyone had closed up shop. This time of day was perfect, and I made my way through the building, blending inconspicuously from shadow to shadow. Here in the quiet darkness, I could focus better, play scenarios through my mind and search for any weaknesses in security. The final walk-through brought me to the fifth floor where I stood now in front of her office.

Dr. Victoria Carr, Ph.D. was written across the frosted glass in gilded script, almost indistinguishable now in the near-dark, and I unlocked the door using the key Benny had given me. It swung open without a sound, granting access to her inner sanctum. It amazed me, sometimes, that a woman so cold was in the business of helping people to sort out their emotions and address their vulnerabilities.

I hadn't seen her all day—not that I was watching for her. It was merely an observation. I paused in the doorway, and the memory hit me with startling clarity. Benny had mentioned it this morning in passing, but it hadn't even registered. Dr. Carr's office had been closed today. I wished I'd remembered that sooner so I could've gotten out of here a little earlier. Not like it mattered anyway. The only thing on my agenda for the evening was to head back to my little fixer-upper and chill alone in front of the TV. If I was really motivated, maybe I'd do some work around the house.

I stepped inside, quietly closing the door behind me as I scanned the small space. The lobby was fairly spacious with large, comfortable couches and potted plants that made it feel more like a living room than an office. A couple of abstract paintings hung on the walls and a large window overlooked the city, the lights twinkling in the dark sky.

Directly opposite was a short hallway. One door on the right, two on the left. And one directly at the end of the hall. *Hers*. It was like seeing the light at the end of the tunnel—I didn't want to venture closer, yet I couldn't deny the pull.

The first door on the right led to the receptionist's office and small kitchen area for employees only. As far as I knew, only Dr. Carr and her receptionist, Phyllis, worked here. A gentle jiggle to the handle confirmed that it was locked up tight, everything safe and sound. A restroom and a small closet graced the left side of the hallway and I opened each door, checking to make sure the rooms were empty.

A muffled sound caught my attention and my ears perked up. Keeping my tread silent on the industrial grade carpet, I slowly walked toward Dr. Carr's office. The door stood open, the room lit by the glow of the city lights spilling slim shafts of light onto the floor through the blinds over the windows.

Pausing just outside the office, I pulled my sidearm from the holster at my waist and held it low in front of me. Craning my neck around the doorjamb, I searched the darkened corners of the room, watching for movement, listening for anything out of place. Someone was here—I could feel it. Every instinct on alert, I stepped into the room, simultaneously pushing the door open wide with my left hand.

Gun trained, I swiveled toward the soft sound of protest as the door collided with the tiny form curled up on the floor. Dr. Carr sat huddled in the shadow of the door, dozens of papers and a discarded manila file folder scattered around her feet. Legs drawn tightly to her chest, she lifted her head to regard me and, even in the dim light, I could see the glistening trail of tears running down her cheeks. I held her gaze for a long moment before she pillowed her forehead on her hands where they lay clasped over her knees.

Son of a bitch. Her tears filled me with a combination of fury and protectiveness. Fury at whoever had caused them and the protective instinct to want to swoop in and make things better. Staring down at the prickly doctor, I debated what to do. Maybe I should just turn around and leave. What were the odds she'd accept my offer to help anyway? After all, she'd made it abundantly clear that she didn't like me. The feeling was mutual.

But shit, I couldn't just leave her like this. After seeing her initial aloofness on the news after the murder, then being carved up by her scathing tongue at our disastrous first meeting, I hadn't expected this from her. Her posture spoke of helplessness and fragility like she bore the weight of the world on her shoulders. No one deserved that.

Slipping my pistol into its holster, I took a step closer and squatted next to her. "Ma'am?"

A tiny hand shot out and shoved my shoulder. "Stop that! I hate being called ma'am."

She didn't even bother to glance up, but I smirked nonetheless. "Just a sign of respect, *ma'am*."

This time, her head jerked up, her moist eyes filled with fire as she glared at me. "We both know you're full of shit. You don't even like me. What do you want?"

"Just making sure you're okay."

She studied me, her expression unreadable. "Why?"

I raised my eyebrows at the ridiculous question. "You're the doctor, you tell me."

"Nothing you need to worry about."

Her voice was clipped, and it set my teeth on edge. I was half a second from wishing her luck when I forced myself to take a deep breath. I knew I was going to regret this, but... "I'm actually not a bad listener," I said. "You know, if you want to talk about it."

Her icy eyes stared into mine and for a second, I forgot to breathe. A million emotions lurked in the granite depths, tugging at my soul. I could practically see the chasm widen as her fiery façade cracked, her anger at me forgotten. Fresh tears filled her eyes and her head drooped, her words broken as she spoke. "She's... gone."

Goddamn it. Her face automatically burrowed into the crook of my neck as I scooped her into my arms and sank into the corner of the couch. Threading one hand into her hair, I wrapped the other around her waist and pulled her close. It was impossible not to notice the way her body curled into mine where she was settled in my lap. Victoria's hourglass figure was infinitely more appealing than the stick-thin women who'd routinely hung out in the bars off base in hopes of catching a Marine for the night. Her soft curves were a perfect contrast to my much harder, more muscular body. Her bottom pressed into my groin and I shifted her slightly, my forearm brushing her breast as she cuddled closer.

She felt delectable, and I wanted to run my hands over her, explore the sinful body she kept hidden under those shapeless suits. But that wasn't what she needed right now. Instead, I curled my arms protectively around her and pressed the gentlest of kisses to her temple. A soft, heady fragrance wafted up to my nostrils, reminding me of vanilla frosting. Unable to resist, I brushed my nose over her hair, breathing in the intoxicating scent.

We remained that way for several minutes, until her tears slowed. I coasted one hand down her spine. "You okay, Doc?"

Her head bobbed against my throat and a small hand extricated itself from where she'd tucked it between us, palm up. "Tissue?"

I glanced toward the small box on the corner of her desk. "Too far away, sweetheart. I can't reach them without getting up."

She leaned away from me slightly and nodded, using the pads of her fingers to dab away the stray tears clinging to her cheeks.

I lifted my shirt away from my chest. "Use my shirt, I don't mind."

Victoria huffed a mirthless laugh. "I wouldn't do that."

"Really," I said dryly, "I insist. Not like it could get much worse."

Confusion lit her face for a moment as her gaze met mine then dropped to my shirt. Her brows furrowed and she blinked several times. "Is that... purple?"

I snorted. "Company called it Royal Blue. Fucking heinous, is what it is."

"It's just... so... purple." A strangled sound escaped her

throat, and Victoria covered her mouth with her hands, eyes dancing with mirth.

I'd never heard her laugh before, and the sweet, breathy sound sent a strange sensation swirling through my chest. Her laughter was infectious, and I couldn't help but smile too. "Yeah, yeah. Laugh it up, sweetheart."

Giggles finally under control, she pressed one hand to my chest. "I'm sorry. I don't mean to laugh at you, but... purple is just *so* not your color. You're too..." Her eyes flicked to mine then dropped again as her voice trailed off.

"I'm too... what?" How did she see me?

Her fingers played with a button at the top of my shirt and she bit her lip before speaking. "Masculine."

I lifted a brow. "Better than the alternative, I suppose."

She cracked a tiny smile at my joke, but it slid from her face a second later, replaced with unease once more. I hated that look. I opened my mouth to say something—anything— then snapped it shut again. She didn't like me. And I didn't like her. But damn, she was beautiful.

Several long, dark tresses had come loose from her typically severe chignon, softening her features. One tendril curled down around her shoulder, dangling temptingly in front of me like forbidden fruit. Almost before I could stop myself, I reached out and fingered the silky strands. Victoria sucked in a sharp breath, and I froze. What the hell was I doing? Tucking the lock of hair behind her ear, I dropped my hand and clenched it into a tight fist.

Swallowing hard, I willed my arousal away. I couldn't believe I was getting so turned on by a woman who, just a few days ago, had ripped me a new one with her Queen Bitch act. Not only that, I couldn't afford to muddy the waters. This first new contract was a huge deal to QSG, and Con would murder me if I made a mess of things before we even got off the ground. I needed to get my shit together, get my mind off the woman in my lap.

Still, I couldn't leave her all alone. She was obviously broken up over something, some*one*, but she seemed the type to keep her emotions well-hidden. Otherwise, why would she be crying all alone on the floor of her office at nine o'clock at night?

"My offer still stands." She threw a curious look my way, and I lightly squeezed her waist. "If you want to talk, I'm all ears."

Victoria's mouth turned down in a sad frown, her chest deflating and shoulders curling inward in defeat. "One of my patients. I couldn't... it wasn't enough." A tear slipped from the corner of her eye and rolled down her cheek. "She just... gave up."

A second tear joined the first and I brushed them away as she continued. "I keep replaying our last conversation over and over in my head. Why didn't I see it coming? Did I say something that caused her to...?"

"Absolutely not." My voice was harsher than I'd intended, and she jumped a little. I skimmed my hand up her back in a soothing motion. "It's hard to understand a person's choices. It's like the old adage about walking a mile in someone else's shoes. You may never know what happened. Some people can't see the light at the end of the tunnel. Giving up is so much easier than fighting. Trust me, Doc, I've seen it first-hand."

She nodded and swallowed hard. Clearly the woman's death had affected Victoria deeply. It was clear now why she was always so restrained. If she allowed her emotions free rein, they would slowly destroy her. Instead, she kept them under lock and key, refusing to acknowledge them.

I studied her. We'd gotten off on the wrong foot, but now that I'd seen the woman underneath the icy façade, I wanted to get to know her better, peel back the layers and find who she really was.

"How many of them just... give up?"

Sadness seeped into her beautiful features. "It doesn't happen often, thank God. But... you spend all this time getting to know someone and they become important to you, you know? It's like losing a friend, except worse. Rachel depended on me to help her and… I let her down."

Fresh tears sprang to her eyes, and I mentally swore as I framed her face with one hand. "I'm sorry you're hurting, Doc. It's never easy to lose someone."

I brushed my thumb lightly over her cheek, unable to break the connection between us just yet. My gaze dropped to her lips, and I curled my fingers into the soft flesh of her waist. Her lips parted slightly as she closed the distance between us, and my heart sped up. God, I wanted to kiss her. I dipped my head, lips mere millimeters from hers—

Shocked by what I was about to do, I jerked back.

Her wide, horrified eyes met mine and she reared back as if I'd slapped her. "Oh, God! I'm so sorry, I shouldn't have—I didn't mean—"

"Doc—"

I reached for her but she pushed off the couch and staggered awkwardly to her feet. "Just pretend that didn't happen. It's been a bad day—well, a bad couple of weeks, really, and—"

"Victoria." I followed and settled my hands on her hips, drawing her to a halt and cutting off her nervous rambling. It was the first time I'd called her by name, but it sounded so good, so right. Her gaze remained glued to the floor, and I could practically feel the heat of embarrassment radiating from her body. "Look at me."

Reluctantly, her eyes slowly traveled up the length of my body until they met mine.

"You didn't do anything wrong." Her teeth cut self-consciously into her lower lip, and I pressed my fingertips into her lower back, gently easing her forward. "Come here."

Her feet shuffled forward until she was only inches from me, and I cupped her face in my hands. "I want you, Doc, there's no denying that. There's nothing I'd like more than to lay you down and take this sweet, sexy body of yours… But I can't." Her cheeks flamed, and her gaze slid toward her toes. Using my thumb, I gently pressed upward on the underside of her jaw, bringing her focus back to me. I wanted to make sure she understood; I wanted her to hear every single word I said.

"I won't do that while you're upset. You're hurting right now, and I don't want to be another regret tomorrow morning."

I stroked my thumb over the apple of her cheek. "Let me take you home. I'll walk you to your door like a gentleman and leave you my number. If you're still interested tomorrow, you can give me a call. Deal?"

She gave the barest of nods and moved to stand beside her desk. I regarded her for a moment before striding toward the door. I could feel her gaze on my back as I bent to pick up the discarded files.

"Oh!" She let out a soft exclamation, then rushed over to collect the forgotten papers. "You don't have to do that."

I studied her, my gaze traveling from the tips of her toes all the way up to her beautiful eyes. The mixed expression of mortification and discomfort clouding her face was too much. I cupped her chin, forcing her to make eye contact. Uncertainty swirled in the stormy gray depths and she shifted anxiously from foot to foot.

"Do I make you nervous, Doc?"

Her teeth caught her bottom lip, and I felt her swallow hard. "Yes."

I slid my free hand over the curve of her hip then around to her lower back. My fingers burned where they rested just above her bottom, and images of all the dirty things I wanted to do to her flickered in my brain.

Before I could speak, she continued. "I just... I don't understand. Why are you here?"

"I was making rounds when I heard you."

She let out an exasperated huff. "I know that. I just meant, you know, why are you *here*?" She gestured between us, her voice wavering with apprehension.

I couldn't do anything except answer honestly. "I saw you there and I knew I couldn't just leave you like that."

Victoria pulled away and wrapped her arms around midsection, steel infusing her voice. "I don't want your pity, Mr. Lawson."

"Doc, pity is the absolute last thing you'd get from me."

She studied me for a moment before nodding. "Well then, I suppose I should thank you. If you'll excuse me, I need to head home now. I have an early day tomorrow."

It was a lie. She was in here every morning at 9:00 sharp, with her first appointment usually beginning at 10. But she needed time and space to process everything—and so did I. Wordlessly, I held out the stack of files, and her gaze flicked to mine before she pulled them from my grasp. Turning away, she stowed them in the filing cabinet, collected her purse from the bottom of her desk, and checked each drawer to make sure that everything was locked up tight. She glanced back at me, her mask of indifference firmly back in place.

Damn it. "Would you like me to follow you home?"

She straightened her dress and swept her hair back into a semblance of order before speaking. "No, thank you. I'll be fine."

I nodded. "See you tomorrow."

Fuck. I couldn't let her leave like this. If she walked out the door now, I knew I'd never see her again. This one shared moment wasn't enough—I wanted more. I refused to allow her to go back to haunting me like a specter, elusive and unobtainable. I watched her stride determinedly toward the door before speaking again.

"What about my thank you?"

Confusion clouded her steely eyes. "I did thank you."

"No." I shook my head. "You said, 'I suppose I should thank you,' but you haven't."

"Oh. Well. Thank you." She cleared her throat uncomfortably as I took a step toward her.

"Come on, Doc, I think you can do better than that." I kept my gait slow and measured as I closed the distance between us.

"I... What are you doing?"

I was in front of her now, staring into those magnetic gray eyes. "I want a proper thank you."

My hands went automatically to her hips, my fingers sliding over the curve of her ass as I pulled her toward me. She came willingly, albeit dazedly, as if she'd never experienced the intimacy of a man's touch. A feeling of possessiveness washed over me at the thought. One hand cupped her bottom as I pulled her flush against me, while the other coasted up her body to cradle her jaw. Releasing her eyes, my gaze dropped to her lips and I bowed my head, catching her mouth with mine. I kissed her gently at first, experimentally, waiting for her to pull away.

She didn't. My heartbeat kicked up when, instead, her arms came to rest on my shoulders, her fingers sliding around my neck, lightly brushing the hairs at the base of my skull. She tugged me closer and I happily obliged, deepening the kiss. Her lips parted, allowing me to taste her, to take the lead. She seemed unsure of how to react to my attention and I almost smiled. Certainly she'd been kissed before but if she felt at all the way I did, then I could understand her delirium. She literally took my breath away. The fusion of our lips was intoxicating, and I allowed the burning passion to take over, turning me mindless with pleasure as she melted into me.

Sweeping my tongue across hers, I buried one hand in her hair, cradling her head. Kissing for me had always been a necessary evil, a form of foreplay before sex. But this kiss, with this woman... I couldn't get enough. Every touch of her lips swept me further from reality to a place where only Victoria and I existed. I tore my mouth away and trailed kisses over her cheek and down the line of her jaw. Nipping her bottom lip, I flicked my tongue soothingly over the plump, swollen flesh.

My senses gradually returned as I drank in her beautiful features. Her eyes were closed and her lips were parted slightly, damp and shiny from our kisses. I could pick her up right now, carry her to the couch and make love to her, but that wasn't what I wanted. Our first time needed to be in a bed, somewhere I could spend an obscene amount of time worshipping her.

I slowly eased her away, and Victoria blinked sensually at me, the gray depths still glimmering with lust. I knew it would only be another moment or two before reality intruded and she'd pull away. Dropping a kiss on her forehead, I skimmed my hands over the expanse of her back.

"That was one hell of a thank you, Doc. I hope you'll still feel indebted to me tomorrow because, to be entirely honest, I'm really looking forward to doing it again."

Victoria's cheeks flamed red even in the dim light, and I couldn't help but smile. Her hands slipped down my arms then dropped to her sides as she took the tiniest step backward. "I... I should get going."

I watched her for a moment. "Want me to walk you out?"

Her head shook briskly, causing more tendrils of hair to fall loose around her shoulders.

With a gentle brush of my fingertips over her cheek, I tucked the strand behind her ear. "All right. Be careful."

She nodded but refused to meet my eyes as she shifted her purse back into place. "I will."

"Night, Doc."

My gaze was drawn to the hypnotic sway of her hips as she hurried from the room, and a grin broke over my face. The shy little doctor was so much more than I could've ever imagined. The icy façade hid a fiery, passionate woman, and I couldn't wait to see what else lay beneath the surface.

CHAPTER ELEVEN

Victoria

I strode into the welcome air conditioning of the bistro, my gaze sweeping over the small room. Kate sat tucked away in a corner booth, bright afternoon sunlight spilling over the table, glinting off her auburn hair. Feeling my eyes on her, Kate looked up and waved. Her infectious smile was impossible not to return, and I felt an answering grin tugging at my mouth as I wound my way through the tables.

She pulled me into a hug as I approached. "Hey, I'm glad you could make it."

I squeezed her back, then slid into the booth across from her. "Me, too. It's been a little crazy recently."

Her expression turned serious. "So I heard. What happened?"

I relayed the details of the past couple of weeks until the waiter stopped by to take our orders. The bistro was a regular lunch spot for us, and he took our orders with a knowing smile before heading back to the kitchen.

"Anyway." I turned my attention back to Kate. "Johnathan brought up a good point. He suggested it might be a good idea to have some extra security at the healthplex until we figure out what's going on. He even suggested I start dating again."

"And, of course, Johnathan thought it should be him,"

she interjected with a roll of her eyes.

"He just wants me to be safe."

Kate snorted. "Please."

"He's... protective," I hedged.

"Jealous." She raised an eyebrow, and I sighed.

"He asked me again about joining his practice."

Her eyes widened. "Please tell me you said no!"

"I told him I'd think about it."

"Vic..."

I held up a palm.

"I know what you're going to say. I have no intention of joining with Johnathan, either in my professional life or personal. But it shut him up for a while."

She studied me for a moment before heaving a sigh. "Look, Johnathan seems nice enough, but he's obviously infatuated with you. He follows you around like a puppy yearning for your approval."

Johnathan was always inviting me to dinner, to the opera or a new art exhibit. Which wasn't a bad thing—if he could accept the fact that we'd only ever be friends. I was pretty certain, though, that he would be harder to dissuade than most. It bothered me sometimes that he thought he knew what was best for me. He was a nice person, and he was a great doctor, but I felt no intimate attraction to him.

"Why don't you just tell him how you really feel and put the guy out of his misery?" Kate asked. "Otherwise, he's going to keep hoping that one day you'll give in and finally go out with him."

And therein lay the crux of the problem. "I've tried to tell him. Or, at least, I've dropped subtle hints about not dating friends and coworkers."

"Men don't do subtle. You'll have to just come right out and say it. Or better yet"—Kate raised her water glass in a kind of mock salute—"start dating someone else."

I picked up my own glass of sweet tea and drew little designs in the condensation coating the glass. My fidgeting drew her attention, and her eyes narrowed.

"Okay, spill. Something's going on, I can tell."

I'd known Kate since our sophomore year of college, and she knew every detail of my sordid past. She understood my outlook on love and relationships, but she still encouraged me to get out and meet people. Aside from my two semi-serious relationships in college, I'd only been on a handful of dates since opening my practice. The dates had felt stilted and awkward, and after the third dinner spent mostly in silence, I'd begun to think I'd never feel truly comfortable with a man. Until Blake.

"So, you know the new security guard that Benny called in?"

"Oh, yes. That man is gorgeous." Her eyes widened as she glanced across the table at me. "Oh, my God! You like him, don't you?"

I opened my mouth just as the waiter stopped by the table to deliver our food. After he left, I speared a piece of lettuce and lifted it to my mouth. "Well, do you remember me telling you about Rachel?"

Her eyes filled with sympathy. "Yes, I'm so sorry about that. How are you doing, by the way?"

I shrugged. "Better. I'm still disappointed, in both her and myself, but I'm coming to terms with it. I can't help everyone, but I can try to learn from my mistakes. Hopefully, I can better help the next person."

"Good for you. I'm glad you understand it wasn't your fault."

I swallowed a bite of salad before clearing my throat. "Anyway, after her service I went back to my office. I was upset and Blake—the security guard—found me. We talked for a few minutes and..." Heat flooded my cheeks at the memory of his hands roaming my back, his lips on mine. "We kind of... kissed."

A huge grin spread over Kate's mouth. "Really? It's been a long time since you've been interested in a guy."

"He asked me out."

"And?" She stared at me. "What did you say?"

"Well…" I glanced out the window and watched a bird flit from bush to bush in search of food. I finally turned back to her. "I've kind of been avoiding him."

Kate studied me. "I know it's hard for you to trust guys. I'd probably feel the same way if I were you. But that was a long time ago. Maybe it's time to move on. If you really like this guy—Blake—why not go for it?"

It was the same advice Johnathan had given me. Except Johnathan obviously thought he should be the logical choice, not someone else. Blake made me feel things. What, exactly, I wasn't sure… But I wanted to find out.

He'd been a complete gentleman and, though I'd felt his eyes following me around the healthplex over the last few days, he hadn't pushed me. I caught glimpses of him from time to time as he patrolled the building, but I hadn't worked up the nerve to talk to him again.

"I don't know. I'm not sure it's a good idea."

The morning following our encounter, I found a note on my desk. A phone number had been scribbled along the bottom under the words "Debt Collector." It had made me smile, and I'd tucked it in the top drawer of my desk, only to pull it out several times this week.

I wished I had the confidence to do as Kate said and take what I wanted. I'd hidden a part of myself away for so long I wasn't sure I even knew how to be a desirable, attractive woman. I knew the relaxed, dark suits didn't look good, but they were comfortable. And safe. They provided a layer of protection against men who only wanted sex. Most couldn't see beyond the baggy fabric to the person underneath. Except… Blake had. He'd been the first man to look at me—to really *see* me—in a long time.

"I've been thinking I might go shopping," I said slowly. "Maybe get some new clothes."

Kate was silent for a moment as she regarded me. "For you? Or for him?"

My spine tightened defensively. "I'm doing this for me."

"I understand." She nodded. "I think that dressing in

something more... flattering... will really help to boost your confidence."

I tried to push down the sting of hurt her comment had inflicted. "I know."

"You know I mean that in the best way possible," she added softly. "It's been almost ten years. Maybe it's time to stop hiding."

It was true; I had been hiding. I'd closed myself off for so long that I'd forgotten who I really was. I wanted Blake to be attracted to me. I wanted him to desire me. But I was tired of being restrained, defined by my past. The idea of moving on, putting it all behind me, was scary and exciting all at the same time. Years ago I'd been confident and happy. And I desperately wanted to be that person again.

*

"Are you sure this isn't too tight?"

"Are you kidding me?" Kate circled me. "Women would kill for a body like yours. If I had half the curves you do, maybe my husband wouldn't have cheated on me with that little blonde bimbo."

I turned to her, sympathy swelling up and making my chest feel tight. "I'm so sorry."

"Why?" She shrugged. "It's really a blessing in disguise. I was young and dumb and getting married was a mistake. It took me a while to realize it, but we're both better off."

"Is he being a jerk about it?"

"A little bit, but my lawyer is a total shark and the proceedings are going really well. We've determined that Steve's going to buy out my half of the house and I get to keep Peanut," she said of her tiny Bichon Frise. "We're still negotiating what to do with the practice. I've worked too hard to get where I am today to let him take that away, too."

"Is it uncomfortable working together?"

"Not really." She shook her head. "We've scheduled our appointments so we work opposite days. That way we don't have to run into each other."

"So there's no chance of reconciliation?" Kate and Steve had been together for years, since undergrad. I couldn't imagine just walking away from someone I'd once loved.

She shook her head. "We both know where we stand. Of course, it helps that the bimbo is knocked up."

I whipped toward her. "You never told me that!"

Kate lifted one shoulder. "I just found out about it myself. He's planning to marry her as soon as the divorce is finalized."

She hid the hurt well, but I could see the pain in the depths of her clear blue eyes. It was obvious that Steve's infidelity had done a number on her. I prayed she never had to go through that.

With that thought in mind, I turned back toward the mirror in the dressing room. Was this whole endeavor even worth it? Was dating worth all the effort if I might one day end up like Kate and Steve?

Kate met my gaze in the mirror and shot me a reassuring smile. "Thank God we're older and smarter now. You won't make the same mistake I did."

I forced a tight smile as I examined my reflection. The beige pencil skirt clung to my curves and ended just above my knees, and the white blouse accentuated my waist while still looking professional.

"Trust me, this is perfect," she continued. "We need to get you out of drab, dark colors. You need something neutral to show off your natural beauty."

I rolled my eyes. "What natural beauty?"

Kate lightly smacked my arm and I let out a little sound of protest as she jerked my shoulders back. "Hey!"

"Look in the mirror," she ordered, ignoring me. Reluctantly, I did as I was told. "Your hair is gorgeous. It's never been dyed, and it contrasts beautifully with the cream top. The gray of your eyes really pops when you're not in all black."

She stepped in front of me. "We're not here to change who you are, only to enhance what you've been hiding for years. You have amazing features, Vic. You just need to believe it."

I glanced in the mirror again. "You really think so?"

"Oh, honey." Her eyes softened. "I wish you could see yourself the way the rest of us do."

I bit my lip as I studied the reflection in front of me. It was so easy to pick apart my own features, to see only the bad instead of the good. Now that she mentioned it, my eyes did seem brighter, and my hair looked glossier and more radiant. I nodded a little, and made a silent promise to myself. From now on, I would focus only on the positive things.

The next three hours were a whirlwind of activity as we picked out several dozen outfits and pairs of shoes. A trip to the beauty store yielded a mass number of cosmetics that I wasn't sure I'd ever master. I'd played with eyeshadows and lipsticks as a teen, but over the last decade I'd forgone most beauty products in lieu of keeping my face natural. I didn't see the point in getting all dolled up for no one.

I stared at the mirror, examining the flawless finish the makeup artist had wrought. My skin glowed, and my cheeks looked flushed with the barest hint of pink. The trace of eyeliner blended with the shimmering neutral shadow on my eyelids, giving them a sultry look. I felt like a new and improved version of myself. The thought of Blake seeing me like this made my heart race.

"You look beautiful."

"Thanks." I blushed at the compliment as Kate looked me over. "I love it."

A grin spread over her face. "And so will he." She glanced at her watch. "I've got to get home and let Peanut out. Would you mind if I took off?"

I glanced at the bags surrounding my feet with a smile. "I think I have plenty to do this evening."

"Are you sure you don't mind?"

I waved her off. "No, really. I'll be fine. I might go back to the department store anyway. I think I changed my mind about those shoes."

I had no idea where I'd ever wear them, but I hadn't worn high heels in years. Maybe I'd get dressed up just for myself and head to the art gallery for something to do, try out my new look.

Kate lifted her brows appraisingly. "It's always good to have a pair of fuck-me heels when you need them."

I shook my head with a smile. Not that I was considering using them in that manner. Maybe. "You're a bad influence."

"You like it."

With one last hug, Kate took off and I gathered my bags. I walked sedately through the mall, window shopping as I went. Pausing in front of Victoria's Secret, I checked out the mannequin on display in the front of the shop. Lingerie was one thing I didn't need. I'd always been a fan of pretty underwear, and they made me feel sexy, even if no one else ever got to see them. They were my one indulgence, but today I was on a different mission. I turned away and strode to the back of the department store and picked up the shoes. I'd tried them on earlier for Kate, deliberating over them for almost twenty minutes before putting them back on the shelf. I'd never spent this much on shoes in my life, but it felt good to spoil myself after so many years of hiding behind layers of functional but decidedly unflattering suits and loafers.

Carrying the box to the counter, I went over the mental checklist Kate and I had mapped out. Clothes, shoes, makeup. I'd made an appointment tomorrow at a local salon to spruce up my haircut. After paying for the shoes and thanking the cashier, I gathered my things and awkwardly turned around, bumping into the man behind me in the process.

"Oh, excuse me. I'm sorry." My gaze flicked up to the man's face and widened in surprise as his own eyes shone with appreciation.

"Victoria. Wow, I didn't recognize you."

Greg Andrews's gaze slid slowly down my body before returning to my face. I barely repressed a shiver of revulsion. "Hello, Mr. Andrews."

"You can call me Greg." One corner of his mouth lifted,

and I smiled politely but didn't correct myself.

"How have you been?"

"Better now." His eyes roved over me again. "Can't say I've ever seen this side of you before. I like it."

I pressed my lips into a firm line at his errant compliment. "Have you had a chance to speak with Dr. Martin yet?"

Irritation flashed across his face but he quickly suppressed it. "I called you last week, you know. The receptionist wouldn't put me through, but I wanted to apologize. I can be a bit hot-headed at times and I overreacted. I'd like to come back next week if you have an opening."

"Well, thank you for the apology. I appreciate it. Unfortunately, I'm not accepting more patients at the moment," I lied.

His face darkened. "Well, from what I heard, you just lost a patient. Doesn't that open up a slot?"

I stiffened and swallowed down the tears burning the back of my throat. How could the man be so callous and unfeeling? "No. Thank you for your interest, though. I'll forward your information to Dr. Martin and have him contact you."

His hand shot out and grasped my elbow as I turned to leave. "I'm asking nicely, Victoria."

Fear snaked down my spine, but I fought it off. I would not let him rattle me. I threw a pointed glance to where his hand was still curled around my arm. "Is that what you're doing? Please let go."

He released me but the fire in his eyes didn't diminish. "I want to come back."

"I'm afraid that can't happen. Please excuse me." With a polite nod, I turned to leave.

"See you soon, Victoria." His tone was cold, and his words sent ice sliding through my veins. Refusing to acknowledge him, I hurried from the store casting surreptitious glances over my shoulder occasionally to make sure he wasn't following.

The words were too similar to the ones I'd heard just a

week and a half ago, and they still had the power to shake me to the core. Rushing to my car, I tossed the bags in the back then climbed inside and locked the doors behind me. Only several miles down the road was I finally able to take a deep breath. I stretched my fingers before clenching them around the steering wheel again and tried to shrug the tension from my shoulders.

I glanced in the rearview mirror as I turned into my allotment, watching for anything out of the ordinary. Seeing nothing out of place, I let out a shaky sigh. When would I stop looking for threats? Maybe the better question was, would I ever feel safe again?

CHAPTER TWELVE

Blake

I was halfway to the security office when the front door swung inward with a soft *whoosh*. I shot an obligatory glance over my shoulder and immediately did a double take, blinking several times to make sure my eyes weren't deceiving me. As if it had a mind of its own, my body slowly turned toward Victoria. The sight of her knocked the breath from my chest as she swaggered forward, hips rolling sensually with every step.

Holy shit. I had to be hallucinating. This wasn't the Victoria I knew. Her three-inch heels tap-tap-tapped across the floor, increasing my heart rate with every staccato beat. Long, dark tresses hung freely around her shoulders with a slight curl at the ends, bouncing as she walked. The red V-neck blouse showed off the tiniest hint of cleavage and nipped in at her trim waist, and the black skirt she wore hugged every curve, stopping just above her knees. And sweet baby Jesus... those shoes.

I gaped at her, frozen in place, as she closed the distance between us with each step of those fuck-me heels. Her eyes met mine for a brief second before she dropped them to the floor and bit her lip, her expression bashful yet flirtatious. Was she even aware of what she was doing to me? Unable to move, still not quite believing this gorgeous woman in front of me was the same doctor I'd held in my arms last week, I stood rooted in place as she brushed past me and punched the button for the elevator.

What the hell? Following every movement, I watched her step inside before turning toward me with a seductive flip of her hair. The provocative smile she shot my way as the doors closed made me want to lunge after her, pull her into my arms and ravage her mouth, run my hands over every curve exposed by those sexy new clothes.

Who the hell was this woman and what in Christ's name was she doing? Nearly a week ago she'd sat splayed across my lap, meek and insecure. Today, she strode across the room like the world was hers for the taking, along with everyone in it. This woman could bring a man to his knees with a single look—and I'd be the first to fall at her feet.

Since I'd known her, Victoria had covered herself basically from head to toe in shapeless dark suits that did nothing for her. Today's outfit was the polar opposite, flattering and highlighting her best features. What had happened over the weekend to bring about this radical change? Ice streamed through my veins as an unwelcome thought hit me square in the chest. Could she have a date tonight? Something akin to envy washed over me, leaving a bitter taste in my mouth.

She intrigued me, triggered my protective instincts, and although I didn't *know her* know her, my body did. Deep down, my body had recognized hers and the chemistry between us was so thick I could have cut it with a knife. I'd been with a good number of women but none who stirred him down to my very soul as Victoria did. Now that I'd gotten a taste, I wanted more.

Still unsettled, I swiped my key card through the slot on the wall and stepped into the room. Benny called this the security office, but he didn't do much back here except glance occasionally at the screens linked up to the cameras positioned around the building, watching clients come and go. I'd ordered another half-dozen cameras, one to be installed on each floor—except Victoria's—and a couple more at the main points of interest. The wiring and components were all sitting in a box in my office at QSG. Once the cameras arrived, I hoped to get everything hooked up by the end of the week. I wanted to make sure that Victoria was safe, even after I was done here.

"Anything happening today?"

The building manager shook his head. "Nope. How about you?"

I let out a sigh. The job paid well, but I was getting a little burnt out with nothing to do. Not that I should complain. Any day spent watching the sexy doctor come and go was fine in my book, and today was better than the past week. Part of me couldn't help but wonder if her worries were unfounded. Maybe the murder had been a fluke, just a streak of bad luck on her part. There had been no communication since then, and the expense to keep me here would be astronomical by the end of the temporary four-week period that I was scheduled to stay on.

I'd missed a call from Con this morning and I needed to touch base with him. Just a week ago, he'd offered to take over my position here. There was just one little problem with that... She was five-foot-two with pouty lips and long brown hair that I wanted to wrap around my fist while I explored every inch of her petite, curvy body.

I hadn't spoken with him over the last few days, so he knew nothing of my encounter with Victoria last week in her office. There was no way I couldn't see her anymore, especially after today. The only question was, did I stay on as security or let Con take over so I could see her outside of work and not be associated with the bad things that had happened recently? Would it be better to be the lover or the savior?

Maybe I could be both. The last thing I wanted was to not see her at all during the day and miss my opportunity with her. If I picked up another gig that took me away from her, would she forget all about me? No, I couldn't risk that. I'd stay on for now until I got a better feel for things.

Pulling out my phone, I tapped Con's number. After two

rings, the call connected.

"What's up?"

"Not much. Everything's been quiet."

"Glad to hear that," he returned.

I took a deep breath. "Hey, change of plans. I'll stick to the original contract." Benny didn't know anything about my original plan to let Con take over, so I didn't elaborate.

Con's end was silent for a few moments before he spoke. "You sure?"

"Yep."

"Did something happen that I need to be aware of?"

Other than the fact that I'd kissed my client and told her I wanted to fuck her? "Nope."

"Okay." His voice was hesitant, and I could practically hear the wheels spinning, trying to figure out the real story. "Grab a beer later?"

Let him grill me once I'd tossed back a couple too many? No thanks. "Maybe another night. Rain check?"

"Keep your dick in your pants."

"It wasn't..." I stopped before I could incriminate myself further.

"That's what I thought. You sure you don't need me to come in?"

Anger burned in my stomach. "No, I've got it."

"Keep me posted."

The line went dead, and I shoved the phone into my back pocket with a huff of irritation. Motherfucker. I glanced at the computer screen over Benny's shoulder, watching as Dr. Kate Winfield made her way through the doors, her husband on her heels.

Benny made a low sound in his throat. "Think there's trouble there?"

I glanced at the screen where Steve Gerber stood toe-to-toe with his wife in what appeared to be an intensely heated conversation.

"I'll go check it out." It would give me something to do and get Victoria off my mind for a few minutes, at least.

Pushing open the door, I strode into the lobby just in time to see Steve grab Kate roughly by the arm and jerk her toward him. Red flashed across my vision and I was across the room before I realized it. "Hands off!"

Steve immediately released Kate and jumped back at the sound of my voice. His eyes darted wildly in my direction, a mixture of surprise and loathing filling their depths.

Disregarding the asshole for the moment, I turned to Kate. "Is everything okay?"

"I... I'm fine." She smoothed down her blouse and pushed her hair behind her ears. "But he has to go."

"I'm not going anywhere." Steve grabbed at Kate again and I planted a hand firmly against his solar plexus, shoving him backward.

Steve coughed roughly from the contact, and I pointed at him. "Touch her again and I'll lay your ass out. Understand?"

"Who the hell do you think you are?"

"Security. I'm here to make sure our staff and clients are safe." The man's eyes glimmered with hate but he gave a jerky nod, and I stared him down for a moment before glancing back at Kate. "What's going on here?"

"He's not supposed to be here. We're going through a divorce right now and today is my day for appointments, but—"

"Until the paperwork is finalized, I can go wherever the hell I want, whenever I want," Steve bit out. I shot a warning look his way, and Steve fell back a step with a glare at his soon-to-be ex-wife.

"Anyway," Kate continued, "he was waiting outside and followed me in to harass me about the proceedings. You need to leave," she directed at her husband.

"Not until we talk."

Kate threw her hands in the air. "We have nothing to talk about. You cheated on me with your new girlfriend and knocked her up. Go to hell, Steve, and take the bimbo with you."

"Don't be a bitch," Steve shot back. "You're just pissed

that she's younger and more beautiful than you."

Uncomfortable at witnessing the details of what was obviously a very messy divorce, I intervened. "Dr. Gerber, I think it would be best if you leave. If you put your hands on your wife again, I'll have you arrested for assault."

"But—"

"It wasn't an option. You're leaving."

He threw one more angry glare his wife's way. "This isn't over." He pushed the door open angrily and stormed outside.

I turned back to Kate. "You okay?"

She nodded, but her hands shook. "I'll be fine. Thank you."

"If something like this is happening, we should be aware of it so we can put precautions in place."

Kate dropped her chin. "I know, I'm sorry. Things were going okay for a while, but... Ugh, I can't wait until this is over."

I nodded. "I understand. This is a public space, so I can't stop him from entering without a restraining order, but I can keep him away from you if that's what needs to happen."

"Please. I just... He's not dangerous, he's just an idiot. I don't want to deal with him at work, too."

"Has he been bothering you at home?"

She shrugged. "Just little stuff. He's been calling a lot, showed up a couple times."

"Listen." I pulled a card from my pocket and handed it to her. "If you think you need someone to watch over your place for a few days, deter him, let me know. I'll recommend one of my buddies. They'll take care of him."

A smile curved her face as she slipped the card into her purse and adjusted the strap over her shoulder. "Thanks. I'll keep your offer in mind."

I studied her for another moment. "You sure you're okay?"

"Yes. Thank you again." She took a few steps away before turning back. "Victoria was right. You're a good man, Mr. Lawson."

Momentarily taken aback, I froze, unable to respond. Finally, I managed a little nod. "Thank you, Dr. Winfield."

She strode away, leaving me to ponder her words. Victoria had been talking about me? That was a good sign, right? Hell yeah, it was. A slow smile spread across my face. It was time to make some rounds, see if I could catch a glimpse of my pretty little doctor.

CHAPTER THIRTEEN

Blake

I unlocked the door and stepped into the brightly lit interior of the newly remodeled office. The smell of fresh paint and carpet wafted up to me and I inhaled deeply. This place was lightyears away from what it'd looked like barely a month ago.

I shot a glance toward the reception desk to my right. A desktop computer sat on the Formica countertop, waiting to be hooked up, along with an array of wires and miscellaneous office supplies.

Con strode around the corner, his steps slowing as his eyes fell on me. "I thought I heard the door. Come on back."

"Place looks great, it's really coming along."

Con nodded as he headed down the hallway toward his office. "Still have to bring in all the furniture and get everything hooked up, but we should be up and running in another two weeks or so."

He strode into his office and gestured at me to follow. "Abby will be here next week, and two of the guys just flew in a couple days ago."

I nodded absently and dropped into a seat. "How'd the meetings go?"

"Not bad. I was able to get our name out there, make a few contacts, so hopefully we'll get some business here soon.

In fact"—Con swiped a piece of paper off his desk—"I may have a new job for you if you've changed your mind about working at the healthplex."

I tipped my chin. "What's that?"

"Some local up-and-coming pop star needs security for an event—"

"Hard pass."

Con stared at me. "Do you have something else lined up?"

"I've only got a couple weeks left with Victoria. I'll just stay on."

One dark brow lifted. "Victoria?"

"Dr. Carr," I amended.

"*Victoria.*" The way Con said her name raised my hackles. "The same woman you couldn't stand a week ago."

Shoving down the irrational anger, I tried to roll the tension from my shoulders. "She's not that bad."

"Apparently."

His sarcasm was not lost on me. "I made a promise and I'll stick it out."

"I have no doubts about that," he muttered before turning away and striding behind his desk. He sank into the chair and pinned me with a look. "You're like a brother to me."

"I—"

"Which means I will fucking kill you if you shit where you eat."

I rolled my eyes. "Don't be dramatic."

"Don't be stupid," Con shot back. "If you want to fuck her, by all means, do it. Just wait 'til the contract is up. But for God's sake, don't ruin a good thing for a piece of ass."

Anger surged through me. "Watch your fucking mouth."

"Is that how it's going to be?"

My body literally quivered under the force of the fury rippling through my veins, and I crossed my arms over my chest in an effort to contain it. "I don't know what you're talking about."

Con stared at me. "You want her."

I couldn't deny that. But I was a man of my word. I would stay on until I was done and keep my hands off... even if it physically hurt to even consider it. "I told you I won't touch her."

"Do you really think some piece of tail is worth—?"

"Enough."

His mouth lifted in a smirk and too late, I realized the comment for what it was. He let out a sigh. "Look. I trust you, I just don't trust her."

I opened my mouth to protest, but Con cut me off. "It's not her personally, I just don't trust anyone. I don't want to end up with our asses in the wringer before we even get off the ground."

I understood that, even though I disagreed with his assessment of her. "I know. She's not like that, though. She's... I don't know."

"You like her."

It was more statement than a question, and I shrugged. I didn't honestly know what I felt for her. Lust, definitely. There was something else, though, too. She intrigued me. "Like you said—she's off limits so I'll keep my distance from now on."

I knew it was the right thing to do, but it was going to be hard as hell. She was like an addiction I couldn't kick. It had started last week in her office. She'd felt so fucking good in my arms, had opened up so much in that half hour we'd spent together in the dark, just the two of us. It was like we'd ripped away the barrier separating us.

And now, with her new clothes and come-hither attitude... Damn. I initially thought she might have a date last night, and I was loath to admit the little surge of jealousy I'd felt. But then she'd shown up this morning in an equally sexy new outfit and thrown a coy glance my way. If she was trying to get my attention, then she definitely had it.

Something must have shown on my face because Con's eyes narrowed. "Something happen that I need to be aware of?"

I wiped my expression clean. "Nope."

"Bullshit."

"Fuck off, Con."

"Goddamn it. I knew I should've taken over when you first came to me. Did you pull a disappearing act like usual?"

The anger was back, simmering just below the surface. I curled my hands into fists by my side. "I didn't sleep with her."

Yet. The unspoken word hung in the air, and Con's eyes narrowed.

"But you plan to." He leaned back in his chair and laced his fingers together over his midsection.

"Is this a fucking interrogation now?" I glared back at him.

"Yes. This is business, not pleasure. All you have to do is keep your dick in your pants for a while."

"Trust me, asshole, you don't have to worry about that."

A slow grin spread over his mouth. "So that's the problem. Wondered why you were so bitchy."

"Fuck off."

"Sounds like that's exactly what you need. Go get some, just not one of our clients."

"I don't want some random piece of ass."

"She's that good?"

"Con..." I swore to God, if he kept this shit up...

He laughed. "Wow. I never thought I'd see the day."

I clenched my molars together, desperately trying to wrangle my patience. "What now?"

"The woman. You like her."

"I already told you—"

"I heard what you said." Con's head tipped to the side, those dark eyes pinning me in place. "But I'm more interested in what you didn't say."

He wasn't wrong. I hadn't even slept with the woman and she already had me tied up in knots. Damn it. The sooner we figured out who'd called her and what the psychopath wanted, the sooner I could deal with this thing between Victoria and me—whatever the hell it was.

"I don't know. Haven't spent enough time with her to know for sure. But she's not just some piece of ass, so don't bring that shit up again."

Con just raised a brow. I rolled my eyes. "I won't jeopardize the business. Promise."

"Okay."

"Okay."

We stared at each other for a long minute before Con pursed his lips. "So... no on the diva, then?"

"That would be a 'hell no.' I'm not going to play babysitter for some bratty little girl."

He made a face. "Well, I'll be damned if I'm going to do it. The other guys better show up by this weekend so I can put one of them on detail."

"It would serve your nosey ass right." I smirked when he made a face. "Did you get those fucking horrible shirts replaced yet?"

"Being stateside has turned you into such a pussy."

Despite his words, he reached below his desk and extract something from a box, then tossed it my way. Holding the shirt up, I inspected the solid black polo with Quentin Security embroidered in white over the chest, the logo on the left sleeve. "At least I won't get laughed at in this one."

Con's dark stare flicked back to me, and I wanted to recall my words. "She's nice," I admitted.

One dark brow lifted. "Nice?"

"Don't make it sound so horrible. She's had a streak of shit luck here recently. I feel bad for her."

"Is that all it is?"

Was that it? I already knew the answer was no. I admired her, wanted to know more about her—what she liked, what made her tick. I'd left my number, but she hadn't called, hadn't said so much as a word to me since that night. Each time I saw her in the lobby, she'd duck her head and practically sprint to the safety of the elevator. But the look she shot me once she was inside... It spoke volumes.

"No."

I couldn't explain it myself, but I knew there was more to her—to us—than just mutual attraction. And I wanted to know just what it was.

CHAPTER FOURTEEN

Victoria

I glanced at my watch and counted down the time until Kate would get there. Not quite half an hour. I dropped into the chair and turned my attention to the unanswered messages cluttering my email. Most of it was junk—marketers trying to sell stuff, updates from various journals and magazines, as well as other non-work-related stuff.

I clicked through them on autopilot, my mind drifting down to the first floor of the building. To *him*. The look he'd thrown my way Monday when I strode across the lobby in my new sexy high heels and red blouse had turned my cheeks almost the same color as my shirt.

He'd watched me like a panther stalking its prey, his assessing eyes canvassing every inch of my body, looking like he wanted to devour me. I grinned. He'd been barely able to restrain himself when I came in this morning, catching himself only after he'd taken several steps toward me. From the hungry look he'd given me, I knew it was driving him crazy. But he'd put the ball in my court, and he was waiting for me to make the first move.

Now that I had his attention, though, I wasn't quite sure what to do. I didn't flirt with men—I didn't know how. I'd continue to put myself out there, tempt him, slowly draw him in and then... then what? Was I ready to take the next step?

I drew in a sharp breath. Yes. It was time to move on. I was done hiding behind flimsy excuses and ugly clothes.

I'd never been the instigator, never played hard to get. The man addled my senses, turned me inside out. All I knew was, I needed more—more of his touch, more of those addictive kisses that rocked me to my core. The memory of his mouth on mine, his hands low on my hips, sent a rush of anticipation curling through me.

"Miss Victoria?"

I jerked my head up, heat blossoming over both cheeks. "Yes?"

Phyllis smiled. "I'm headin' home now, miss. You'll be all right by yourself?"

"Oh. Yes, yes." I waved her off. "Please just lock the outer door when you leave. I'm almost done here anyway."

"All right, dear. You be careful and I'll see you in the mornin'."

"Thank you, Phyllis."

I smiled as the woman departed with a wink, the outer door closing with a snap less than a minute later. Pushing thoughts of Blake from my mind, I cleared up the last few emails and shut down the computer, then checked my phone. Still no Kate. Since the office door was locked now, I'd expected her to call once she got up here, but I figured her last appointment had run late.

Gathering up my things, I made my way out of the office and locked up. My gaze darted between the elevator and the door to the stairwell. I really should take the stairs. The cardio would do me good, but... I glanced down to the three-inch heels adorning my feet and sighed. The elevator it was. I punched the button for the second floor and relaxed against the railing as the car began its descent.

The doors parted with a soft ding and I stepped into the dim lobby on Kate's floor. No one remained in the waiting room and the eerie silence grated on my nerves. Straightening a chair as I passed, I walked toward the door leading to the inner office. A handful of lights were still on, and I glanced through the rectangular window in the door, hoping to catch a glance of a familiar face. I waited a beat, then knocked loudly, hoping to get someone's attention. The door rattled loosely in its frame and I jumped back. Tentatively, I grasped the handle. Under the slight pressure, the door swayed toward me.

That was odd. Just like in my office, the doors were supposed to be locked at all times, for the safety of the staff as well as the patients. Why would Kate leave it unlocked? Maybe she'd guessed I would come down since she was running late. Grasping the door handle, I jiggled lightly but it remained frozen in place, the locking mechanism still engaged. So why had the door opened on its own?

Ice slithered down my spine as I peered at the striker plate on the door, the catch jammed so it wouldn't close properly. I peeked around the door, but the labyrinth of hallways and patient exam rooms remained quiet. Cautiously stepping into the inner office, I closed the door softly and approached the first exam room on silent feet. The light was off but I peeked in, heart racing, half expecting someone to jump out at me.

Seeing nothing out of place, I continued down the hallway toward the back of the building where Kate's office was located. Calming my racing heart, I forced my nerves to quiet and took several deep breaths. The stress of the last few weeks was definitely catching up to me, making me anxious and jittery. I just needed to wind down and relax a bit, and tonight would be the perfect solution. A couple of drinks with Kate would go a long way to relieving my anxiety. We'd both been under a lot of stress lately—me with the murder a couple weeks back followed by Rachel's suicide and Kate with her ongoing divorce. We both deserved tonight. Maybe I'd even drop a hint to Blake on the way out, let him know where we'd be in case he wanted to show up. A little liquid courage never hurt, right?

A soft cry stopped me in my tracks, and my head swiveled left and right, trying to discern where the sound had come from. A combination of fear and trepidation kept me from calling out as I moved quickly but quietly toward Kate's office where the lights blazed brightly. The deep baritone of a man's voice floated toward me, but I couldn't make out the words.

I rested one hand on the doorframe before peering around the corner. A man dressed in all black stood with his back to me, and the metallic object clutched in his left hand glinted under the harsh glare of the fluorescent lights. Kate lay on the ground at his feet, auburn hair fanned around her head, highlighting the gash that split her forehead.

My soft gasp alerted the man to my presence and he spun around. His face was covered by a mask, obscuring his features except for the brown eyes that appeared almost black as he scowled and took a step forward. A scream caught in my throat as I dropped my purse and fled back down the hallway, my only thought of getting away from him and getting help for Kate. I rounded the corner at a dead run and sprinted toward the door. Afraid to slow down, I threw all of my weight against it, and it slammed against the outer wall with a loud bang.

I tossed a quick glance over my shoulder, but the man was nowhere to be seen. Praying he was making his escape and not hurting Kate, I bypassed the elevators and shoved open the door to the stairwell. The high heels slowed me down, and as I rounded the last landing, the heel of my right shoe skidded precariously on the concrete. Desperately trying to regain my balance, I grabbed for the railing as I pitched forward. Propelled by the momentum, I tumbled down the stairs and landed in a heap at the bottom with a miserable groan. My back and bottom ached from where they'd bounced against the sharp angles of the stairs, and my palms and knees were red and skinned from scraping the hard floor. Adrenaline forced me unsteadily to my feet, and I yanked open the door to the lobby.

"Help!" I ran toward the small security office near the reception area, and a tall, broad form filled the space as the door swung open. "Blake! Thank God, we need to hurry!"

He caught me as I flew at him, his hands wrapping around my upper arms, pulling me close as I fisted my hands in his shirt. "What's wrong?"

"She's hurt!" I clutched at him, my breathing erratic, pulse pounding from the adrenaline flowing through my veins. "We need to get help!"

"Talk to me, sweetheart. What happened? Who's hurt?" He eased me away, eyes searching mine.

I curbed the urge to fling myself back into his arms. "Kate. I went to her office to meet her and there was a man standing over her and she was laying on the floor. Her head was bleeding and—"

"What did he look like?"

"I don't know, he had a mask. I..." I winced as I brushed my scraped hands over my blouse and he grabbed my wrists, holding my palms up for examination.

"What the hell happened?"

"I fell down the stairs." At his hard look, I quickly elaborated. "It's nothing. Just a few scrapes. I'll be fine, really. We need to get to Kate."

His eyes quickly swept over me, catching on the reddened flesh of her knees. "Have Benny clean you up and call the police," he ordered. "I'll go check on her."

Blake took three long strides to the security office and yanked open the door. "We need an ambulance—Dr. Winfield has been hurt. I'm going up to check on her and see if I can find anything. Can you clear the building and send them up to the second floor when they get here?"

The smaller man gave a sharp nod and reached for his phone. "On it."

Blake turned to me. "Stay here. I'll be right back."

"I'm coming with you." I started toward the stairs, but he caught my elbow and pulled me back to him.

"Let me make sure it's safe first."

I shook my head. "I need to be there for her, she's my friend."

"Doc—"

"No. I'm coming with you. I need to be there for her if..." *No*. Kate had to be fine—I refused to contemplate the alternative.

Blake let out a heavy sigh. Grabbing my hand, he pulled me toward the stairs as he pulled the pistol from its holster on his hip.

He studied me for a moment. "You sure you want to come?"

I lifted my chin. "Yes. I need to."

He nodded. "All right. Follow my lead."

Pushing me behind him, Blake pulled open the door and peered inside, checking each corner before cautiously entering the stairwell. On quick feet, he made his way up to the second floor. "Stay behind me, back to the wall."

I mirrored his stance and in tandem, we worked our way up to the second floor. Tossing a look over my shoulder, I bumped into Blake as he stopped to survey the floors above him before continuing on.

"See something?" His voice was low as he spoke, and his eyes swept our surroundings before returning to mine.

I shook my head. "No, just... You know."

"Give me your hand." He held out his hand and I slipped my palm into his. He tucked my hand into the belt circling his lower back then reached behind him to pat my hip comfortingly. "Hold on to me."

I clung to the thick leather as we proceeded up the few remaining stairs and Blake paused outside the door of the second floor. He peered through the rectangular window before slowly cracking the door open an inch. I tried to peer around him, but his large frame blocked my view. I clenched the belt tightly, and he shifted a little.

"Easy," he murmured. "I happen to like my equipment right where it is."

I couldn't help but smile at his unexpected humor, and I relaxed my hold a bit. Blake pushed the door open wide enough for us to slip through and he led the way into the lobby of the second floor.

"Where is she?"

"Her office. Are you familiar with this floor?"

He nodded. "All the way in the back to the left?"

"That's it."

He strode toward the reception area, head swiveling left and right, searching for anything out of place. When they reached the door, I laid a hand on his shoulder. "Someone tampered with the lock so it wouldn't close. That's how I got in."

His lips flattened into a straight line and he used his free hand to untuck his shirt. Lifting the hem, he wrapped the fabric around the knob and pulled. The door swung open easily, and Blake shook his head when he saw the jammed mechanism. "Simple but effective. Maybe the police will be able to lift some prints."

"Crap." At his questioning glance, I elaborated, "I touched the handle when I came in."

He shook his head. "Likely won't matter anyway. If he went to this extent to jam it, he probably wore gloves. They can print you just in case to eliminate you, but I can't begin to imagine how many people have touched this knob today alone."

Disgusting. I instinctively wiped my palms on my skirt. Blake kept his back to the wall as he peeked inside and examined the hallway. Everything remained silent and still, and he pulled me inside. Quickly peering into each room we passed, we made our way to Kate's office. I sank to my knees beside her and pressed a hand to her cheek.

"Kate, honey, everything's gonna be okay. Just hang in there. We're going to get you some help." Pressing two fingers to her neck, I searched for a pulse. "Pulse is weak, but it's there."

"We need to get some pressure on that wound, stop the bleeding," Blake commented from above me. "I'll be right back."

He jogged out of the room and returned less than a

minute later, a roll of gauze in hand as well as a large square of tissue-like material. As he passed the thick material to me, I recognized it as a drape sheet to cover patients during an exam.

"Sorry." He threw an apologetic look my way. "It was all I could find. All the cabinets were locked. Use that first—head wounds bleed like a bitch."

I nodded. The gauze would come in handy later, once the flow of blood had slowed enough. I applied the large square to Kate's forehead, pressing gently. The sound of approaching sirens floated up to them, and Blake pulled out his phone as it vibrated its soft rhythm.

"Lawson." He was silent for a beat as he listened to the person on the other end. "Thanks, Benny, I'll intercept them."

Turning to me, he dropped to one knee. "They're on their way up right now, and I have to go meet them at the elevators. Will you be okay here for a minute?"

I bit my lip. The thought of being alone made my heart stutter in my chest.

"I'll stay right in the lobby so I can hear you if you need anything." He reached out and squeezed my shoulder gently. "I promise."

"Okay." The word came out whisper soft and Blake shot me a grim smile.

"She's a fighter. Just keep talking to her."

Standing, he strode from the room, leaving me alone with Kate.

"Who did this to you?" I whispered. "He won't get away with it. Blake and the police will find him."

I realized in that moment just how much I believed him. There was something about Blake that I trusted. He was more than just a marine, more than a security guard. This wasn't just a job to him—he genuinely cared.

A commotion in the hallway drew my attention and I reluctantly scooted away as the paramedics filed into the small office. Blake gestured for me to join him where he stood with two police officers, and I made my way to his side.

"Dr. Carr actually found her. Victoria, can you tell them what you told me?" He watched me intently as I relayed the details.

"He was average height, maybe a little taller than you." I pointed to the older police office before continuing. "But he wore a mask so I couldn't see anything except his eyes. They were dark brown."

So dark brown they were almost black. I shuddered and Blake settled a hand at my lower back. His thumb moved back and forth in gentle sweeps, and the silent support comforted me.

One patrolman looked me over. "Weren't you recently involved in a murder?"

I stiffened and Blake shifted me a fraction closer, into the protective shelter of his body. "I was notified by the killer, that's correct."

"And do you think these incidents could be related?"

"I... I'm not sure. I can't see why anyone would hurt Kate when I was in the same building. If he wanted to hurt me, I think he would have."

"We'd like to ask you a few more questions," the officer stated. "Would you mind coming down to the station with us?"

I dropped my gaze to where the EMTs knelt by Kate, checking her vitals. "Now? But..."

I wanted to help them catch the assailant, but I needed to be with Kate more, to make sure she was okay.

The cop must've read my thoughts because he nodded. "Tomorrow would be fine."

I shot him an appreciative glance. "Thank you. I'll be there tomorrow afternoon."

Dropping his hand away, Blake directed his attention back to the officers. "Building was clear. Would you like to take a look around anyway?"

Both officers nodded and Blake turned to me. "Will you stay with the medics, show them back to the lobby?"

At my nod, he lightly ran his fingers down my arm. "I'll

meet you down there in a few minutes."

One of the officers passed me the purse I'd dropped earlier, as well as Kate's, then the men ambled away. A vibration came from inside one of the bags, but I ignored the phone's persistent alert. I walked with the paramedics to the elevator and rode down to the ground floor. The phone vibrated again as I stepped into the lobby, and I dug through my purse, looking for my phone.

Just as the medics wheeled Kate outside and loaded her into the waiting ambulance, I pulled my phone free. Several missed calls lit the screen, all from Johnathan. It rang again as I was holding it, but I hit the button to silence it. I'd call him back later, once Kate was taken care of. Blake and the officers exited the stairwell, and I'd just taken a step forward when a man tore through the front door of the building.

"Victoria!"

I offered Johnathan a weak smile as he strode toward me. "What happened? I've been calling and calling."

"I know." I held up the phone. "I'm fine, but someone attacked Kate in her office."

His eyes widened. "God. Is she okay?"

"I don't know." I drew in a shaky breath. "I have to go to the hospital with Kate. I have all of her stuff."

"Of course." He looped an arm around my shoulders. "Come on, I'll take you."

He tugged me toward the doors, and I threw an apologetic glance over my shoulder at Blake. His watchful eyes were pinned on Johnathan's hand where it rested on my shoulder, looking very much like he wanted to rip the other man to shreds. Muscles tight with tension, mouth set in a grim line, Blake's eyes slowly slid over to meet mine. He searched my eyes, and I gave a slight shake of my head. His lips turned down in a frown as I allowed Johnathan to pull me outside, and I let out a sigh. I'd have a lot of explaining to do later.

CHAPTER FIFTEEN

Victoria

I shifted again in the uncomfortable vinyl chair and let out a little sigh. Thoughts spun through my mind as I tried to piece together what had happened and why anyone would want to hurt Kate. The logical suspect was Steve, but was he really so upset with Kate over their impending divorce that he'd stoop to hurting her? It was a possibility, I supposed. It would save him a lot of time and money in legal fees. Then there was the life insurance. Without kids, Steve would surely be her beneficiary.

I peered through my eyelashes across the hospital waiting room where Steve sat jiggling a leg restlessly. He looked anxious, worried, but he'd always been good at concealing his true emotions. He'd played the doting husband for years before Kate had caught him with another woman. Maybe he was a better liar than anyone knew. I'd heard about their argument yesterday morning. Could Steve actually be responsible for this?

Johnathan drummed his fingers on his thigh, and I turned to look at him. "You don't have to stay, you know. I can call a cab."

"No, no." He shook his head. "I'm not leaving you here all alone after everything you've been through today."

I sighed. "Kate's the one who's hurt, not me."

He crossed one foot over the other. "I'm sure they'll take good care of her."

"You didn't see her, Johnathan. She's lucky to be alive right now." I rubbed my arms to dispel the chill that had crept down my spine. If it wasn't Steve, then who could've done something so horrible?

The door to the waiting room swung open, emitting a doctor clad in blue scrubs. "Are you Kate Winfield's family?"

I jumped from the chair and strode toward the doctor, anxiety gnawing at my insides. Before I could open my mouth, Steve jumped in. "Is she okay? How bad is it?"

"She has a mild concussion, which is to be expected, and she received seventeen stitches for the laceration on her forehead. The X-ray showed no broken bones, but we'll want to do a CT scan to make sure there are no internal injuries. She's being prepped now, so we should have an answer in an hour or so. Barring that, she should make a full recovery."

"Thank God!" Relief washed over me, and I watched as Steve laced his fingers behind his head and bent at the waist. I laid a gentle hand on his back and he straightened, turning his gaze to mine, tears swimming in his eyes.

Whatever I suspected him of evaporated at that moment, and I pulled him in for a quick hug.

"She'll be fine," I whispered. "I know she will."

He tightened his hold and nodded against my neck before pulling away and wiping the dampness from his eyes. "When will we be able to see her?"

The doctor glanced at the clock on the wall. "They have her scheduled for the CT in less than half an hour." He turned to Steve. "I can only allow one person back there at this time, and only for a few minutes. I'd like to get the scan done as soon as possible to ensure there are no additional injuries."

I handed Kate's purse to Steve, and he clutched it to his chest. "You go. I'll stop by after work tomorrow."

"I'll keep you posted. She'll want to see you." With a final nod, he followed the doctor through the doors and down the long hallway to the patient rooms.

I let out a slow exhale, then turned to Johnathan. "I wish I'd been able to see her, but thank God she's okay."

Despite everything Steve had done, it was important that he see Kate first. He was her husband, after all, even if he seemed to have forgotten that minor detail a few months ago. I could tell from his reaction that he still cared about Kate. He might not be in love with her anymore, but he still wanted to make sure she was safe and healthy.

Johnathan placed a hand low on my back and guided me toward the door. "You could have been seriously hurt tonight, too. You're still in shock, and you need your rest. Let's get you home."

I allowed him to lead me out to the parking garage, and I followed numbly. For once, I didn't object to his nearness. My thoughts immediately flew to Blake and the way he'd held me last week, so snug and secure in his arms, offering solace when needed, but mostly just being there to listen. I let out a sigh. I really wished he was here now, but he was probably still tied up with the police.

I was grateful they hadn't pushed for me to come in tonight. Tomorrow would be a busy day between appointments, setting aside time to go speak with the detective, and stopping by the hospital to see Kate. The mere thought drained me and I smothered a yawn.

"You must be exhausted." Johnathan ran a hand up my back. "Why don't you stay with me tonight?"

I couldn't begin to tell him all the reasons that would be a terrible idea. I really needed to come clean with him soon. Even without looking at him, I could tell from the slight increase in pitch that I'd find hope in his eyes if I looked at him. And that was the last thing I wanted. I wasn't attracted to Johnathan, at least not in that way. Viewed objectively, he would probably be considered handsome with his dark brown eyes, and prematurely graying hair that gave him a mature, distinguished look and made him seem older than his thirty-some years. Not so tall that a woman had to crane her neck to look up at him, but not so short that she felt like a giant next to him.

Not that I had that problem. Being very average herself, I looked up to almost everyone. And the height difference hadn't mattered at all last week as I'd straddled Blake's lap. The position had put my mouth even with his, perfect for kissing. His beard was thick but trimmed close to his face, and the well-maintained whiskers had brushed over my skin, tickling the nerve endings. The thought sent a delicious shiver down my spine.

Johnathan's sporty, low-slung Porsche came into view and he held the door wide as I slipped inside. I tipped my head back against the seat and shut my eyes as he closed the door then rounded the car and slid into the driver's side. I prayed that he'd let the question slide, but I could feel his eyes on me as he started the car.

"You shouldn't be alone tonight, Victoria."

I turned toward him and studied him warily. "I'm really exhausted, and I have a ton to do tomorrow."

His mouth turned down in a frown of displeasure, but he pulled out of the parking garage before speaking again. "I'd feel much better if you weren't alone. Do you really want to go home to an empty house tonight?"

The thought of going home, wondering if every creak and groan was the house shifting, or if someone was lurking in the darkness just waiting for me was unsettling. No, I really didn't want to be alone tonight.

He seemed to read my thoughts and stretched a hand over the console, slipping his palm into mine. "Stay with me. You can use the guest room."

With a tight smile, I pulled my hand free. "If you're sure it won't be an imposition—just for tonight."

Dismay tugged at his features and I almost felt bad for him. I'd noticed that he was more touchy-feely than usual—a hand on my knee, his arm around my shoulders. Was Johnathan slowly trying to move in, put himself in my path so I would have no choice but to acknowledge him? Not tonight, but one day soon, I'd have to tell him I just wasn't interested in him romantically. Maybe Kate was right—if I started dating Blake, maybe Johnathan would just kind of disappear on his own. Hopefully he'd take the hint and move on with someone else.

I stared out the window into the darkness, watching street lamps whiz by in a blur of light. Twenty minutes later, we turned into a subdivision and pulled around the circular driveway in front of Johnathan's house. The stately home was the epitome of a wealthy doctor's house with its intricate brickwork and meticulous landscaping, lit by dozens of soft white lights.

Fancy car, fancy house. Instead of being impressed, I viewed the image as a whole with an odd sense of detachment. I'd been here before, of course, but this was the first time I'd really *looked* at it, and now I saw it for what it really was: a show. Johnathan had come from nothing. Growing up poor, he'd left that life behind to make something of himself. And he'd done well—very well—for himself. He could afford pretty much anything he wanted now, and he always needed the newest and the best of everything.

I had no such issue. My parents had been well-off growing up, and I'd never lacked for anything. Leah's parents had been incredibly wealthy, giving their only daughter everything she could ever dream of. But money hadn't saved her, and it couldn't bring her back. I didn't need expensive things to be happy—I was glad every day just to be here, to be alive. I loved my little house with its big backyard. Living in a giant monstrosity like this would just be overwhelming. I had no desire to play the little doctor's wife, even if I continued to practice. Johnathan would be a great catch for some lucky woman. But it would never be me.

Drawing a deep breath, I pushed open the door and stepped out.

Johnathan retrieved his briefcase from the backseat, then rounded the car and guided me up the front steps. "How are you feeling?"

I lifted one shoulder. "Fine, I guess."

"You've had a tiresome day. You need to relax, maybe take some time off."

Like that would happen. I hadn't had a vacation in almost six years, and it didn't look like that was going to change any time soon. I couldn't afford to just leave my patients for a week or more. Johnathan traveled all over, attending seminars, sometimes speaking. It suited him, but I preferred to stay home during my time off. A glass of wine and some TV or light reading was infinitely better than jet-setting all over the place in my mind.

He led me inside the house and strode down the hallway to the guest bedroom on the main floor. Flipping on a light, he allowed me to enter first. The room was lovely, the walls a pale blue with cream linens. Everything looked expensive and high quality, but cold and impersonal. I'd seen hotel rooms with more personality.

I offered him a small smile. "Thank you for letting me stay tonight."

"You know you're welcome to stay here any time." His dark brown eyes bore into mine and guilt turned to lead in my stomach. I couldn't deal with this much longer. He would only continue to make advances, gradually try to wear me down and convince me to go out with him. Unfortunately, I didn't have the energy tonight to deal with it. I aimed for polite gratitude, but the smile felt tight and foreign on my lips. "Well, good night."

"Good night." He remained frozen in the doorway for another moment, looking very much like he wanted to say something else.

I placed a hand on the doorknob, hoping he would take the hint. Something flashed quickly across his features before he nodded. "See you in the morning, then."

He took a step backward, eyes locked on mine as he reluctantly retreated into the hallway. Before he could come up with another reason to stall me, I closed the door and flipped the lock into place. I walked to the large bed and flopped back on the fluffy mattress with a sigh of relief. I really shouldn't be here tonight, but it was better than being at home, all alone with nothing but my thoughts to keep me company.

And the last thing I wanted to think of right now was what had happened at the healthplex. I'd replayed the evening over and over while I'd sat in the waiting room at the hospital, agonizing over different outcomes. People said hindsight was 20/20, and I couldn't help but run different scenarios through my mind. I'd wasted twenty minutes checking emails that could've waited while some monster had been stalking Kate. I should have called her right after my last appointment. Then maybe she never would've been in the man's path. If I had gone down sooner instead of waiting, maybe I could have prevented it. Worst case, I could've intercepted him and frightened him off before he'd hurt Kate. Maybe if...

There were too many outcomes to contemplate. Pushing off the bed, I strode into the bathroom and twisted the handle on the shower. Water flowed out, and steam rose into the air. I rolled my shoulders, pushing the stress from my muscles. Scouring the cabinets, I turned up a travel-sized bottle of shampoo and a small bar of soap. Stripping out of my clothes, I climbed into the shower and stood under the warm stream of water, allowing the invigorating spray to pelt my skin.

Fatigue pulling at me, and I quickly soaped my hair and body before rinsing off and wrapping up in a fluffy towel. I couldn't bring myself to care about my hair and I fell into the large bed naked, leaving it to dry while I slept.

I tossed and turned for several hours and finally woke just after dawn, feeling more tired than I had when I'd gone to bed. I donned my clothes from the day before and made my way to the large kitchen.

Johnathan and a pot of coffee greeted me. "Good morning. Did you sleep well?"

Not wanting to hurt his feelings, I pasted on a smile. "Wonderfully, thank you." I gestured to the coffee pot. "May I?"

"Of course." He nodded to a cupboard to the left of the

sink. "Mugs are in there."

I retrieved a cup and filled it with coffee, then took a long sip as I leaned against the counter. An uncomfortable silence settled over the room as I drained my coffee cup, studiously avoiding Johnathan's intense gaze. I waited with bated breath, hating the silence but dreading another conversation with him. Finally, I cleared my throat. "Would you mind stopping by my house before we head to the office? I'd like to change first."

"Absolutely. Are you ready?" I nodded and set my empty mug in the sink. "Let me just get my things."

We stopped by my house just long enough for me to change and do a quick makeup job, then made our way to the healthplex. As Johnathan pulled alongside the brick building, he reached across the console and took my hand.

"If you need anything, I'll be here."

I smiled, fighting the urge to pull away. "Thank you."

I put my hand on the door handle, but he spoke, stalling me once again. "Please be careful."

My heart softened as I turned back to him. His eyes were serious, his face sincere, and guilt ate away at my insides. Johnathan was a good guy—wealthy, sweet, caring. On paper, we made sense—we were almost a perfect match. I wished I could feel more for him.

I squeezed his hand. "I will."

Climbing from the car, I made my way into the building. Catching a glimpse of Blake across the lobby, I felt heat climb up my neck into my cheeks. Had he seen me get out of Johnathan's car? Oh, God, what would he think?

Unable to look at him, I averted my eyes and hurried to the bank of elevators. I could practically feel his gaze burning into my back, and I stabbed the button to summon a car. The elevator to my left pinged almost immediately, and the doors opened. I stepped inside and raised my eyes just in time to meet Blake's intense gaze before the doors slid shut. Was that disappointment I saw in those stormy hazel depths? Anger, maybe?

I let out a shaky breath and slumped against the wall, tipping my head back and closing my eyes. Damn it. I never should have gone home with Johnathan last night. There was something between Blake and me—the way he looked at me, the way he'd held me. It meant something. Maybe I'd give it a couple days, try to approach him and smooth things over.

A quiet ding sounded as the elevator doors whooshed open, depositing me on the fifth floor, and I ambled down the hallway to my office. Phyllis's face appeared in the doorway, and the older woman yanked the door open with a small exclamation before pulling me into her arms.

"Thank goodness you're okay!"

I fell into Phyllis's warm embrace and wrapped my arms around the older woman, soaking up her strength and compassion. Tears sprang to my eyes. I hadn't realized how much I'd needed the hug this morning.

Pulling out of her hold, I swiped my fingertips under my eyes, drying the errant tears that had managed to escape.

"Oh, you poor thing," Phyllis lamented. "Go sit down, and I'll make some tea for you."

Phyllis had already disappeared into the kitchenette, and I headed to my office and dumped my bag into the bottom drawer of the desk. Avoiding the couch where Blake and I had sat just a few days ago, I sank into one of the plush armchairs and closed my eyes.

I heard Phyllis enter the room and glanced up to see the woman carrying a tray with two steaming mugs. She set the tray on the small, round table between the chairs then handed me a mug. I gratefully wrapped my hands around the warm porcelain. I let the tea steep another moment before removing the bag and setting it on the tray between us. Working in comfortable silence, Phyllis did the same.

I took a small sip, allowing the liquid to warm me from the inside out. I closed my eyes and savored the feeling, but my thoughts kept drifting; first to Kate, then to Blake.

As I'd tossed and turned last night in the guest room of Johnathan's house, I realized that I wasn't uncomfortable because I was afraid—no, the discomfort was caused by the man sleeping only a few rooms away. Guilt assailed me, and I needed to address the issue before it consumed me completely. Johnathan was a good friend, and it had been kind of him to offer me a place to stay, but I felt horrible for taking him up on his offer knowing I could give him nothing in return. More than ever, I knew he hoped I would finally agree to go out with him. Instead, it had reinforced my decision to tell him the truth—that there would never be anything between us.

I'd stared at the ceiling until the gray light of dawn began to push away the shadows of night, replaying the events of the evening in my mind over and over. Despite the unsettling events of the past couple of weeks, first the phone call from the murder scene, then the altercation with Greg, I'd been more scared for Kate than myself. After all, the man had made no attempt to follow me when I'd run for help. For some reason, the attack against Kate was personal. He'd wanted to hurt her, but he wasn't desperate or deranged. Instead of chasing after me to keep me silent, he'd fled even knowing that I'd run for help.

Why? What had Kate done to attract someone of that nefarious sort? Was someone infatuated with her? That made even less sense. If someone was obsessed with her, they shouldn't want to harm her. The nature of the assault itself screamed that it was personal but, aside from the divorce, I couldn't begin to think of what may have prompted the violent act. Kate hadn't been with any lovers since she and Steve had split up. She'd been too torn up over his infidelity, and she'd told me once that it would be a long time before she could trust a man again. Sex was an act of commitment for her, just as it would be for me.

Ruling out a disgruntled lover, who else could it be? Steve, of course, but he'd seemed genuinely distressed last night. I wasn't an expert on behaviors, but I spoke with enough people on a daily basis—I knew when someone was lying or hiding something. The only thing I'd seen in Steve's eyes was grief and worry. I'd told the detectives I would stop in this afternoon to give my statement, so I'd tell them what I thought and see what they could dig up. They were more highly trained and better equipped for that kind of thing.

Now that I knew Kate was safe, my thoughts turned to Blake. Even when I'd been beside myself with fear, he'd put me at ease, made me feel safe. I couldn't stand the thought of not seeing him again, never feeling the way I had when he'd held me. His eyes had swept over me, inspecting every inch, and my palms tingled at the memory of his thumb stroking softly over the tender, scraped flesh. I turned my hands over and examined the reddened skin, the tiny abrasions already beginning to heal. I just had to convince him that there was nothing between Johnathan and me. What he'd seen was an act of friendship only.

"What happened?"

I traced a finger over the sensitive flesh and offered a small shrug. "I think Blake saw me get out of Johnathan's car this morning."

A lengthy silence ensued, and I met Phyllis's expression of confusion. *She was asking about Kate, not...*

My cheeks burned with embarrassment, and I quickly spoke up to cover my blunder. "Someone attacked Kate last night. It was pretty bad."

Phyllis raised her brows. "I caught most of that story on the news this morning, but it sounds like your version of events is much more interesting. Not that Kate isn't important," she rushed to add.

A small smile curled my lips. I may as well just tell her. Besides, some good womanly advice might come in handy.

"Well, it's kind of a long story." I relayed the events of the previous evening, pouring out every detail. "Anyway, I didn't want to be home alone last night, so I stayed at Johnathan's. He brought me back to work this morning, but I think Blake saw me get out of the car."

She finally spoke. "So, by Blake, I assume you're refer-ring to Mr. Lawson, our very handsome new security guard?"

I dropped my eyes to my lap, and I toyed with a non-existent piece of lint on my skirt. "Yes. His name is Blake."

"And since when are you and *Blake* on a first name basis?" A mischievous smile curved the receptionist's mouth and I couldn't help the answering grin that spread over my own.

"Since he kissed me last Tuesday."

Her mouth rounded into an 'O' of surprise. "Why didn't you tell me?"

"Because..." I sighed. "Because I wasn't sure what to do. He left me his number, so I think he likes me." I was silent for a moment. "We got off to a bad start, but... he's a good guy."

Realization dawned clear and bright on Phyllis's face, and she gestured my way. "Would Blake have anything to do with the recent change in your wardrobe?"

I blushed. "A little. I was just... tired of blending in with the walls."

"Good for you. I, for one, am glad to see the last of those frumpy suits." With a glance at her watch, Phyllis patted my hand and rose to her feet. "Your first appointment begins in twenty minutes. I'll let you get settled."

Grateful for the reprieve, I moved to one of the large windows. Bright morning light spilled onto the floor, and I stepped into the rectangular shaft. I gazed out over the city bustling below, watching as people went about their day. I knew that Blake had been hired through a group called Quentin Security. I'd vaguely remembered seeing the logo on the chest of that God-awful shirt I'd cried into just over a week ago. The memory made me smile and, just as quickly, it slid from my face.

I knew nothing about him. His job here was only temporary. Once his post was up, where would he go? For that matter, where did he live? Would he travel all over the state on different security details, just disappear from her life as if he'd never existed?

Voices in the outer office drew my attention, and I knew my first appointment of the day had arrived. A glance at the clock on the wall told me they were almost fifteen minutes early. Eager to do something other than ruminate on what might, or might not, happen with Blake, I invited the first patients—Mr. and Mrs. Walters—into the office with a smile.

Three excruciating hours later, I sat back in my chair and rubbed my temples. I felt as if I'd been through an emotional wringer, and I hadn't even reached the pinnacle of the day yet. Already, I'd had to play referee during several altercations between Mr. and Mrs. Walters, and console two weeping patients—one of whom was Mrs. Walters herself, as well as my second patient of the day, Mr. Norris.

On the cusp of retirement, Philip Norris was apparently having his two-thirds life crisis. We'd had a progressive half hour before he'd broken down and sobbed uncontrollably for the remainder of their session. I empathized with the man. I worried too, occasionally, that I'd end up in his shoes—more than halfway through life, all alone. On days like these, I longed to have someone to go home to, someone who would welcome me with open arms, cuddle me close and kiss away the sadness.

Along with that train of thought came the memory of Blake's eyes burning into mine this morning. I let out a heavy sigh. So much for pushing him from my mind. Pulling open the bottom drawer of my desk, I extracted my purse and locked up my files before striding into the reception area. Phyllis was watering the plants near the windows and turned to me with a smile.

"All done for the day, Doctor?"

I nodded. "Here, anyway. I still have to go to the police department, then stop by the hospital and check on Kate."

Phyllis affected a sympathetic look. "Would you like some company?"

Touched by the offer, I smiled. "I couldn't ask that of you. Besides, I have no idea how long it will take."

"All right," she conceded, "but if you need anything at all, just let me know."

"I appreciate it. And thank you again." I cleared my throat. "Especially for the advice."

With a wink, Phyllis ushered me out the door, and I rode the elevator down to the lobby, heart racing in anticipation. Would I catch a glimpse of Blake, or was he busy making rounds? The doors slid open and I stepped from the small compartment, already scanning the large open area. Disappointment settled in my stomach when I realized the room was empty. I'd just reached the front door when footsteps echoed in the hallway to the left, and Blake rounded the corner.

His steps hitched, and I froze with one hand on the door. Our eyes locked across the room, tethered by some invisible connection that seemed to go soul-deep. My hand dropped from the door and I took a step toward him just as Benny called Blake's name from the security office. His eyes darted to the left then flicked immediately back to me. He held my gaze for another moment before nodding, and I released a sigh as he turned away and strode toward the building manager. Maybe there was hope, after all. He hadn't looked upset or angry—he'd just been his normal, intense self.

Nearly half an hour later I found myself glancing around the bustling police department downtown. The harried-looking officer waved me over to the enclosed desk and spoke through the glass. "What can I help with, ma'am?"

"Hello." I shifted uncomfortably on her feet as I introduced myself. "I'm looking for Mister, um, Detective Sanchez."

The officer nodded and pressed a button to unlock the door. "Come on in, he's expecting you. Have a seat and he'll be out in just a minute."

"Thank you." Pulling open the steel door, I entered the room and took a seat in one of the hard, blue plastic chairs lining the hallway.

I hugged my purse as I glanced around the busy space. The incessant ringing of phones and sounds of shuffling papers filled the air, countered by the din of low voices. Several long moments later, a short, dark-skinned man with graying hair rounded the corner, and I recognized him from our previous interactions.

"Dr. Carr, how are you today?" He held out a hand as he approached, and I slipped my palm into his for a quick shake.

"Fine, thank you. How are you?"

His eyes looked tired. "Just a normal day here. Come on back."

I followed the man to a small office off the large bullpen area. The office was crowded, most of the free space taken up by the wide, scarred desk and two tall, beige filing cabinets, both dented and beginning to rust in places. I took a seat in another of the standard issue chairs and leaned forward, eager to get the interview over with.

Navigating his way through the narrow space, Detective Sanchez settled into the chair behind his desk and picked up a pen and yellow legal pad.

"Dr. Carr, could you please walk me through the events of last night?"

I took a deep breath and relayed the events, Detective Sanchez intermittently asking questions. "I'm not sure why," I began slowly, "but it felt like I knew him."

"Why do you say that?" The detective tipped his head to one side, his eyes boring into mine.

"I just got this... feeling. I kind of wonder if that's why he didn't come after me. Maybe he didn't want me to recognize him."

"You're sure the suspect was male?"

"Absolutely." There was no question in my mind.

"And do you have any idea who might want to harm Dr. Winfield?"

I paused. "I'll be honest, the first person who came to mind was her husband Steve."

"And why is that?"

"Isn't that the way it always works?" My mouth quirked into a tiny smile. "It's usually someone close to the victim: the husband, the boyfriend."

Sanchez's expression didn't change. "Occasionally, that's correct."

"Well," I continued, "I can tell you this—Kate and her

husband, Dr. Steven Gerber, are in the middle of a divorce right now, and I know he harbors some animosity about the proceedings." Detective Sanchez nodded as if the logic behind that was perfectly understandable. "As of now, they are still sharing the office at the healthplex, but I know they're working to determine who gets to keep the practice. They did have an argument in the lobby a couple days ago." I paused as Sanchez jotted down notes. "But I don't think Steve was responsible for this."

The detective's features remained bland. "And why is that?"

"I just... I know it sounds strange, but I saw him at the hospital. He looked... ravaged." The detective lifted a brow, and I held up a hand. "I know what you're going to say. But I deal with people on a daily basis, most of whom are dealing with serious emotional issues. In my personal, and professional, opinion, I believe his reaction was sincere."

Sanchez studied me for a moment before heaving a deep sigh and leaning back in his chair. "We'll have to follow up with him as a precaution anyway. Is there anyone else you can think of? No lovers?"

I shook my head. "No, not that I'm aware of. I can't be one hundred percent certain, of course, but Kate was really hurt by Steve's infidelity. I don't think she's been seeing anyone, but you'll have to ask her for sure."

"Alright. Well, I think that's everything we need, unless you can think of anything else?"

I hesitated, twisting the straps of my purse between my fingers. I released a deep breath and met the detective's eyes. "I don't know if this is in any way related, but a few weeks ago I released a patient from my care. I caught him antagonizing another patient of mine, Rachel Dawes, who took her own life shortly after."

Pity and anger flashed across Sanchez's face in quick succession, and he held the pen poised in midair. "Name?"

"Greg Andrews." I watched as he scribbled the name on the legal pad. "He obviously wasn't happy with me at the time.

I referred him to a colleague of mine, Dr. Johnathan Martin, but apparently Mr. Andrews never reached out to him."

"Have you had any contact with Mr. Andrews since the altercation in your office?"

"Last weekend." I nodded. "I was at the mall when he approached me. He asked to come back as a patient, but he got angry when I refused. He made some nasty remark and stormed off."

"Nothing since then?"

I shook my head. "No."

"Think it could possibly have been him?"

"I just don't know. The men's builds are similar, but with the mask and everything…" I lifted my hands. "I can't be certain."

"Thanks for coming in. We'll contact you if we have any additional questions."

"Of course, anything to help." I paused, and Detective Sanchez lifted his eyebrows in silent question. "I, um… I was just wondering if you had any news on Monique Henderson's murder."

He regarded me shrewdly before responding. "We're following some leads, but we don't have anything concrete yet. Have you been contacted since that night?"

"No. I just worry." I met his eyes and bit my lip. "I don't want there to be a second victim."

He let out a commiserating sigh and laced his fingers together over his stomach. "I don't either. Until we catch this guy, just be aware of your surroundings and let us know if anything happens."

"Thank you." I rose from the chair and shook his outstretched hand.

I left the station and headed to the hospital. I stopped at the front desk to get Kate's room number and followed the attendant's directions to the sixth floor. Peeking my head around the doorway, I saw Kate laying in the stark white hospital bed, Steve in a chair by her side.

His head lifted and he waved me in. Climbing to his feet,

he pulled me into a hug.

"Hey," Victoria said, pitching her voice low so we wouldn't wake Kate.

Steve gestured to the chair he'd recently vacated. "Here, have a seat."

"How has she been today?" I sank into the uncomfortable chair and glanced at Kate before returning my gaze to him.

"Good, just really tired. No internal bleeding and her brain scan showed normal activity, so they don't believe there's any permanent damage. She'll be weak for a bit, but she should be out of here tomorrow."

"That's wonderful."

Kate shifted on the bed and her eyes fluttered open. A small smile crossed her face. "Hey."

I stood and leaned over the bed to pull her into a gentle embrace. "How are you feeling, honey?"

Kate lifted a hand to her head and laughed low in her throat. "Like I got hit by a train."

Sympathy zinged through me. "Do you remember what happened?"

"Bits and pieces. I remember finishing up with Mr. DeLuca and going back to my office to get my things, but it's a little fuzzy after that."

"Someone attacked you in your office. I don't know exactly what they used, but he hit you pretty hard. You lost quite a bit of blood."

Kate nodded. "That makes sense. I remember hearing your voice, but it sounded really far away, almost like a dream."

Steve laid a hand on my shoulder, his eyes fixed on his wife. "Victoria saved your life."

"I just wish I'd checked on you sooner."

Kate shook her head. "Don't blame yourself. Thank God you were there at all."

"I'm going to go down and get some coffee, let you two talk for a few." Steve stepped forward and kissed Kate on the cheek. "Victoria, do you want anything?"

"No, thank you." I smiled at Steve as he left the room, then turned to Kate. "He's playing the doting husband pretty well."

She rolled her eyes, immediately picking up on my underlying question. "Amazing how almost losing something can make you realize how badly you've messed up."

"Are you going to try to work things out?"

"No." Kate closed her eyes for a moment. "I don't think I can ever forgive him. And, even so, I don't think last night changed anything for him, either. He's been nice, but I'm pretty sure his plans are still the same."

I nodded. "Maybe he feels like he owes her. He did get her pregnant."

Her gaze dropped to the sheet. "I heard him take a call a little while ago. He thought I was asleep, but I overheard him talking to her. He told her he loved her."

"I'm sorry." I didn't know what else to say. "Everything will work out the way it's supposed to, I'm sure of it."

"Speaking of, you owe me some gossip," she joked.

I knew she was trying to push away the sadness, so I allowed the change of subject. I dropped her head to the bed. "Oh, Kate. I think I messed up." I told her all about Johnathan insisting I go home with him.

Kate's lips pressed into a firm line as I continued. "As if herding me out of there last night wasn't bad enough, we left my car there so he had to take me back to work this morning. And naturally..."

"Blake saw you show up with Johnathan," she finished. The corners of her mouth turned down. "I know he's your friend, but... I think this will just get worse unless you do something about it."

I dropped my gaze, knowing she was right. "I know. But I think he truly does have my best interest at heart."

She looked like she wanted to say more, so I eagerly changed the subject. "Do you think you'll get released tomorrow, then?"

Kate shrugged. "I feel fine, so as long as everything looks good, I don't see why not. I'm ready to get the hell out of here and sleep in my own bed."

I laughed. "You've only been here one night."

"One night too many." She grimaced. "Hospital beds suck. I have a whole new appreciation for long-term care patients."

"You can come stay with me."

"No way." Kate shook her head. "I wouldn't impose on you like that."

"Don't be silly, of course you can. You're my best friend." I crossed my arms over my midsection. "You really should have someone around, just in case. I don't know who the creep was or what he wanted, but he came after you for a reason."

"I'm not too worried about it. My condo's in a pretty safe area." She shrugged. "Plus, I haven't had a chance to update anything, so my old address is listed on almost everything. Unless someone would try to follow me home, they'd have a hard time trying to find me."

I opened my mouth to say more, but motion outside the door caught my eye as Steve entered the room. I turned to Kate. "Listen, I'll let you get some rest, but I'll stop by tomorrow to see you. We'll talk then."

With another quick hug, I said goodbye and headed home. I disengaged the alarm and kicked my shoes off with a little sigh of relief. All I wanted to do was drink a glass of wine and unwind on the couch, maybe get caught up on a couple of shows. Dropping my purse and keys on the side table, I walked down the hallway toward the kitchen. A strange tension hung in the air and my steps slowed as I glanced around. Something felt... off.

I peered through the archway of the living room, my gaze flitting around the room. Nothing appeared to be missing, but I couldn't help the prickle of unease that slithered down my spine. My eyes landed on the coffee table and I examined the cluttered surface. My fingers trailed over the magazines and books stacked haphazardly in one corner. They looked slightly out of place like someone had riffled through them then tried to put them back just the way they'd found them.

I turned slowly in place. Something was wrong here. Backing toward the door, I snatched up my purse and strode from the house, digging my phone out as I went. After everything that had transpired over the past couple weeks, it was all too much.

Standing outside on the lawn, phone in hand, I hesitated. The police wouldn't be able to do anything. There was no evidence of a break in, nothing missing that I'd seen. I tapped my nails against the screen and bit my lip. There was only one person I could call.

CHAPTER SIXTEEN

Blake

I turned into the driveway and pulled alongside Victoria's silver sedan, heart in my throat. This was not at all how I'd imagined our next meeting. I'd driven like a bat out of hell the whole way here, breaking every law imaginable in my need to see her. I still wasn't entirely sure why she'd called me of all people, but I wasn't going to look a gift horse in the mouth. She'd sounded terrified on the phone, her voice vibrating with fear even as she'd tried to remain calm. Throwing the truck in park, I hopped out and was already jogging toward the front porch before the door fully closed behind me.

Victoria popped up from where she sat on the bottom step and I froze. My eyes raked over her from head to toe, taking in the tension in her body, the way her arms were wrapped protectively around her waist. "Thanks for coming."

"Of course." I ached with the need to pull her into my arms but stopped myself just in time. I flexed my hands at my sides. "Want to tell me what happened?"

She glanced off to the side. "It sounds silly, but I got home and things just felt... wrong."

I ambled closer, keeping my steps slow and measured as I closed the distance between us. "Is anything missing or out of place?"

"I... I'm not sure. I mean, I don't think anything is

missing, but it feels like someone went through my stuff, like it's not exactly the way I left it."

I examined her for a moment before responding, watching as she rubbed her hands briskly over her arms as if to dispel a chill. Considering it was almost eighty-five degrees outside, I seriously doubted it was the weather. She'd been through a lot lately, and I understood her discomfort. "I'm going to clear the house. Do you have your keys?" She automatically extended her hand toward me to pass them over, but I wrapped my hand around hers and curled her fingers closed over the keyring. "I want you to get in the car and lock the doors. I'll let you know when it's safe to come in."

Her eyes flared wide. "I'm not leaving you in there alone."

"I can handle myself."

"I'm going with you."

I studied her for a second. "If you're sure."

I held out my hand and she slipped her palm into mine. A sense of déjà vu swept over me, reminding me of the events that had transpired just twenty-four hours ago. With Victoria on my heels, I cautiously made my way up the porch to the small house. Ears and eyes alert, I stepped inside.

Parallel to the hallway leading to the back of the house, a set of stairs lay directly in front of us, and I glanced up to the second level. Seeing nothing amiss, I turned to the right and passed through the large archway to the living room. I canvassed the room and moved on to the kitchen, dining room, and downstairs office. Although everyday clutter dotted the surfaces, nothing appeared to be out of place. Moving upstairs, I checked each bedroom and bathroom, every closet and possible hiding place.

I paused at the top of the stairs and gave Victoria's hand a reassuring squeeze. In the fading light of the evening, her face looked drawn and haunted. "Everything looks good to me. How about you?"

Her mouth twisted, and her cheeks were tinted red with embarrassment. "I'm sorry I wasted your time. It was silly and—"

I slid an arm around her waist and pulled her close. "If it means making sure you feel safe, it's not a waste of time."

She resisted for a moment before relaxing against me, then tucking her head against my chest. I breathed her in, loving the way she felt in my arms. I'd lied to Con. I wouldn't—couldn't—stay away from her. There was some indefinable quality that connected us, and though I'd only known her for a week-and-a-half, I wanted more—more of her sweet kisses, more of her shy little looks. I wanted to know everything about her.

I pushed her gently in the direction of her room. "Why don't you go change and I'll start some dinner?"

She threw a bemused look my way but went willingly. I jogged back downstairs, checking to make sure the front door was locked as I passed before heading toward the kitchen. I rooted through the pantry and fridge for ingredients and had just added everything to the skillet when a soft sound drew my attention.

I met Victoria's eyes across the room and gestured to the small table situated in the corner breakfast nook. "Have a seat, it'll be ready in just a few minutes."

I served up the food and grabbed two bottles of water from the fridge, then placed everything on the table in front of Victoria. Expression bewildered and a bit disturbed, she picked up her fork and began to eat. After several moments, she finally broke the uncomfortable silence.

"This is nice, thank you."

"You're welcome."

"I've never eaten here before."

I glanced at her. "At home?"

She shook her head. "At this table." Her words were soft, like she was afraid of revealing too much. "I don't cook much. Even when I do, I usually just eat in the living room on the couch."

She traced a finger over a dark woodgrain running through the table. "It's just me, so... there's not usually much reason to cook."

I studied her for a moment before scooping up another forkful of food. "Your boyfriend hasn't stayed for dinner?"

Her cheeks pinkened. "I don't have... I've never..."

She couldn't have shocked me more if she'd tried. "Really? You've never invited a man over for dinner?"

She didn't answer, just dropped her embarrassed gaze to her plate, and a strange surge of pleasure washed over me. "Well, this is a first for me, too, then. I can't say I've ever enjoyed dinner this much. I was in the field so long that I haven't had much chance to spend time with a beautiful woman."

A delicate red flush made its way up her neck and across her cheeks, and the sight brought a smile to my face. I loved it when she blushed like that. "I mean, I go home to see my mom when I have a chance. I love her and all, but it's just not the same."

I winked at her and Victoria chuckled, a soft, sultry sound that sent sparks of awareness straight to my groin.

"Now I know you're lying. A guy like you would have no problem getting any woman you want."

I tipped my head. "Just one."

Victoria's brows drew together and I almost laughed. After the kiss in her office last week, I was certain she knew where I stood. She, however, was a mystery. I'd seen her exit a car this morning that clearly wasn't hers, and the driver had looked suspiciously male. Was it the same guy from last night? And was he just a friend, or was he... more? She'd just admitted that she didn't have a boyfriend and that a man had never stayed over.

Deciding not to press for the moment, I changed the subject. "How are you feeling?"

She shrugged. "A little sore from my tumble down the stairs, but I'll be fine."

"Did you get to see Dr. Winfield?"

"I stopped by the hospital today." Victoria forked up some chicken. "Everything's good, but the cut required a ton of stitches."

I grimaced at the memory of the injury. "I'm sure. It looked awful."

I could sense the change in her as we spoke of the incident, and I didn't want her to draw away again. I needed to keep her here in this moment, with me. "Tell me about yourself, Doc."

Her posture stiffened and her eyes dropped to her plate. "Not much to tell. What about you? How long were you in the military?"

I took another bite of food to cover my surprise at her abrupt deflection. Swallowing, I cleared my throat. "Sixteen years."

Her eyes flared with surprise. "That's a long time. Couldn't you have retired soon?"

I shrugged. "Yeah, but I'm getting old and I decided it was time to get out. My body can't handle that kind of shit anymore."

"So you moved home?"

"Nah." I shook my head. "My parents are back in Wisconsin. A buddy of mine from the Marines had this idea to start a private security firm, so I jumped on board. I didn't know what I was going to do once I was discharged, so his offer came at the perfect time."

She tipped her head, studying me with those perceptive gray eyes. "Have you been adjusting well?"

Was that her only interest—to see me as a patient rather than a prospective lover? I lifted a shoulder. "Yes and no. We all have our demons, it's just a matter of not allowing them to control us."

She tensed, fork suspended in midair, an array of emotions passing over her face. Curious about her reaction but not wanting to pry, I leaned back in my seat and studied her. "Did you grow up here?"

She met my eyes and shook her head. "I'm originally from Ohio."

"So, what brought you to Texas?"

She shifted uncomfortably. "I needed a change. My

grandparents live near Snyder, so I moved down here about ten years ago, went to school at UT, and I've stayed ever since."

Her story was succinct, and I instinctively knew she'd left out a lot of very important details. Determined to win her trust, I teased, "Couldn't have picked somewhere a little cooler?"

At that, she smiled. "It can get really cold in Ohio in the wintertime, so it's kind of a welcome change to have warm weather all year round. On the other hand, I do miss having a white Christmas."

"I can imagine. Winter in Wisconsin lasts about six months, or so it seems. I've only been here for a few weeks, so we'll see how I feel a year from now."

She smiled. "I had no idea you'd just moved here."

"Yep. Just over a month now. Con—my buddy—and I met down here to check out a building he'd bought in the Industrial District. It pretty much had to be gutted, but he hired a construction company to come in and renovate the place. It's almost ready to go."

"Are you finding your way around okay?"

"So far. Although I really don't have much reason to go out. Maybe once I settle in more." I smiled at her. "Are you offering to show me around?"

She blushed. "Well, I just thought... Never mind, it was silly." She stood and picked up her plate, then rounded the table.

Shit. I hadn't meant to embarrass her. "Victoria."

Snaking a hand out, I grasped her wrist, freezing her in her tracks. The plate slipped from her fingers as she recoiled, and it shattered with a crash. I immediately released her, shocked at her response. "I'm sorry. I shouldn't have done that."

Her entire body was rigid with tension, and I could hear the difference in her breathing. I couldn't begin to comprehend what had just happened, but I decided not to push at the moment. I slowly rose from the chair. "I'll get this cleaned up if you tell me where the broom is."

"No, I—" Her voice broke and I cut her off.

"Doc, look at me." She reluctantly met my gaze. "It was my fault. Let me take care of it."

She swallowed hard. "I have a broom and dustpan in the pantry."

I nodded. "Why don't you head up to bed? I'll crash down here on the couch."

"You're staying?" Victoria's voice shook.

"I was planning to. Unless you prefer I leave?" I leaned a hip against the table and studied her.

After a moment, she shook her head. "You can stay if you want."

I nodded. "I'm going to clean up then check the windows and doors. If you need anything, you know where to find me."

Victoria silently faded from the room, and I pondered her reaction. What the hell had set her off? Even earlier this evening when I hugged her, she seemed perfectly fine. But the moment I'd grabbed her wrist, everything had changed. Her anxiety stemmed from more than just a recent scare—it was a deeply ingrained response. She refused to talk about her past, glossing over the details and jerking away from my abrupt touch. What had happened to her?

I made quick work of cleaning up the kitchen then made my way through the house, checking each door and window to make sure they were locked up tight. Satisfied that everything was good, I headed into the living room. Sinking onto the couch, I dropped my head back and stared at the ceiling. Was I reading her totally wrong? Was she not interested in me or was it something else, something that ran deeper, tied into a past she didn't want to talk about? I listened to her move around upstairs. The water turned on, presumably for her shower, and I stifled a groan.

Propping my feet on the coffee table, I turned on the TV then flipped through channels until I came to a crime show. The lamp on the end table kicked off at eleven o'clock, triggered by an automatic timer, and I turned off the TV with a sigh then settled in for a night of restless sleep.

Although the couch was large and comfortable, I tossed and turned, unable to fall asleep. Sometime around midnight, I heard a soft creak on the stairs. Seconds later, Victoria's wraith-like figure appeared in the doorway of the living room. She stood there, shifting from foot to foot for several moments before she finally spoke, her voice soft and timid.

"Blake?"

"Yeah?"

"I'm sorry I freaked out on you earlier."

I pushed to a sitting position. "Do you want to talk about it?"

Silence descended heavily over the room and I held my breath, afraid that she would flee to the sanctuary of her room if I made one wrong move.

She hesitated for a moment before drifting toward the couch and propping a hip on the armrest. I turned to face her, examining her silhouette in the darkness, highlighted by the moonlight coming through the window.

"You know Monique Henderson's killer contacted me from the murder scene?" I nodded at the rhetorical question and she took a deep breath before continuing. "He didn't ask for me, exactly."

I froze. Why the hell would she lie about that? QSG had been called in specifically because of the murder. We'd been under the impression that she was at risk because the killer had contacted her. If she was playing some kind of twisted game... Anger burned through my gut. Before I could speak, Victoria continued.

"I had a bad experience back in high school. I didn't want to finish out the year up there, and I moved down here my senior year. I just had to get away." She stared at the floor, unwilling to look at me, lost in some memory ten years old. "My real name is Bekah Baker. He asked for me—for Bekah. He knows who I am."

I sucked in a breath as a red haze filled my vision. *Christ.* She should have said something sooner. If I'd known some asshole was stalking her, had been after her for God knew how long, I could've been better prepared. This changed things completely.

"Jesus, Doc, why the hell—" I abruptly cut off when she flinched. I dragged in a deep breath before continuing, this time more calmly than before. "Do you know who it is?"

She shook her head. "No. The police never found out back then"—she waved her hand as if to emulate the past— "and Detective Sanchez told me earlier they don't have any suspects yet for Monique's murder."

Goddamn it. I wanted to push for the truth, demand she tell me every detail of what had happened, but I forced it down. "Doc, look at me."

Reluctantly, she lifted her gaze to mine. Even in the dim light, I could see the haunted look was back in her eyes, and protectiveness welled up. "I won't let anything happen to you. I will always keep you safe."

She hesitated for a minute before finally nodding. "Would you mind if I... sat with you for a bit? I can't sleep."

"Of course."

She slinked closer, taking a seat next to me and curling her feet beneath her. I forced myself to relax, though anger still thrummed forcefully through my body. I was upset that she hadn't told me, but I couldn't really blame her. She was scared, and she obviously didn't trust anyone, not even me. But I would change that. "Not tired?"

She shook her head. "Still too worked up. I'm sorry you came all the way over here for nothing."

I stretched one arm over the back of the couch. "I told you before—it's worth it to me if it made you feel better."

"Thank you." She shot a sweet smile my way, turning my insides to fire.

"Any time. And, Doc?" I studied her for a moment. "I meant what I said."

She averted her gaze, and I imagined the pink flush tinting her cheeks. Deciding not to push her any further this evening, I gestured toward the TV. "Do you want to watch something?"

"Sure. Whatever you want is fine."

I flipped the TV on and settled into the corner of the couch. Victoria sank back into the cushions, her shoulder just inches from my hand. Needing to touch her, I stroked my thumb over the flesh of her upper arm. From the corner of my eye, I watched her body stiffen at the initial contact. I kept my touch light and soothing, and her muscles gradually loosened as she eased into me. After a few minutes, I felt her body start to relax, and I shifted her closer. Her breathing slowed, turning deep and even, and I knew she was asleep. Trying to jostle her as little as possible, I turned off the TV then scooped her into my arms. She nestled against my chest with a soft, sweet exhalation, and she curved one arm around my neck as I headed upstairs.

Her bedroom lay at the end of the hall, the subtle vanilla scent pulling me closer. I propped a knee on the edge of the mattress and reluctantly deposited her in the middle before pulling the covers over her.

"Blake?" Her voice was raspy, and she groggily reached for me.

I grasped her hand and gave it a light squeeze. "I'm right here."

"Don't go."

A war raged within me. "Are you sure?"

Her head bobbed in a disoriented nod, her voice heartbreakingly soft and vulnerable. "Stay. Please."

"I'll be right here." I stretched out on top of the covers, folding my hands behind my head.

I stared at the ceiling for a long time, wondering about the woman beside me and the past she kept hidden before finally falling into a fitful sleep.

CHAPTER SEVENTEEN

Blake

Light slowly infiltrated the dark and I blinked several times, disoriented for a moment as the events of last night flickered through my mind in rapid succession. Something in my peripheral vision caught my attention. Turning my head slightly, I smiled. Victoria had crept closer while she slept until she was snuggled up against my side. Her head lay on my pillow, just inches from my face, so close I could kiss her.

At some point during the night, she'd whimpered and begun to struggle against the confines of the sheets. I'd slid in next to her, pulling her close and holding her tight until she'd calmed and fallen back to sleep. The heat from her body surrounded me, and the sensation made me want to pull the covers over our heads and not surface for days. Levering to a sitting position, I reluctantly slipped out from under the covers and stretched, my vertebrae popping as they shifted back into place. The faint rustling of sheets drew my attention and I turned to find Victoria propped up on an elbow, her sleepy gray eyes trained on me.

"Morning, beautiful."

She smiled. "Hey. You stayed."

I braced one hand on the bed as I leaned toward her. "I told you I would."

She shrugged. "I thought it might have been a dream."

I shook my head. "Nope. I'm still here."

Her eyes drifted over my torso, clouded with confusion. "Are you in your underwear?"

I chuckled. "I stripped down in the middle of the night. Sleeping with you is like being in bed next to a furnace."

She blushed profusely and I brushed a stray lock of hair off her forehead. I didn't want to ruin the good mood by bringing up her tossing and turning, so I kept my tone light. "Trust me, sweetheart, I wasn't complaining."

Her blush spread lower and I grinned at her obvious discomfort. She seemed more embarrassed by her own reaction than the fact that I'd climbed under the sheets without an invitation. I decided to press my luck. "We'll just have to turn down the air conditioning next time. You know, after a real date."

"You... want to go out with me?"

This woman... She truly had no idea how beautiful she was. "If you're willing to give me a shot, hell yeah."

Quick as a flash, her entire demeanor changed and her teeth sank into her lower lip. "There's something..."

I immediately thought of the man who'd shown up Wednesday evening and dragged Victoria away before I'd even had a chance to speak with her. "Are you seeing someone else?"

Her head tipped slightly to the side. "What?"

"The guy who stormed into the healthplex the other night—are you two dating?"

It took a moment for her brain to connect the dots and understanding lit her eyes as she shook her head. "No, that's not... We've never dated. Dr. Martin is a colleague and a friend."

I wondered if the man knew that. He seemed awfully territorial for just a friend, but Victoria didn't seem too interested in the guy, or I figured she would have called him last night. Still, the memory of her climbing out of a strange car yesterday morning, a man at the wheel, was burned on my brain.

I shut it down before I could overthink it and changed the subject. "I have to head home so I can shower and change. Will you be okay getting to work?"

She nodded. "I'd prefer we show up separately anyway."

I understood, but the comment stung a little nonetheless. "Okay."

She slid from under the covers and stood next to me, arms wrapped around her waist. "Do you want some coffee before you go?"

I examined her for a moment, my eyes sliding over her body of their own volition. Her curves were outlined by the thin camisole and shorts she wore, and I felt my resolve begin to waver. I wanted to run my hands all over her and make her forget all about the other man. I couldn't figure her out. Was she telling the truth about him or not?

Her eyes seemed sincere, large and gray in her face, and she just stared back, waiting on my response. Trying to get a read on her was like trying to nail Jell-O to a tree. Finally, I nodded. "That'd be great, thanks."

Pulling a robe from a chair in the corner, she slipped her arms inside and tied the sash tightly around her waist. We descended the stairs in silence, and the atmosphere remained tense and uncomfortable as Victoria began to make the coffee. I was just about ready to forego my daily shot of caffeine when she finally spoke up.

"I... I just wanted to say thank you. Again."

I fought the urge to smile, remembering how her previous thank you had ended. "It was no big deal."

"So..." She fiddled with a cup on the counter, her expression one of intense discomfort. "Were you serious about wanting to go out with me? Or were you just being nice?"

I regarded her warily. "What do you mean?"

She bit her lip and shook her head. "Never mind."

I reached across the counter and hooked a finger under her chin, forcing her to meet my stare. I could feel her throat move as she swallowed hard. I was afraid to let myself hope as well, but the stupid emotion burst into my heart as her cheeks pinkened with embarrassment. "Tell me what's going through that head of yours, beautiful."

"I just... I'm not good at this kind of thing—dating, talking with guys. I get all awkward, and... weird." She blew out a little breath. "I was kind of hoping you weren't just saying you wanted to go out. I mean, people say that all the time, but then..." She shrugged and dropped her gaze back to the slab of granite that separated us.

I released her and circled the bar. Sliding my hands up her arms, I cupped her elbows and pulled her close. "I always mean what I say."

She lifted her face and stared up at me for several seconds, seeming to weigh my words. "Okay," she whispered.

I dropped a soft kiss on her upturned mouth, and her eyes fluttered closed. I kissed her once more, breathing in her sweet scent before reluctantly releasing her. "All right, beautiful. I'll let you get ready for work. See you in a few?"

She nodded. "Sounds good."

I laced my fingers through hers and tugged her toward the front of the house. Pausing by the door, I turned to her. "Be careful and make sure to lock up behind me."

"I will. And, Blake? Thank you."

"Any time." I locked my hands together at the base of her spine, pulling her close and kissing her again. She fit me perfectly, felt so good within the circle of my arms, that I didn't want to let her go just yet.

She rolled her lips together before meeting my gaze. "Would you like to come over for dinner again?"

The question was tentative, like she thought I'd turn her down. But I wasn't giving her up now, not when I was just starting to figure her out. "Of course. I'll see you back here at seven."

Her sweet smile made my heart ache. I dropped one more kiss on her lips before shooting a wink her way and stepping out into the bright morning light. I glanced over my shoulder to where she stood outlined in the doorway. A soft smile on her face, she made for a beautiful sight—one I hoped I'd see a whole lot more of.

＊

The sun had just begun its descent, disappearing over the back of the house as I pulled into the driveway and parked next to Victoria's car. I unfolded from the driver seat, then rounded the hood of her car. "Why don't you park in the garage?"

She rolled her eyes. "Johnathan asked me the same thing. I don't mind parking outside."

At least we agreed on that score. "I think it might be better if you parked inside. That will at least keep someone from knowing if you're home or not."

Her head tilted up to meet my gaze, so close that her breasts barely grazed my midsection. "You'll keep me safe, won't you?"

My hands automatically went to her hips and pulled her flush against me. "Always, beautiful. You can count on it."

A slow grin spread over her face and I bent my head, capturing her lips with mine. It went on for several long moments until her hands slid up to my chest and gently pushed. Pink tinged her cheeks and she dropped her gaze to the ground before looking up at me again. "We'd better get inside; we're giving my neighbors a show."

I glanced to the left where an elderly man stood across the street watering his flowers. I lifted one hand in greeting and the older man returned the wave with a smirk. "Come on, let's head in."

Placing a hand on her lower back, I guided Victoria up the stairs to the front door. Following her inside, I closed and locked the door before heading toward the kitchen. We tossed together a quick meal and afterward, Victoria up cuddled next to me on the couch as we watched TV. Her body felt tense and she bit her lip, a faraway look in her eyes. Finally, I muted the television and turned her in my arms.

"Okay, Doc. What's on your mind?"

Her head swiveled toward me, a guilty look on her face. "Oh, I… It's nothing, never mind."

"Doesn't look like nothing." I studied her for a moment. "You can talk to me if something's bothering you."

"I was just wondering…" Her gaze dropped to her hands where she picked at an imaginary piece of lint on her pants. "Where do you think things are headed?"

The question caught me off guard. "With us?"

Her head jerked up. "I mean, I know it's too early to label anything, but I thought… I don't know what I thought." She let out a sigh and scrubbed her palms over her face. "I'm making a mess of this already."

"No, you're not." She looked so damn vulnerable that I wanted to pull her into my arms and comfort her the only way I knew how. But she needed the reassurance of words. I reached out and turned her chin toward me, waiting for her eyes to meet mine. "If you're asking whether I'm interested in you—in a serious relationship with you—the answer is yes."

Instead of looking relieved, Victoria seemed to pale even more. "I just… there's something you should know."

I stiffened as our previous conversation came to mind. Though she'd insisted she didn't have a boyfriend, her demeanor screamed that it was something I wasn't going to like.

Her hands drifted down to her lap again where she wrung them together nervously. "I don't even know how to start. Oh, God, this is so awkward."

She sucked in a harsh breath before letting it out, and she stared at her hands as she spoke. "Remember how I told you I had a bad experience in high school?" I didn't bother to answer the rhetorical question, and she continued. "Well, it was really hard for me to open up to people after that—especially guys. I went on dates, but I never really trusted anyone enough to be… intimate."

She'd never…? Emotion slammed into me—pride that she'd made such an important decision, elation that I might be her first, but also fear. Mostly fear. What if she trusted me to be her first and she hated it? Would she despise me because of it? Shit, I was getting ahead of myself.

Words escaped me for a moment, and she turned to me with a pained expression, misinterpreting my silence. "If you don't want to see me anymore, I'll understand."

"No!" Her eyes widened, and I forced myself to relax. "I'm sorry. No—that was the absolute last thing on my mind."

She bit her lip, watching me warily, and I took a moment to gather my thoughts before speaking. "I didn't mean to overreact. You just... caught me by surprise."

A deep scarlet raced over her skin, and I picked up her hand, gently squeezing her fingers in silent apology. "It's an important decision, and I'm glad you told me. I promise I won't ever push you to do something you don't want."

Relief crossed her features, quickly followed by something I couldn't quite discern. Before I could ask, she turned to me. "Will you stay again?"

My gut twisted, but I forced myself to nod. Regardless of what happened between us, I'd still make sure she was safe. "Of course."

She examined her toes before turning back to me. "I was thinking you might stay... with me."

With her, in her bed. Hope flared again—that silly, stupid, yet oh-so-welcome emotion—and I pressed a gentle kiss to her forehead. "I'd love to."

CHAPTER EIGHTEEN

Blake

This woman was going to be the death of me. My heart gave a hard thump, and my blood turned to fire as my gaze swept over her. She'd changed into another skimpy white tank top, and she sat there in the middle of the bed staring at me, looking like the most delicious fantasy.

Catching my eye, she flipped the covers back with a nervous smile. Maybe I wasn't as far into the Friend Zone as I'd thought. Not about to let her renege on the offer, I yanked my shirt off and shucked my pants before sliding under the cool gray sheets next to her. Victoria's eyes widened momentarily before she averted her gaze and turned toward the nightstand. She flicked off the lamp, bathing the room in darkness.

I stretched out on my side of the bed, staring at the ceiling, feeling every dip of the mattress as she shifted. Why had she asked me to stay with her again? Was it just for protection? Or was it more than that? She'd looked so vulnerable admitting her attraction to me this morning, but she'd been giving off mixed signals all night. She'd withdrawn after admitting she was a virgin, and I couldn't quite figure her out. Maybe I'd just give her some time, slowly earn her trust. I wouldn't take advantage of her, but neither was I willing to give up on her just yet. As much as I hated it, I'd just have to wait for her to come to me.

Which happened sooner than I expected. The sheets pulled taut, and the mattress dipped as Victoria shifted so close that her hip touched mine. Taking it as a sign, I rolled to my side and pulled her against me. Draping an arm over her hip, I slid my hand beneath the hem of her tank top and settled it on her stomach. She snuggled closer, fitting her body to mine and burrowing her head into the space beneath my chin. I tightened my hold on her and our bodies moved together, chests rising and falling with each breath in an easy, comforting rhythm. I was almost asleep when she spoke.

"There's a reason I've never had sex."

The seriousness of her tone immediately jerked me awake. I stroked my thumb over her stomach, silently letting her know I was listening, encouraging her to continue.

"I did something really stupid. Looking back, I can't believe how naïve I was." I felt her head shake in self-deprecation against my chin. "It was years ago—almost a decade ago now. God, I can't believe it's been that long."

She was silent for a moment, lost in the memory. "My friend Leah and I stopped at Blockbuster to pick up a movie one night the summer before senior year. When we left, there was a guy standing on the sidewalk. He said he needed a ride."

A sense of foreboding slithered down my spine, but I remained quiet.

"Leah didn't want to give him a ride, but I insisted. Our families were both very religious, and we'd been raised to be good Christians. If someone needed something, you did whatever you could do to help. Leah kept telling me no, but I ignored her. I didn't want to listen..."

She drew in a shaky breath and shifted restlessly, a testimony to how much the past still affected her. I dropped a kiss on her shoulder. "You don't have to tell me if you don't want to."

"No, I do, I just..." Her voice wavered and she sucked in another breath. "I've only told a couple people about that night. It's part of the reason I wanted to be a psychologist, you know. After what happened... I wanted to use my personal experience to help other people." She let out a bitter laugh. "Look how that worked out. I obviously couldn't help Rachel."

Christ, she still blamed herself for that? "Sweetheart, whatever happened to you and whatever Rachel was going through were two entirely different situations. Rachel was suffering from something of her own, right?" I felt Victoria's slight nod and continued. "You may have made a mistake, but it wasn't your fault that something bad happened."

"I just..."

"Tell me what happened."

She let out a harsh exhalation and I brushed a kiss over her temple to temper the command. She snuggled closer before continuing. "Well, he said his friends had played a joke on him and left him behind, so I offered him a ride."

She touched her fingers to her lips. "He had a facial deformity—a cleft lip. I felt bad for him, you know?"

Yeah, I could understand that completely. The guy had probably used it to his advantage to prey on Victoria and her friend.

"He said his name was Marc, but..." She took a deep breath. "I'm sure he lied about that, too. Leah complained the whole time about what a terrible idea it was. He said he lived just outside town, and it felt like we'd driven forever until we finally turned down this long, dark road. I had a bad feeling, so I stopped the car and told him I couldn't take him any farther.

"I should have known; I should have seen it coming." Another deep breath. "He pulled a knife from out of nowhere and held it to my throat then made Leah tie me to the steering wheel. I knew we wouldn't make it out of there, and I screamed at Leah to run, to save herself. He left me in the car and took off after her into the woods. I sat there for probably close to an hour, praying to God that she'd managed to get away. When he finally came back, he cut me loose and forced me into the woods, too."

I couldn't help the way my hands clenched into fists. He couldn't imagine what she'd experienced, the sheer terror she'd felt. And she'd been—what?—all of seventeen at the time? She was just a kid trying to do the right thing and help someone out. I forced myself to relax, splaying my fingers once more over the soft skin of her stomach. If my touch was firmer, more possessive, she didn't complain.

Victoria spoke again, her voice breaking. "I... I couldn't see where I was going, and I tripped. He turned on the flashlight and..." Her voice turned to a whisper. "I didn't even recognize her at first. There was so much blood. I think I screamed, but I don't remember, I just ran as fast as I could. I didn't know where I was going, I just knew I had to get away."

I closed my eyes and swallowed, simultaneously wanting her to stop talking yet get it off her chest.

"I ran and ran until I came to an old train trestle. He'd caught up with me by that point and he grabbed my hair, cornered me. I was pressed up against the railing, begging for him to stop, to let me go. He said, 'I'm sorry it has to be this way.'" Her motions were illuminated by the pale light filtering through the gauzy curtains covering the window, and she raised a hand to her neck. "He had the knife to my throat and I knew I had to do something. I kneed him, and the next thing I knew, I was falling. I'd never been so scared in my life, and I knew right then that I was going to die."

The anger I felt on her behalf was almost overwhelming. I wanted to track down the asshole responsible and rip him limb from limb. My voice came out rough. "How did you get away?"

"I happened to fall near the middle of the bridge where there was a support pillar. It had stormed the day before, and a bunch of tree limbs and debris had gotten caught there. I landed near them, and somehow, they kept me afloat. I laid there, listening to him walk back and forth over the bridge, talking to himself for probably half an hour. I stayed as still as I could, moving my head just enough to keep it out of the water so I could breathe." She shuddered. "Finally, he left. I don't know how long I waited after that. It seemed like forever. I swore he'd come back for me, but he never did. He must have figured I was dead. I climbed out of the river and followed the train tracks—looking for a house, a road, anyone who could help. I saw headlights just as I was coming up to a road and I ran like a crazy person, waving my arms around, trying to get them to stop."

She let out a self-deprecating laugh. "I must've scared the poor woman half to death. I was wet and covered with mud, my clothes torn. I refused to get in the car with her, and I just stood there crying hysterically, begging her to call the police. Thank God she had a cell phone. She was nice enough to wait with me until the cops came. I told them what happened, where Leah was…"

I laced our fingers together, then pressed a kiss to the spot where our hands were joined. "Oh, baby. I'm so sorry you had to go through that."

She squeezed my hand in return. "I wonder all the time why God chose me. I shouldn't have lived that day, but somehow I did."

I gently rolled her to her back and stared down at her. "He knew you'd do great things, Doc. You're a survivor; not many people can say that. Better yet, you use your experience to help others. He chose you because you're an incredible, amazing person."

Tears slipped down her temples, dampening her hair, and I brushed them away.

"Seriously—you know it wasn't your fault, right? Not what happened to you back then, and certainly not what happened to Rachel."

"I know." Eyes downcast, her reticent tone was a direct contradiction to the words she spoke.

I released her hand and pushed to a sitting position and scooped her into my lap. I held her close, just as I had a week ago, reflecting on how much had changed in just a few short days. She'd stirred something within me, something I never knew was missing. "Thank you for telling me. It means a lot that you trusted me with that."

She leaned her head into my chest, cuddling closer. "It

THE DEVIL YOU KNOW | 153

was hard to have normal relationships after that. I tried dating in college, of course, but I couldn't trust anyone enough to let them in until…"

Her words trailed off and hope bloomed in my chest. "Until?"

"You know, I really didn't like you when we first met."

Her comment elicited a startled bark of laughter. "Yeah, I kinda got that impression, Doc."

"I just…" She sighed. "When I walked through the door and saw you… It sounds weird to say, but I felt *something* before I even met you. Lust, maybe? I can't explain what it was, but I immediately thought 'he would never be with someone like me.'"

I tipped her face up to see her better. "You're beautiful. You should never feel that way."

"I couldn't help it, and I instantly got defensive. It was easier to pretend I hated you than to feel that little spark of… whatever it was. You stood there in your suit, looking like you just walked off a billboard and gave me this little smirk. I thought you were making fun of me." I opened my mouth to speak but she cut me off. "I know how I looked, Blake. I hid under those baggy clothes, trying to hide my figure."

"You're perfect, no matter what you wear or how you look. What brought on the change?" I held my breath, almost afraid to hear the answer, and I couldn't help but grin when it finally came.

"You." Her head dipped in embarrassment. "Kind of, I mean. I just wanted to get your attention."

I chuckled. "Oh, sweetheart, you definitely have that."

I could practically feel her blush. "Kate finally talked me out of hiding behind my old clothes and helped me pick out some new things."

"Do the new clothes make you feel better?"

She hesitated before nodding. "They do, actually."

"Then that's all that matters. There's nothing sexier than a confident woman."

When she remained silent, I changed the subject, shifting

her the tiniest bit closer. "I could get used to this, you know."

"What's that?" Her voice was soft and tentative.

"Being here with you. I know we've only known each other for a couple weeks, but I have this crazy need to see you, touch you all the time. It's hell having to work in the same building as you all day but not be able to pull you aside and kiss you whenever I feel like it." I lowered my voice. "I'm glad you asked me to stay."

"Me, too."

I dipped my head and brushed my lips across hers, teasing the seam of her mouth with my tongue, and she opened for me, returning the kiss with equal fervor. Caught up in the passion of the moment, I skimmed one hand up her side and cupped her breast. She stiffened, and I immediately dropped my hand away.

"Sorry."

She burrowed her nose against my neck, inhaling deeply before speaking. "No... I... Please."

"Please what?"

She grabbed my hand and pulled it back to her breast.

"I need to hear you say it." My heart beat frantically as I waited for her to answer, the silence almost interminable.

"I want you to... touch me."

Her plea cut through me like a knife. I gently lay her back on the bed then stretched out next to her. Propped on one elbow, I coasted my fingers down her arm from shoulder to wrist, then back up again. Across her collarbone, up her neck, my fingers blazed a trail over her skin, slowly acclimating her to my touch. I wouldn't make love to her. As much as I wanted to bury myself inside her, it was a new experience for her, and I wouldn't pressure her. I had plenty of other methods of pleasure to share with her instead.

Goosebumps broke out over her skin as I coasted down-ward, my fingertips gliding over each rib, the dip of her waist, and across her hip. Inching her shirt up, I teased the silky skin of her stomach before slowly making my way up to her breast. A little shudder rocked her body and her head dropped back in ecstasy as I circled her nipple.

"If you want to stop, sweetheart, just tell me."

She shook her head and opened her mouth to speak. Instead of words, a soft moan escaped and I bit back a smile. Smoothing my hand over her waist I grasped the hem of her shirt, then pulled it upward.

"I want to see you." Levering to a sitting position, I drew the material over her head and off, exposing her exquisite body. My gaze trailed over her torso, examining the indent of her waist where it flared out at her softly rounded hips, then up to the swells of her breasts. I leaned in and dropped a kiss on the arc of one. "God, you're gorgeous."

She turned her face away in embarrassment, and I redirected her gaze to mine. "Do you trust me?"

I held my breath for a moment as she searched my eyes. "I trust you."

Her hands stole around my neck, curling into my hair and tugging me down for another kiss. I ground my mouth down on hers before remembering my vow to take it slow. Pulling back a fraction, I gentled the kiss and trailed my lips over her jaw, down her throat, between the valley of her breasts. I sucked one tight peak into my mouth, and she writhed beneath me. I teased her other breast, circling the nub until her flesh tightened under my ministrations.

I took her mouth again, skimming my hand lower and slipping under the waistband of her shorts. Her legs moved restlessly as I found her hot center and stroked her through the satiny material. She tore her mouth from mine and threw her head back as she arched under my touch.

The sight of Victoria, eyes closed in ecstasy, chestnut waves tossed wildly over the sheets, was nearly my undoing. Looming over her, we locked eyes as I hooked my fingers in the fabric and slowly pulled the shorts down her legs.

The sight of her clad in only a pair of black satin panties made my heart beat double time and my mouth water. She bent her legs, tucking them in close for modesty, and I shook my head, a tiny smirk playing about my mouth. I wouldn't let her hide from me anymore.

Catching one foot in my hand, I pressed my lips to her instep before kissing my way over her ankle, up her calf, along the inside of her thigh. At the apex of her legs, I nuzzled her core through the material of her underwear.

Her breathing hitched as I slipped one finger beneath the fabric and pulled them down her legs. One foot slipped free of the panties, then the other, and I settled beside her, chest to chest. My lips caught hers again in a scorching kiss as my fingers trailed up her thigh, over her hip, and down to her core. My hand slid through her curls to cup her mound with gentle pressure. Her breathing quickened and she threw her arms around my neck.

A ragged moan welled up in her throat as I slipped one finger inside her, massaging the sensitive folds. Her legs fell open in invitation and I stroked in and out, gradually increasing the tempo until she came with a ragged cry, her muscles clenching, holding me tight. She looked so beautiful lying there, breathing heavily, hair disheveled, that I couldn't help but smile. Her eyes finally opened and they met mine, the gray depths immediately wary even in the dim light.

I dropped a reassuring kiss on her lips before she could allow the doubt to intrude and ruin the moment. "You okay, beautiful?"

She nodded, eyes still locked on mine. "I'm... great."

I stroked her hip bone. "Good. We should get some sleep."

"What about..." She propped herself on an elbow and gestured toward my groin. "Aren't you...?"

Oh, yeah. I was hard as a rock and ready to go. But I needed to earn her trust first, and I was too wound up at the moment to control myself. I shook my head and shifted her so she lay next to me. "Tonight's all about you. Now, c'mere."

Pulling her closer, I tucked her against my side, spoon-style, so her head rested just below my chin. I dropped a kiss on her hair and splayed my fingers possessively over her stomach. I had her right where I wanted her, and I wasn't about to let her go.

CHAPTER NINETEEN

Blake

I glanced around the sunny kitchen as Victoria measured coffee into the basket of the percolator and turned it on. The window above the sink looked out over a small, but well-maintained backyard. The grass was green but I knew it would be hard and brittle to the touch, dry from the intense heat of the sun. It was one thing I didn't think I'd ever get used to. Back in Wisconsin, the grass was lush and soft; here it was like walking across a green Brillo pad.

Victoria's house was decent sized and well taken care of. Unread mail was heaped in a small pile on the corner of the counter and several plates and glasses, including my own from last night, filled the sink. She took good care of the place, but she wasn't a neat freak. I liked that about her. I wouldn't have to worry about her losing her shit if I left something out of place.

My mom and two sisters had beaten good habits into me growing up, and what they hadn't taught me, the military had. I'd been on my own for over a decade, but I couldn't deny how nice it was to be here with Victoria. I liked the idea of sharing responsibility—taking care of her, and of her taking care of me.

"How long have you been here?"

Victoria pulled a small glass container of sugar from the

cupboard, then glanced over her shoulder at me. "In Texas?"

"This house."

"Oh." She set the container on the counter and strode to the fridge. "About two years now." Yanking open the door, she pulled out a bottle of hazelnut creamer, then gestured to a jug of milk. "How do you take your coffee?"

"Black, just a touch of sugar."

With an affirmative nod, she closed the door and set the creamer on the counter. Turning to face me, she crossed her arms over her chest. "You've been here for a month?"

"Yep. I bought a little fixer-upper on the outskirts of town. It was cheap and I figure I can flip it once I find something I really like."

It was actually only about three miles from the health-plex, so it was an almost perfect arrangement. Right after I'd accepted Con's offer to work for QSG, I'd contacted a realtor in the area and purchased the small ranch. With a little work, the place could be really nice, and I hoped to turn a decent profit once the renovations were complete. The neighborhood was older and fairly quiet, which suited my needs well.

Given a choice, I'd rather be in the country where I had a little space to myself. It'd be hard to come by, being this close to the city, but maybe I'd eventually find a little plot of land somewhere more rural. Although the house was conveniently located, I enjoyed my privacy and would prefer to have some space to roam around. I didn't want neighbors right next door. I wanted to be someplace where I could walk outside in my underwear because, well... why the hell not?

I stared out over the backyard, at the roofs of the houses just over the fence at the edge of her property. This was ultimate suburbia. Each home sat on a quarter- to half-acre, with only small hedges or trees to separate one lot from the next. Still, it was nice. I imagined it was perfect for Victoria, young and vibrant as she was. She probably attended cookouts and block parties with the neighbors, waved to them as they passed on the street or walked their dogs.

"It's nice here."

"Thanks. Everyone seems to be pretty friendly."

"Have you met many of your neighbors?"

She shook her head. "Only a couple. I pretty much keep to myself."

I nodded. "Where I grew up was mostly woods. We had almost twenty acres, and I knew it like the back of my hand. I spent every season hunting or fishing, building forts and putting up tree stands. My dad and I were always out just after midnight on Thanksgiving, ready for the first day of hunting season."

She grinned. "I can see that. My parents would never dream of doing anything like that."

I shrugged. "It's not for everyone. It's tedious and time-consuming, freezing your balls off fifteen feet in the air, trying not to move too much, just waiting for a buck to wander by."

"Sounds cold and tiresome."

"It can be. But the thrill of the hunt is what it's all about." I winked at her and she cocked an eyebrow.

"Is that what they call hunting these days? Sitting in a tree drinking coffee and just waiting for a deer to wander by?"

I narrowed my gaze, but the teasing smile didn't leave her lips. "It's a lot harder than it sounds."

She lifted her hands in the air, fingers spread wide, her expression playful. "I'm just saying, it sounds pretty easy to me."

"Oh yeah?" I took a small step toward her and her arms dropped to her sides. "I don't think you appreciate the extent of my tracking skills."

"I..." Her eyes darted to the side and she let out a shriek as I lunged forward. My fingers grazed the material of her robe as she sprinted toward the living room, her musical laughter filling the air. I caught up to her just as she reached the couch, and I wrapped my arms around her from behind. She wriggled like a worm on a hook, laughing and pleading incoherently as I hauled her against my chest.

"See? Who's laughing now?"

Her head dropped back, and a peal of laughter filled the air. I took advantage of the position, kissing the exposed column of her neck and gently raking my teeth over the sensitive flesh. The laugh died in her throat and a soft sigh escaped her lips as she turned to putty in my arms. Trailing kisses up her neck, I set her on her feet then spun her to face me.

Her hair fell around her face in gentle waves, and her luminous gray eyes sparkled up at me, cheeks pink from exertion. Why the hell had I ever thought she was cold and unfeeling? Victoria was soft and sweet, and she fit me perfectly, all soft curves to my hard planes of muscle. The passion she'd shown last night told me I'd barely scratched the surface. If I ever had the opportunity to make love to her—and God, did I want to—I knew her desire would set the bedroom on fire.

Cupping her chin in one hand, I watched her eyelids flutter closed as I traced the contour of her jaw with my thumb. I dipped my head and pressed my lips to hers. The tingle of our chemistry ignited a fire inside me that shot sparks of awareness all the way down to my toes. I pulled back and let my gaze wander over her beautiful face.

Husky breaths escaped her parted lips and they quivered slightly as if lamenting the loss of my mouth on hers. I traced one finger along the slight point of her chin, over the apple of one cheek, up to the sculpted, winged eyebrow over her right eye. I met her gaze, heavy-lidded with lust, and I captured her mouth again, unable to resist tasting her once more. A low sound left her throat and I swallowed it as my tongue swept over hers.

Her hands swept over my shoulders, encouraging me to continue. Lips never leaving hers, I bent and slid my hands beneath the curve of her ass. I swept her into my arms and settled in the corner of the couch, arranging her so she was spread over my lap.

I speared my fingers into her hair, cradling her skull and tipping her head for better access as I plundered her mouth. She writhed against me, heat from her center pressing against my groin. I abandoned her silky soft hair and trailed my hands down her back, inching the hem of her robe up her thighs and stroking the soft skin along the crease of her hip. The fabric parted and I delved inside, eager to touch her, skimming my hands along the curve of her full breasts.

She inhaled sharply as I brushed her nipples, and they instantly hardened under my touch. Her body went rigid and I froze, praying I hadn't pushed too hard. After last night, I was dying to touch her again, to run my hands and mouth over every inch of her.

"You okay?"

She let out a shuddering breath. "I... yes."

Her forehead dropped forward to rest on my shoulder and I banded my arms around her lower back, holding her tight. I kissed the tender spot just below her ear, my breath stirring the wisps of hair there as he spoke.

"Sorry, sweetheart."

She shook her head. "It's just..."

It was too much, too soon, and she needed reassurance that she could trust me. Last night had opened the door, but she still had a long way to go. Whether it took days or weeks or years—I wanted to be the one to guide her. I cupped the back of her head and tipped her slightly away, catching her gaze. "We've got plenty of time. Not gonna rush you."

A sweet smile lifted the corners of her mouth. "Thank you."

"Nothin' to thank me for. But," I dipped my head and searched her eyes, "I do want to see you again."

"When?"

"Soon. Dinner tonight?"

Lower lip still caught between her teeth, she let out a soft exhalation and nodded. "Okay."

"Good. I'll pick you up around seven. Wear a dress."

One sleek brow shot toward her hairline. "What do you think this is, 1950? Why do I have to wear a dress?"

"So I can check you out." I grinned as I slid one hand over her knee and up her thigh.

She laughed and lightly smacked my chest but didn't say anything else. I studied her for another moment, a strange combination of emotions radiating through my chest. I recognized part of it as lust for the beautiful woman in my lap. Another was joy that she'd allowed me into her life, trusted me with her body—and maybe even her heart. That remaining feeling eluded me, though. It ran deeper, more powerful than the other two; I felt it down to the tips of my toes. Whatever it was, I wanted a hell of a lot more of it.

CHAPTER TWENTY

Victoria

My phone vibrated on the counter, and I swiped my thumb over the screen as I lifted it to my ear. "Hello?"

"Victoria, how are you?"

"I'm fine, Johnathan. How about you?" I shifted the phone so it lay cradled between my ear and shoulder as I moved around the kitchen.

'Fine' was a drastic understatement. My body still pulsed with unrequited desire, and my skin buzzed like a live wire where Blake had touched me. He'd walked out the door half an hour ago, but the warm, fuzzy feeling he'd stirred inside me had yet to subside. From the tingling of my skin, I doubted it would go away anytime soon. And the thought of dinner with him tonight, maybe going back to his place... A welcome heat spread through my chest then lower to my core, making me feel needy and restless.

He was so different from any other man I'd ever dated. He seemed to intuitively know exactly what I needed; he pushed me out of my comfort zone but still managed to respect my boundaries. The last line that lay between us had become slightly blurred. Did I want Blake to be my first? Trepidation mixed with anticipation coursed through my veins when the immediate answer popped into my mind. *Yes*. I could practically feel the heat rising in my cheeks as I envisioned him in my bed, suspended over me—

"Did you hear about the exhibit the art gallery downtown will be hosting?"

Johnathan's question tore me from my daydream, and I forced myself to focus. "I didn't. Are they featuring anyone good?"

"I'm not really sure. I just read about it this morning, and I thought maybe we could go tonight."

I froze. Should I tell him about Blake? Probably not yet. I didn't want to hurt his feelings, and this was a conversation best had in person. Johnathan *had* been the one to suggest I start dating again, but he'd more than likely meant I should date him. No, for now, I'd just keep quiet until I figured out exactly how to break the news.

"Oh, I'm sorry, I can't. I promised Kate I would come see her today. She's supposed to get released sometime this afternoon."

It wasn't a lie, exactly, just... not the whole truth. A trace of disappointment lined Johnathan's tone when he spoke again. "Do you think you'll be there all evening?"

"Possibly. I hate the thought of her being there all alone. They've been monitoring her for internal bleeding and keeping a close eye on her head for any trauma she may have sustained. Last I heard, everything was normal. They kept her just as a precaution, but she should be fine to come home today."

"Wonderful."

I couldn't tell if the statement was genuine or if there was a hint of sarcasm in there. Either way, it didn't matter. A thought popped into my head. "Did Greg Andrews ever contact you?"

"No. In fact, I left a message for him a few days ago but he never returned my call."

Damn. I really hoped he'd gotten the message. I had no desire to ever have another run-in with him. "Well, then, I wouldn't worry about it. I think we were beyond what he initially came for and he was hanging on out of habit."

Johnathan made a thoughtful noise on the other end. "Do you suppose he was infatuated with you?"

"Could be."

I'd told Detective Sanchez of the possibility of Greg Andrews lashing out, but the idea just didn't seem to fit. Of course, nothing was ever as it seemed. Sometimes people hid their deepest secrets right below the surface.

"Well, you should be extra careful, especially in light of recent events. I love you, Victoria. I just want to make sure you're safe."

I cringed at his words. Though I'd told him before that I loved him as a friend, I had a feeling his love went a whole lot deeper. I swallowed hard before speaking. "I'm sure everything will work out."

He was silent for a moment when I didn't return his sentiment. "Well, maybe I'll give you a call tomorrow and see if you're interested in dinner or something."

"Sounds great."

I disconnected the phone and set it on the counter. "Damn, damn, damn."

I really needed to come clean—and soon. Guilt was already weighing down my conscience and I couldn't bear to see him hurt. He'd been my shoulder to lean on, and he'd given me some great advice over the past couple of years. He didn't know the whole story, but then few people did. He knew I'd been held against my will and that I managed to escape, but I'd left out all the gory details about Leah's murder. I'd opened up to Kate one night, years ago, finally spilling every detail. But Johnathan was a man. A friend, yes, and a great doctor—but still a man. I hadn't quite crossed that hurdle of being able to trust him enough to fully open up.

Why, then, had I told Blake?

I glanced at his coffee cup where it lay in the sink next to mine. I'd known him for barely two weeks. What in the world had prompted me to air my dirty laundry? Because he made me feel... everything. Safe. Happy. *Loved.*

I promptly cut off that last train of thought. It wasn't

love. Attraction, certainly—but not love. People didn't develop those kinds of feelings in just a couple of weeks. As a doctor, I knew it was nothing more than lust driving us. As a woman… I desperately wanted it to be more.

✳

I smiled at Kate as I stepped into the room. "How are you feeling?"

"Ready to get the hell out of here." She sat in a chair by the window, her pale face accentuated by the bruise on her forehead. "I still don't know why they kept me an extra day. Complete waste of resources."

I smiled as Kate rolled her eyes dramatically. It kind of surprised me, too. Usually hospitals pushed people through recovery and out the door to open up the bed for the next patient. Maybe it was more of a professional courtesy than anything, or maybe there really was more trauma than the doctors had initially guessed.

"But everything's okay?" Brain trauma was a tricky thing. Sometimes everything appeared to be okay initially, but latent injury manifested itself later.

Kate nodded. "Normal function. Everything's still there, bad judgment and all."

I frowned. "You weren't the one with poor judgment—Steve was. He's the one who cheated and ruined your marriage."

"Maybe," she agreed, "but it was a bad idea to get married in the first place. We were too young."

I didn't know what to say to that, so I kept quiet. Kate piped up a moment later. "My memory from the other night is coming back, too."

"Really?" That was a good sign. "Did you recognize him?"

"No." She shook her head. "But I do remember a little bit of what he said."

"Oh. I didn't realize he'd said anything."

"I hadn't either. But when I woke up this morning, it was the first thing that popped into my head, clear as day."

Her tone was hesitant, and I warily dropped into the chair beside her. "What did he say?"

"He said you were perfect just the way you were."

My brows drew together. "But if you were perfect, then why—"

"Not me." She glanced my way. "You."

"Me?" I jerked back in surprise.

Kate nodded. "He called me a whore. Told me I was corrupting you, that you were perfect just the way you were."

I couldn't suppress the shiver that racked my body. Someone had attacked her because of me?

"My God. I'm so sorry, I had no idea."

Kate grabbed my hand. "It's not your fault. I didn't want to worry you, but this person is clearly obsessed with you. You need to be extra careful."

I bit my lip. "I think you're right. I think someone broke into my house the other day."

I held up a hand as Kate's eyes rounded in shock and her mouth opened to speak. "Nothing was stolen, at least not that I can see. But it felt different, like someone had been there."

"Did you call the cops?"

"No. Blake came over and checked things out for me."

"Oh?"

I couldn't miss the interest in Kate's question, and a smile curved my mouth. "Then he stayed the night. Last night, too." Her mouth dropped open, and I grinned. "And before you ask, he was a perfect gentleman."

Her face twisted into an expression of dismay. "Well, that's disappointing."

"Although..."

Kate's eyes lit up as I told her all about the night before. "Was that your first time?"

I nodded. "We're going to dinner tonight and I think... I think I'm ready."

"It's a big step," Kate said, her voice serious. "You're

sure?"

"Yeah. Blake is…"

"Sexy? Gorgeous? Ripped?" she supplied with a grin.

I laughed. "Yes—to all of those. But he's… different. I want him to be the first."

"As long as you're certain."

"I am."

"Good." She pinned me with a stare. "I want details tomorrow. All of them." Kate pointed at me. "And don't you dare leave a single thing out."

I grinned. "I wouldn't dream of it."

CHAPTER TWENTY-ONE

Blake

"You're not a vegetarian, are you?" I gestured with my fork toward her salad and Victoria shook her head.

"No, I eat meat occasionally."

I thought she'd eaten the chicken I made the other night, but I couldn't be sure. "I hope you didn't choose it because it's the cheapest thing on the menu. I brought you here to spoil you a little, not starve you. Jesus, a bird couldn't get full on that."

Her lips curled into a smile at my teasing tone before she shrugged. "I don't get much of a chance to work out these days, so it's just the lesser of two evils. I have to be careful what I eat."

"You have nothing to worry about. You're beautiful."

"I just... I don't know. I've always been self-conscious. Leah..." She dropped her gaze to the table. "She was the pretty one—the homecoming queen, the one all the guys flocked to. Next to her, I felt like the Ugly Duckling. I've tried to diet, but it's like I can never lose those last ten pounds."

"That's because you're not meant to. Your body is perfect just the way it is." I allowed my gaze to rove over the parts of her I could see. "Curvy, sexy, just begging to be touched. Who wants some supermodel who looks like she'll break the second you touch her?"

I shook my head. "Besides, Victoria, all that matters is what you think. If you're happy with yourself, then screw everyone else."

Our conversation was interrupted by the waiter stopping by to refill our drinks. "Can I get you two anything else, or will that be all? Our chef made a fabulous tiramisu tonight."

I shot her a look. "Dessert?"

Longing flashed in her eyes before she quickly blinked it away. "I really shouldn't."

I stared at her for a moment before directing my gaze back to the waiter. "I'll take it. Thank you."

The man nodded and left, and I turned to her. "You're sharing with me, you know."

A tiny smile broke over her face, even as she shook her head. "You'll regret those words tomorrow when I'm carrying an extra ten pounds on my hips."

"Not a chance. I love your curves." Her head dipped at the compliment and I smiled, amazed at the woman across from me. She was sweet yet sassy, innocent but still the most tempting thing I'd ever seen. "What's your favorite food?"

The question caught her off guard, and she jerked her head up. "Why?"

"I'm curious."

A smile lit her face. "Ice cream, of course. What else do you want to know about me?"

As I studied her, I felt something shift within me. I hadn't realized what I'd been missing until she'd walked into my life. "Everything."

"Well..." She bit her lip. "You know a lot already. I'm originally from Ohio, but I've been here for almost ten years. I love art and music, and I hate sports."

I smiled. I should have guessed, after her remark about hunting this morning. "Do you ever go back home, to Ohio?"

Her face immediately fell. "No."

"Why's that? Don't you miss your parents?" I couldn't imagine being separated from my family for almost a decade with little to no contact. My parents and sisters drove me batshit crazy, but I loved them to death and flew in to see them whenever I could.

She played with a stray crumb on the tablecloth. "We don't exactly get along."

That sucked. "Are they mad you left?"

"Well, they're kind of the reason I moved away." She avoided my gaze completely, and unease settled in my gut. "After everything happened, it was kind of hard having me around, I guess. They're really religious and they saw me as... tainted."

"They what?" My voice was deceptively soft, a direct contradiction to the fury spreading through my body like wildfire. I forced myself to calm down when I saw the expression of shame and disappointment on Victoria's face. *Fucking hell*. Was this the shit she'd spent the past ten years believing? That she'd invited the attack and was now somehow unworthy? I prayed to God I never met them—or the asshole who'd done this to her—because I couldn't be responsible for my actions if I did.

"What happened was *not* your fault." I reached across the table and grasped her hand. "Doc, look at me."

I waited a full ten seconds before her eyes finally met mine, heart threatening to pound out of my chest. "None of it was your fault. Understand?"

Her head bobbed once, but it was less than convincing. "You were a young kid trying to help someone in need. You did nothing to invite trouble then, and you sure as hell had nothing to do with it now. It's not your fault some crazed idiot is stalking you." I turned her hand over and laced my fingers through hers. "You are not tainted, so don't you believe that shit for one second. You are perfect—absolutely fucking perfect. Don't ever let anyone try to tell you otherwise."

Her eyes dropped back to the table, but not before I caught the fine sheen of tears that she tried to blink away. I squeezed her fingers tighter in silent support, and a moment later, she met my gaze again. "Thank you for that."

"I mean it."

"I know." A small smile curved her face. "Kate tried to tell me the same thing a few years ago, but... I think I wasn't ready to hear it then. It still hurt too much. Thank you for believing in me."

It blew my mind that this woman—so smart and so strong—had helped hundreds of other people overcome their anxieties and fears and shortcomings, all while she'd been torn apart on the inside, grieving the childhood she'd lost. The events had been completely out of her control, yet she'd been treated like a leper, cast out of her own family. A sense of protectiveness barreled through me, and I vowed never to let her feel that way again.

"You don't have to thank me for anything. Look at you: you're a survivor. You've made something of yourself. You're an amazing person—because of *you* and no one else. Don't let anyone's opinions—not your family's, not your friends', hell, not even mine—sway you. Ever. You're fucking incredible just the way you are, and I count myself lucky every day to be with you."

Tears swam in her eyes again and I ached to hold her, kiss those tears away, but the approaching waiter cut off that train of thought. With one last squeeze of her hand, I offered her a smile. "Now, no more of that. Tonight is about you and me, and our first official date."

With a smile, the waiter dropped off the tiramisu and the check, and I nodded toward Victoria. "You first."

I scooted around the table and draped an arm over the back of her chair, eager to be close to her. Victoria shot me a shy smile as she picked up her fork and sliced through the creamy layers then lifted it to her mouth. Her lips closed around the tines, and my groin tightened with appreciation.

A vision of my cock sliding between her plump pink lips caused my dick to swell and press against the zipper of my slacks. I knew she was inexperienced, and she'd probably never wrapped her lips around a man's cock before—God, I hoped not—but I couldn't get the image out of my mind. Unable to contain myself any longer, I pulled the fork from her hands and her eyes widened as I lifted my hand to her jaw.

"You have something right here." Using my thumb, I brushed a crumb from the corner of her mouth and pressed my lips to hers. That familiar blush spread over Victoria's cheeks and I couldn't help but grin. "Have I told you recently how much I love kissing you?"

She dipped her head and a self-conscious smile spread over her face. "Me, too."

I leaned forward, capturing her mouth again for another kiss. As I pulled away her head dipped in embarrassment. "What's wrong?"

Her eyes met mine. "Nothing."

She sighed when I lifted a brow. "It's just..." She gestured around the restaurant, presumably at the other patrons. "I've never been good at this kind of stuff. It makes me feel like I'm the center of attention."

"Well, you're just going to have to get over that. I want you to know that I'm in this for you, to show you every minute how much I care about you." God knew the people who were supposed to have loved her and supported her had all let her down. I was damn well going to do my best to make up for it. "Plus, I want everyone here to know you're mine."

She blinked up at me. "Sounds like you're staking your claim."

"Do you have a problem with that?"

She regarded me for a moment. "Not as long as you're being honest. I don't want to be hurt."

I stroked a finger along the line of her jaw before gliding my lips softly over hers. "I would never hurt you. I meant what I said: I just want you—all of you. No ulterior motives."

A sweet smile stole across her face. "It's nice to feel wanted."

My cock throbbed incessantly. God, if only she knew. "You have no idea how much I want you, Victoria. It's killing me to hold back. Good thing I promised to be a gentleman tonight, otherwise we'd already be back at my place."

"Then why don't you?"

I shook my head and pushed down my automatic reaction to her suggestive tone. I already wouldn't be able to leave the table for the next ten minutes until my arousal died down. "I'm trying to do the right thing here. I told you we'd take our time with this, and I'm a man of my word."

She studied me for a moment before settling a hand on my thigh. "I don't want your word, Blake."

I could hear the rush of blood in my ears, and I fought to control my breathing as my muscles tensed under her touch. "What exactly are you saying, Victoria? Because I need to know right now."

Her eyes flickered with uncertainty and her teeth raked across her lower lip before she responded, the words leaving her mouth on a whisper. "I want you."

I stared hard at her. "Are you sure about this? Absolutely positive? Because once we do this…"

She leaned in, her lips mere millimeters from my ear. "Take me home, Blake."

CHAPTER TWENTY-TWO

Blake

I pushed open the front door and allowed Victoria to precede me inside. The door closed with a decisive click and I snapped the lock into place. As soon as the sound reached Victoria's ears, she whirled toward me, eyes wide. Adopting the most casual position I could muster, I propped one foot on the door behind me and shoved my hands into my pockets. She watched me warily like she was second-guessing her decision, and I forced myself to slow down. She knew why we'd come back here—she'd been the one to suggest it. But saying something and following through with it were two very different things.

I offered her a tight smile. Jesus, I felt like an awkward teenager on a first date. "I can take you home if you'd like."

She bit her lip before answering, her gaze darting around the room. "No. I..."

Her words trailed off, uncertainty clouding her features. I pushed off the door and extended a hand to her. "How about we start with the grand tour?"

She glanced around the room. The ranch-style house was older but clean and cozy, and I tried to see it from her point of view. It looked lived-in without being cluttered, and the furniture was large and comfortable. Her perusal of the room brought her gaze back to me and her eyes lit on my hand.

After what I was sure was an intense internal deliberation, she slipped her palm into mine.

I guided her further into the house. "Living room. There's the kitchen and dining room," I added, pointing to the small kitchen at the back of the house.

A short hallway broke off to the left and I stopped in front of a doorway. "I use the spare bedroom as an office."

Although to call it an office was kind of an overstatement. Boxes stood two-deep, stacked head-high around the perimeter of the room, and the only workspace was an equally cluttered desk, papers and paraphernalia scattered across the oak surface.

Victoria glanced inside, and her eyes widened as she let out a startled laugh. "Good lord, are you hoarding inventory for a warehouse?"

"Hey, I have a lot of stuff."

She tipped her chin up, gray eyes sparkling. "You think? And they say women are high maintenance."

I wrapped my free arm around her waist and pulled her flush against me. "Hey, cut me some slack. I just moved in."

"Are you kidding me? This place looks like it belongs on an episode of Hoarders!" She threw her head back on a laugh, but it was cut short as I slipped a hand down to smack her bottom. She danced away from me, retreating farther down the hall, one hand covering the stinging flesh as she pouted prettily. "Ow!"

"Serves you right." I narrowed my eyes and slowly advanced toward her. She bit her lip and threw a quick glance over her shoulder, already taking a step backward. I lunged at her with a low growl, and her high-pitched shriek morphed into laughter as she whirled away and darted into the bedroom.

I took off after her, slowing my pace as I crossed the threshold. She stood across the room, the large king-sized bed between us. "Trapped now, beautiful."

I rounded the foot of the bed with slow, measured steps, all the while watching Victoria's body twitch with anticipation. With a sudden burst of movement, I hurdled the corner of the bed and swept her into my arms. Victoria let out a squeal but managed to evade my clasping hands and scramble free. She was almost across the bed when I grabbed her ankle and pulled her back to me.

Victoria dissolved into a fit of laughter as I rolled her to her back. One knee pressed to the mattress between her legs, I caged her in my arms. Her gray eyes met mine and her smile faded, her gaze suddenly serious and intent.

My heart raced as I stared down at her. Her skin, though perpetually tan from the hot Texas sun, was flushed, and I traced a finger lightly over the apple of her cheeks. Her eyes fluttered closed, and I ran the tip of one finger down the curve of her jaw and over her bottom lip. Victoria's chin lifted instinctively, and I brushed a kiss across the plump flesh of her mouth.

Her eyes slid open and met mine as I pulled back. Her hand lifted to cup my cheek and I turned my chin into her palm, the bristles of my five o'clock shadow grazing her soft skin. "Goddamn, sweetheart. We should stop."

"What if I don't want to?" Victoria's tongue darted out, wetting her bottom lip, and I let out a low growl.

"Damn it, Doc, I'm trying to be a gentleman here."

Her fingers curled into the fabric of my shirt, her voice low and breathy. "Don't."

I met her halfway, ravaging her mouth, and her fingers deftly slipped the buttons free of their holes. The fabric hung loose at my sides and she placed her palms on my chest, the heat of her touch searing my flesh.

"Tell me." It was an order, and her eyes widened a fraction. I needed to hear the words. "Tell me what you want."

The wait was agonizingly long before she finally broke the silence. "You, Blake. I..." She licked her lips and blinked up at me, eyes hooded and sultry. "I want you."

It was almost unfathomable that she would trust me with this. My heart swelled with pride and admiration as I brushed the hair away from her face with one hand. I needed to take my time with her, make sure she enjoyed this first time because I sure as hell planned on doing it more than once. A *lot* more.

I inched her dress up, my fingers gliding over the creamy flesh of her thighs. Her body trembled, and lifted my gaze to hers. "Nervous or... turned on?"

"Both."

The word came out on a breathy whisper, and I couldn't help but smile as I pressed my lips to her hip bone. I stripped the dress over her head, leaving her in a pair of lacy black panties and a matching bra. I lifted a brow and she squirmed under the scrutiny. I leaned forward and dropped a soft kiss on her lips. "You're so beautiful, Victoria. Every inch of you is absolutely perfect."

To reinforce my words, I placed a row of gentle kisses down the column of her neck to her breastbone. Fingering the scalloped edging of the sexy black bra, I pulled the cup down to reveal her lush breast. Her back arched with pleasure and she let out a low moan as my thumb flicked over the sensitive nipple.

"I want to see all of you."

Snaking my hands behind her I deftly unclasped the bra, then slid the thin straps down her arms. She was so beautiful, so perfect—and she was all mine. Desire simmered in my veins, infusing me with a power I'd never experienced before. I felt like I'd splinter into a thousand pieces if she pulled away from me now.

"Are you sure about this? If not..."

Her fingers curled into my hair, silencing my questions as she pulled my head down for another kiss, and I gave in to sweet bliss.

CHAPTER TWENTY-THREE

Victoria

The man could *kiss*. His mouth coaxed me to trust him as he trailed his fingers lower to the apex of my thighs, and I shifted restlessly, nearly mindless with need. My heart beat a million miles a minute—from anxiety or anticipation, I wasn't quite sure.

His fingers slipped beneath the skimpy black lace of my panties, and he inched them down my legs, then slipped them off over first one stiletto, then the other. Turning his attention back to my center, he brushed the tiny bundle of nerves and I let out a low moan, fisting my hands in the sheets.

The sensation was wonderful, better than anything I'd ever imagined, and I allowed my legs to fall open to accommodate his questing fingers. He slid down further still, swiping through my slick folds, and I arched my hips, wanting, *needing* him to touch me there—to touch me everywhere. I couldn't get enough. One long finger slipped inside, and my muscles tightened around him. He was gentle, almost reverent, and it felt unbearably good. He'd awakened my passion last night, and now I needed more.

"Blake." The note of pleading in my voice made me want to cringe, but I refused to regret it. His eyes snapped to mine, almost burning me with their intensity. He looked like he wanted to devour me, and the thought sent a little shiver down my spine. "Blake, please."

He settled his heavy weight over me, bracing himself on his forearms as he stared down at me. "We can stop any time."

I shook my head. No, I wanted him—all of him. There was no going back now. When I told him my story last night, he'd been sympathetic, even angry on my behalf, but hadn't once made me feel vulnerable or blamed me for what happened. Instead, he'd torn down the last of my walls, taken the bad memory and replaced it with passion and something deeper, more intimate than I'd ever known. I trusted Blake with my safety—and my heart.

After this evening, I knew. When he'd looked at me, his expression sincere, I knew in that moment he would never force me, never hurt me. And I wanted him more than I'd wanted anything in my entire life.

He straightened away from me and shrugged out of his shirt, the material sliding over his sculpted muscles and pooling on the ground in a soft heap. My gaze flitted over him, absorbing every detail. The man was gorgeous. Broad shoulders tapered to a narrow waist, the taut muscles clearly defined beneath the tanned flesh. Dark tattoos curled around his biceps and shoulder, winding around to his upper back. Several scars marked his torso and I lightly traced a time-faded line on his abdomen about four inches long.

"How did you get that?"

"Knife."

A small smile curved my lips as I lifted my eyes to his, but his expression was serious. Good Lord, he wasn't kidding. My fingers drifted over his torso, tracing several other marks embedded in his flesh, faded by time.

He captured my palm in his, halting my exploration. "Those scars are from a lifetime ago, sweetheart."

His hazel eyes glowed in the dim light, so honest and sincere. Without another thought, I threw my arms around his neck and pulled him down to me. The kiss was frantic and needy, the deep-rooted desire threatening to sweep me away. Snaking a hand between us, I coasted my hand over the rippling muscles of his abdomen, down to the vee of his pelvis, then halted on the button on his slacks.

I hesitated for a long moment and he pulled back just enough to stare at me in silent question. I shook my head. I'd been terrified for years—scared to live, scared to be free. But Blake had changed all that. He'd taken those fears away and shown me that it was okay to just be... me.

I popped the button free of its hole and eagerly pushed the material down over his hips, taking his boxers with them. Still caged in his arms, I could only reach so far, and I let out a small sound of frustration. He straightened with a chuckle and quickly shucked them, then stepped out of his socks and shoes.

As he stared down at me, I became acutely aware of my nudity. My muscles trembled with the need to cover myself, but I beat back the urge as his hands moved to my stilettos, the only remaining article of clothing covering my body. He slipped one shoe off and dropped it to the floor, and the second shoe disappeared in the same fashion. He kissed the arch of my left foot, and I bit back a laugh as the short hairs of his beard tickled my skin.

His eyes jumped to mine. "What's so funny?"

I bit back a grin. "Your beard tickles."

"Oh?" He dropped his head again and kissed his way up my calf and over my inner thigh, teasing me until I writhed beneath him.

He dropped a kiss on my stomach, then moved over me until he stared down into my eyes. "I love when you laugh."

There was a tenderness in his expression I'd never seen before, and I closed my eyes as emotion rolled through me. It seemed I'd waited a lifetime for this, and I was so glad I had. I blinked my eyes open and met Blake's gaze, dark with desire. "I feel like I've waited forever for this... For you."

"Me, too." His lips caught mine in a gentle kiss, and the tension slowly drained from my muscles. I ran my hands over his biceps as his mouth continued to cast its magic spell over me. I felt him lift slightly away then reach between our bodies to roll on a condom. I was incredibly grateful he'd thought of it because I'd been so delirious with pleasure that safety hadn't even occurred to me. Blake resettled himself over me, sealing us together from chest to thigh and kissed me once more. The thick crown of his erection nudged my core, then slid an inch inside. I gasped, more from surprise than pain.

"Just relax, sweetheart," he spoke against my lips.

The nervousness in my heart slowly melted, giving way to eager anticipation as Blake leaned forward, caging me between thick, powerful arms and pressing me into the bed. His thick length prodded my opening, and I instinctively clenched my thighs around his.

"I'll take care of you." He stared down at me, and his thumb stroked lightly over my cheek. "I promise."

He dipped his head for another kiss, and I momentarily forgot my worries as his tongue teased mine. A thousand thoughts flitted through my mind, the sensations over-whelming in their intensity. My muscles slowly expanded around him, accepting him deeper, and a strange feeling radi-ated through my body—a dull pain combined with the heady deliciousness as he stretched me, commanded my body.

My breath suspended in my lungs as he sank in to the hilt. As quickly as the twinge of pain came, it faded away again. He pulled out before sliding back in, the sensation making me feel almost unbearably full. His pelvis brushed my clit as he stroked into me again and again, and I felt a new tension begin to build. I felt as if I was being pulled in a thousand directions at once—I wanted to speed it up, slow it down, suspend time completely. My body was taut and tense, anxiously waiting for whatever would happen next.

"Relax, sweetheart." Opening my eyes, I saw Blake staring down at me.

I nodded a little, unable to speak, and forced myself to ease my hold on him. He kissed my face, my throat, using his hands and mouth as encouragement as he rocked into me, slow and deep. Each thrust stroked my inner walls, urging me closer and closer to completion.

"Just let go," Blake murmured against my temple. "I'm right here, baby. I'll catch you."

My breath caught in my throat as he changed angles, and I came on a silent scream.

I'd used a vibrator before, but this... This was new. I'd never come so hard, so intensely, before. I clung to him as he increased his tempo and came with a ragged groan. He rested on top of me for a moment before shifting onto his side, pulling me flush against him.

Ensconced in his warm, strong embrace, I shifted my legs and grinned. It had been amazing, so much better than I'd ever imagined. I wanted to melt into him, get closer than skin, and I shifted further into his embrace.

His arms tightened around me. "I'm sorry, sweetheart. It'll be better next time."

How in the world could it be better? He'd been reverent and caring, gentle and loving. I'd been right to trust him with my first time; no one but Blake could've made it more amazingly sensual and sweet.

"It was... perfect."

His lips found my forehead for a soft kiss, and he curled a hand a possessively over my hip. "How are you feeling?"

"A little sore," I admitted.

"How about a soak in the tub?"

Despite my protests, he scooped me up and carried me to the bathroom across the hall. A clawfoot tub sat beneath a large frosted glass window, and he set me on my feet beside it. I studied Blake as he flipped the handle of the faucet and hot, steamy water poured into the tub. His muscles rippled beneath deeply tanned skin, hard-won from all the physical labor he'd endured while in the field.

I'd seen him partially clothed, but somehow this was different. The thin layer separating us had been stripped away, and I'd never felt more exposed. My cheeks burned as I admired his perfect silhouette, and I crossed my arms over my chest, immediately self-conscious.

The motion caught Blake's attention and he turned

toward me, examining my face. "What's wrong?"

I shook my head. "Nothing."

One dark eyebrow rose, silently calling my bluff. He wrapped his fingers around my wrists and gently pulled my arms away from my body.

Mortification welled inside me. "What are you doing?"

"Don't hide from me." I opened my mouth to protest, but he spoke over me. "I know this is new for you, but it's just me."

Didn't he realize that was the problem? He was beautiful in the most masculine way and I... well, I was just plain old Victoria. Mousy and shy with equally uninspiring features and an extra ten pounds that taunted me every time I tried on clothes.

"You're beautiful." He took my hand and placed it flat on his chest, over his heart. My fingers curled against the hardened muscle. He lifted my other hand to his mouth and pressed a kiss to my palm. "And I want to see every inch of you."

Lifting my arm, he curved it around his neck and pulled me flush against him. I could feel him everywhere, from the tips of my toes brushing against his all the way up to his nose nuzzling my hair. He ran his hands lightly down my spine then back up. His palm continued upward, curling around the back of my neck and tipping my face up for a kiss. My reservations melted away the feel of his lips on mine, soft and sweet. He broke the kiss then gave my neck a soft squeeze, those hazel eyes seeming to read deep into my soul.

Stepping over the edge of the tub, he lifted me in and pulled me down as he sat, settling me between his legs. My breasts skimmed the top of the water as I lay back against him, and I sank lower. As if knowing exactly what I needed, he wrapped his arms around me, holding me close. I immediately felt less exposed and my heart warmed at his silent reassurance. As I relaxed into his embrace, his hands left my breasts and traveled over my body, massaging the tension from my muscles. He clasped his fingers around mine, softly brushing the backs of my hands with his thumbs. We remained inter-twined for a long while before he dropped a soft kiss on my temple.

"Ready to get out?"

Reluctant to abandon this tender moment with him, I slowly nodded and climbed from the cool water. He grabbed a towel from a rack on the wall and enfolded me within the fluffy material, briskly running his hands over my body. He wrapped a towel around his own slim hips, then led me back to the bedroom. I stooped down to pick up my panties, but a heavy hand on my shoulder stopped me and I straightened to look at him.

Nervously twisting the material of the towel, I dropped my gaze. "I should probably..."

His large hand cupped my jaw, forcing me to meet his stare. The desire I saw there made my stomach flip and my heart beat double time. "Stay with me."

His words were low and husky, and I shivered at the feel of them as they settled over me. "I'm not sure..."

He held out a hand, silently imploring me to trust him. I stared at it for a moment before dropping the towel and placing my fingers in his. With his free hand, he flipped back the covers and slid into the bed, then tugged me in behind him. As he pulled the comforter over us, I settled against him and tucked my arms in close, not quite sure what to do with them.

"Hand."

I lifted my head to look him in the eyes. "What?"

"Give me your hand."

I pulled my left hand from between us and offered it to him. He kissed my fingers and placed them palm-down over his heart, his own heavy hand resting on top of it. With a secret smile at the unexpected gesture, I lay my head on his chest and breathed deeply. Contentment pulled at me and I closed my eyes, allowing the warmth and protection of his embrace to lull me to sleep.

CHAPTER TWENTY-FOUR

He drummed his fingers on the steering wheel as he gazed at the little house. The vantage point wasn't ideal, but he couldn't risk getting any closer. He'd waited until well after dark to drive past her house then circled back and parked on the opposite side of the street. A single light was on in the living room, but he hadn't sensed any movement in the twenty minutes since he'd been here. It was almost eleven o'clock—she should be home. It was possible she'd gone to bed, but something nagged at him.

Needing to see for himself, he slid out of the car and crossed the lawn, taking care to slink through the shadows. As he approached the house, the light in the living room clicked off. He froze, concealed behind a large rhododendron, and counted to fifty before peering over the sill of the living room window. The TV wasn't on, and the coffee table was devoid of any cups or dishes. It didn't look like she'd been there all evening. Although her car was in the driveway, the house seemed... empty. Lifeless.

Anxiety gnawing at him, he decided to press his luck. He stole through the shadows to the back door. The routine was comforting in its familiarity. He knew every inch of her house inside and out. He'd sat on her couch, run his hands over the clothes in her closet. Lain in her bed.

A smile tugged at the corners of his mouth, spurring him on. Soon, so very soon, she'd be there with him. He'd made significant strides with her these past few months—except for their recent hiccup.

He was still furious with Victoria's friend for trying to change her, but honestly, he didn't altogether mind. He'd always thought she was a beautiful woman. Now that she dressed in more flattering clothes, she was even more so. She would complement him perfectly, and no man would ever touch her—except him. She was meant for him alone.

He expertly picked the lock on the back door and entered into the laundry room next to the kitchen. The alarm beeped its low warning, and he bolted to the front of the house, eager to disengage the system before it announced his presence. He punched in the code and ducked into the dining room, listening intently for movement. When none came, he smiled to himself. The feeling quickly evaporated, the smile sliding from his face. She really should be more careful with her security precautions. It was so easy to bypass things these days. The fact that she'd used a very important set of numbers didn't help either. They represented a date that was intimately familiar to him—and to her. She'd lost her best friend and her innocence while he'd gained... everything.

He'd never truly known power and dominance until that night. That feeling as he held Leah's life in his hands and slowly snuffed it out... it was incomparable. It hadn't been intentional, not really. But when he'd overheard the two of them in the movie store, talking about boys—talking about sex—he hadn't been able to help himself. Leah had been a whore, and he couldn't abide women with no morals.

Victoria, on the other hand... She was one in a million. At first, he'd assumed that she was just like her friend. Although he'd been shocked to discover that she'd survived, he decided it was an act of fate. He existed just on the periphery of her life, watching, waiting.

But he was wrong. She'd never been with a man. He knew from the way she carried herself, the way she interacted with the men she'd dated. Never going on more than a few dates with one man, she was reserved and aloof. He'd realized then that she was waiting for the right man—waiting for *him*. The thought filled him with elation. She'd eluded him once, but now he had her. Almost.

Now that the alarm had quieted, he gazed at his surroundings, listening for any little sound. The house remained still, too still, and he knew it was empty.

Dear God, had something happened to her? Worry spread through him. She'd deviated from her routine and he didn't like it, not one bit. He needed to look around, see if anything stood out. Careful to avoid the windows, he wound his way through the bottom floor of the house. Sticking close to the wall in the living room, he glanced at the lamp that had illuminated the room. Much as he'd guessed, it was on a timer.

He climbed the stairs on silent feet and tiptoed down the hallway to her bedroom. Moonlight spilled in through the windows, aided by the yellow glow of a street lamp, and he gazed around the room. Nothing appeared to be out of place. Her robe lay draped over a chair in the corner, toothbrush tucked into its holder on the bathroom counter. But no Victoria—and no purse.

The realization hit him like a ton of bricks. He hadn't seen a handbag anywhere downstairs, and there was no sign of one up here, either. She'd gone somewhere with someone. Whoever it was had probably picked her up and taken her somewhere. She would be back soon, then.

Wistfully, he glanced at the queen-sized bed. Just one moment wouldn't hurt. He stretched out on the bed, stroking the soft cotton of the comforter, imagining the feel of her next to him. His cheek nuzzled her pillow and he inhaled deeply. She would be soft and sweet and—

He jerked upright and sniffed again, unable to believe he'd missed it until just now. Lifting the pillow, he buried his nose in the fabric. A man's scent, musky and male, assaulted his senses. Rage coursed through his body and red crept into the edges of his vision as his control snapped. His fingers curled into the flimsy fabric and pulled. Stuffing exploded in a puff of white as the fabric ripped, and he flung it to the side.

The second pillow met its demise in a similar fashion, and he tore the tainted sheets from the bed.

She'd had a man here. In her bed—in his *place.*

The thought spurred him on, and he whipped the knife from where it rested against his calf. The long blade gleamed as it slashed down into the mattress over and over until his heart raced and his lungs heaved with exertion. Fury driving him, he stabbed the knife into the wall. Digging around in his pocket, he found the object and hung it from the knife. Pale moonlight fell across it, the gold glinting in the thin shaft of light.

He'd worked too hard for this. He couldn't—*wouldn't*—give up now. She would be his, damn it. He would make sure of it.

CHAPTER TWENTY-FIVE

Blake

Soft hair spilled over my chest and shoulder, tickling my skin, and I shifted the sleepy woman in my arms. Victoria let out a soft grumble and I smiled into her hair. I trailed a finger over each of hers, across the back of her hand and up her arm to her shoulder. Victoria shivered at the contact as I brushed the tiny wisps of hair at the base of her neck and she turned her head, burying her nose against my chest. I pulled her more tightly to me, relishing the feel of her as she snuggled close.

She wiggled as she came awake, and I bit back a groan as her thigh brushed my cock, straining and eager to sink inside her again. I blocked her knee as it came up, then adjusted myself. "Time to get up, sweetheart."

"Mmm." She sighed contentedly, groping blindly for the sheet.

I chuckled and caught her hand in mine. "C'mon, sleepy-head."

Her face scrunched up in consternation as I extracted the sheet from her questing fingers. "What time is it?"

I quirked a smile. Victoria was *not* a morning person. "Almost ten."

Her eyes flew open wide as she tore herself from my arms and bolted upright. "Ten in the morning?"

"That's usually how it works," I teased, reaching for her.

She evaded my hands and, realizing she was naked, grabbed up the sheets and held them to her chest. "I never sleep in this late."

"You were exhausted, and it looked like you needed the rest."

She'd fallen into a deep sleep as soon as she curled against my side, and I'd lain here for the last three hours, alternately dozing and watching her until she woke up, not wanting to abandon her. I'd spent the time enjoying the feel of her next to me and thinking—about the past, about the future, the things I wanted to do, the places I wanted to see... the things I couldn't live without. Victoria was slowly making her way into that last category, and I wasn't quite sure how I felt about that.

I'd only known her for a couple of weeks, but there was something about her that called to me—more than protectiveness, stronger than just simple attraction. Some unnamable force had pushed Victoria into my path, and I'd be a fool to ignore the signs. The more I was around her, the more I liked her, the more I wanted her to become a permanent part of my life.

I wanted to know all about her, wanted to be the person she turned to, not just for help, but for everything—comfort, passion, reassurance, and everything in between. I wanted to sit across the table from her each evening and talk about everything and nothing, and I wanted her to fall asleep in my arms every night.

The Victoria in my bed was a far cry from the Ice Queen I'd met that first day at the healthplex. I loved the way she'd come out of her shell, and I wanted to learn everything about her.

"Do you have stuff to do today?"

"Not particularly. I wanted to go see Kate, but other than that..." She trailed off with a small shrug. "What did you have in mind?"

"For starters..." My eyes skated over her body and a grin split my face. "I want you to get your butt back over here."

I ripped the sheet away from her, and she let out a soft cry of distress. "Hey!"

I rose up on all fours and she held up a hand as I crawled across the bed toward her.

"Blake..." She let out shriek of laughter as I rolled her under me, peppering her face with kisses. "Stop, please!"

I braced myself over her with a grin. "Give me one good reason."

"I haven't brushed my teeth yet."

I rolled my eyes. "That's hardly a good reason."

"It is! Did you know that poor dental hygiene can lead to all kinds of things, including heart disease? It's even been linked to erectile dysfunction."

My brows drew together and I relaxed my stance, leaning backward to rest on my heels. "Is that true?"

"I don't know, but it sounded good!" Victoria rolled away with a spurt of laughter and raced to the bathroom, slamming the door behind her.

I couldn't believe I'd fallen for that. With a grin, I heaved myself off the bed and padded across the hallway to the bathroom.

"I was hoping you might show me around a bit today if you have some free time."

The door cracked open and she peeked out. "Really?"

"I thought you could show me some of your favorite spots. We'll grab lunch and just... relax."

Preferably in bed—after we'd made love again—but she'd figure that out soon enough.

She studied me for a moment. "I was going to stop by Kate's house today to check on her. Do you want to come with me?"

"Of course. I'd like to see how she's doing anyway."

The sweetest smile lit her face, and she stared at me as if I'd hung the moon. I just barely refrained from barging in and sweeping her off her feet, taking her back to bed.

"I'd love to."

"Perfect." I grasped her chin and kissed her once, hard.

"We'll stop by your house real quick so you can change, then we'll head out."

Just under an hour later, we stepped through the front door of Victoria's house. She turned automatically to disarm the system, but silence hung heavily in the air.

"That's strange," she murmured.

"Is something wrong?" I automatically glanced around, but nothing jumped out at me.

"I must have forgotten to set the alarm. I remember being in a hurry because you had just shown up, and..." She shrugged. "I must've walked right out without arming it."

"Do you want me to look around?"

"No, it's okay." She waved off my offer. "I'm sure it was just me. I've been a little sidetracked lately."

"I can see how that'd happen." I pulled her in for a quick kiss. "Go on up and change, sweetheart. I'll be right here. Unless you'd like some help. I'd be more than happy to lend a hand. Or two."

I hooked a finger in the waistband of her jeans and she pushed me away with a laugh. "You stay right here."

"I don't even get to watch?"

She stretched up on her toes for another kiss. "Maybe if you're nice, you'll get to see me tonight."

She threw a saucy smirk over her shoulder, hips swaying with each step as she disappeared from view. I pulled my phone from my back pocket and sank onto the couch with a grin. Damn woman was going to be the death of me.

I'd stopped by the QSG office yesterday and told Con about Victoria's assault back in Ohio. I suspected her captor had been trailing her for years, but the question was—why target her now? She'd changed her name, done everything right to cover her tracks. Since she'd been a minor at the time, her record was sealed. Or, at least, it should have been. Had someone managed to find the original file, or had the killer just now found her by sheer luck? Con was doing some digging into the case and would let me know what he'd found. So far, I hadn't heard anything.

"Blake?" Victoria's voice floated down the stairs, and I called back to her, eyes never leaving the phone.

"Yeah, babe?"

"Blake."

Her voice was soft, deceptively calm, yet I could hear the tension hovering just below the surface. I was already rising from the couch, stowing my phone away when I caught sight of Victoria. She'd paused halfway down the steps, face white as a sheet.

"What's wrong?"

She lifted a shaky hand to point over her shoulder. "Someone was in my room."

"Are you sure?"

She nodded silently, and I slipped my hand into hers. After all she'd been through, there was no harm in making her feel overly secure.

"Is something missing?" I watched her face as she spoke.

"I can't tell."

I lifted a brow at the strange statement. She'd only been up here for a minute or two, how could she have possibly...?

I turned my gaze toward the bedroom and jerked to a stop. "Goddamn it!"

The room had been massacred. Whoever was responsible had spent an inordinate amount of time taking their rage out on her bed. The pillows were shredded, and her mattress had been hacked literally to pieces, most of which littered the floor like a fine layer of snow, covering everything underneath.

"Fuck!" Rage rippled through me and I clenched my fist to keep from putting it through the nearest wall.

Admittedly, I hadn't really taken her claim seriously, thinking she'd just been stressed out and reading too much into things. Turning to the woman in question, I noted her remarkable calm. She was scared, I could see it in her eyes, but she assessed the situation with a steel spine.

Unable to control my rioting emotions, I hauled her against me. "Thank God you weren't here."

She allowed me to wrap my arms around her, but her eyes never wavered from a spot on the wall across the room.

"What's wrong?"

She lifted a shaky finger and pointed. "That necklace."

It hung from the blade of a knife that'd been driven into the drywall just to the right of the bed. "Is it special to you?"

"Not to me." She licked her lips. "Leah."

I stared at her. "Did she have one like that?"

"She was wearing it the night she was murdered."

CHAPTER TWENTY-SIX

Victoria

I stood off to the side, watching the proceedings, numb with shock. I couldn't take my eyes off the necklace. *Her* necklace. The one hanging from the wall wasn't mine, I knew that much. The matching locket was in my jewelry armoire, the clasp broken from so many years of wear. This one was pristine, and it looked exactly the way it had when we'd received them for Christmas, only a few months before Leah was murdered.

I was acutely aware of Blake shooting furtive glances my way every few seconds. It was both reassuring and unsettling. He'd immediately taken charge and called the cops in. Now he and Detective Sanchez stood off to the side, speaking quietly while the others combed the room.

The killer had left it for me, out in the open where I'd be sure to see it. Was he bragging about his accomplishments, or was he indicating that I would be next? The locket hung from the wall, the chain dangling from the blade of a deadly knife. I didn't own anything like it, never had. Even from here, it looked wicked with a heavy-duty black handle. A chill snaked down my spine. Was that the same knife he'd used on Leah?

Anger surged through me. The bastard had been in my house. How long had he been watching me, just waiting for the right moment?

A combination of anger and fear sent my limbs trembling. Within seconds, Blake was at my side. "You good?"

"Fine."

He planted himself in front of me, obscuring my view of the room. "Sweetheart, you should sit down for a minute. Detective Sanchez wants to ask you a few questions anyway."

Briefly closing my eyes, I swayed on my feet and Blake yanked me against him. "We're going downstairs. Now."

"No."

"Yes." His eyes were hard as he stared down at me. "You need a break. Can you walk or do I need to carry you?"

"Blake…"

"Victoria." His tone brooked no argument, and I huffed out a sigh of resignation.

"Fine. I'll go make some coffee, and we can talk in the living room."

I trudged downstairs, and the sound of the men's footsteps followed several minutes later. Unintelligible words floated toward the kitchen as I measured out the coffee grounds and set the pot to brew. My mind remained curiously blank as I loaded three mugs, milk, and sugar onto a serving tray.

I carried the tray out to the living room and set it on the coffee table. Studiously avoiding both men, I returned to the kitchen. I leaned against the counter as the percolator spit out the last out the coffee, then carried the carafe to the living room and set it on the table. Grabbing up a pillow, I hugged it to my chest as I curled into the corner of the couch.

Detective Sanchez shot Blake a quick look before glancing my way. "I'm sorry to see you again under these circumstances, Dr. Carr."

I nodded politely, digging my fingers into the pillow. Blake poured coffee into a mug and peeled the pillow away then pressed the mug into my stiff hands. Despite the temperature outside I felt frozen, and I was grateful for the heat seeping through the porcelain.

"Thank you for coming." I forced the words past the

198 | MORGAN JAMES

lump in her throat.

"So, you believe that the necklace belonged to Leah Wilson?"

I nodded.

His brow furrowed. "And you own one that's identical?"

"Leah and I received those matching necklaces for Christmas. We wore them all the time. When the police found her..." I broke off and glanced away. "They assumed it'd been lost during the struggle, but they weren't able to find it. Now... I guess he's had it this whole time."

"We'll certainly analyze it. You're positive it's not yours?"

I shook my head. "Mine is broken. It's been in my jewelry box for the last year or so, and I keep forgetting to get it fixed."

"Would you mind if we took a look to compare them?"

I nodded reluctantly. "Of course."

"Thank you."

"Would you like me to get it?"

Blake's voice startled me and I turned to him before glancing back at the detective, who nodded. "I'd like to see it."

Blake looked at me for permission and I hesitated, biting my lip. I didn't really want to go back in there. "The tray lifts out. It's in a black box in the bottom."

"I'll be right back." Blake brushed my leg as he stood, and I wondered if it was intentional—just a small connection to let me know that he was there for me. I stared into the cup of creamy hazelnut-flavored coffee and felt a tiny smile curve my mouth. He'd fixed it exactly the way I liked it.

"Since we're alone, would you mind answering some questions?"

I met Sanchez's eyes. "Sure."

"You said you were gone last night. Were you with someone?"

"I was with Blake. We went to dinner, then..." I trailed off, cheeks burning with embarrassment. Fortunately, I didn't have to explain because the detective continued.

"Good. Under the circumstances, I would advise you to watch your surroundings carefully and be aware of your interactions with people. This person clearly knows a lot about you."

"He obviously has some sort of obsession with me, I just can't quite figure out what it is."

Sanchez tipped his head to one side and shrugged. "Hard to tell. You changed your name, moved away. Maybe he's held on to the fantasy all these years."

My stomach flipped, gruesome visions dancing in front of my eyes. "He's going to kill me. Just like Leah, and just like Monique."

"We're going to do everything in our power to keep that from happening." The detective's voice was grim, and I threw a look his way.

"No offense, detective, but you don't have the manpower to watch over me every minute of the day."

"No." Sanchez glanced toward the stairs as the sound of footsteps drew nearer. "But I would advise taking extra precautions, staying with someone you trust for the time being."

Someone you trust... Blake immediately came to mind, and my attention was drawn to the man in question as he moved into the room, a dark expression on his face. He handed the small black box to the detective before settling beside me. A proprietary hand landed on my knee, and I almost smiled despite the severity of the situation.

The box snapped open with a soft click and the detective inspected the locket. He tapped the tablet on his lap, enlarging an image on the screen. He nodded, swiping through photos, murmuring to himself, and I shot Blake a look. Dropping his gaze to my now cool coffee, he extracted it from my frozen fingers and set it on the table. He leaned back against the cushions and draped an arm around my shoulders, easing me into his embrace.

A few moments later, Detective Sanchez gazed over the table. "Looks identical, so I believe you're correct, Dr. Carr."

I'd suspected as much, but the words struck a blow to my heart. This bastard had killed my best friend, and now he'd been watching me, toying with me. Leaving trophies in my house. I wouldn't let him get away with it.

"He'll come after me again, we all know it." At the sound of my voice, both men's heads swiveled toward me.

Detective Sanchez leveled a look at me. "It's likely, yes."

"We could draw him out, make him come to me—"

"No." Blake's hard voice immediately cut me off.

Sanchez's gaze flicked to Blake before returning to me. "I'd like to exhaust every other option before we do anything extreme."

"Whoever this guy is, he's starting to unravel and he's making mistakes." Blake laced his fingers with mine and squeezed gently. "I won't let you put yourself in danger for this asshole. Let the police do their job and catch him. Your job is to stay safe and help other people."

I nodded once, not quite a promise. I would help others— by finding a way to put this guy behind bars.

CHAPTER TWENTY-SEVEN

Blake

"I need a favor."

Con's eyes narrowed suspiciously. "Why do I feel like this is not going to be a normal request?" He caught the black box I tossed his way and flipped it open.

"I need you to find someone to put a tracker in there."

"For Dr. Carr?"

"Yes."

Con shook his head. "Kingsley will never agree to cover this. The expense to keep tabs on her 24/7 will be astronomical."

"He won't have to. It's coming out of my pocket."

He snapped the box closed and leaned forward in his chair. "Tell me what you know."

I settled into the chair and relayed the story. "So, I fixed it up to surprise her. That should be incentive enough for her to keep it on at all times so, on the off chance that I'm not with her, we can keep tabs on her."

"If you're already in her bed then there's no reason to risk this expense. You know it's not going to be cheap," Con warned.

I shook my head. "I don't care. I'll do whatever it takes to keep her safe. Victoria's friend was attacked in her own office. Unless Kingsley extends the contract, which I seriously doubt, I won't be able to watch over her all the time, and I need to make sure she's okay."

He studied me for a moment. "Two of the new guys just got in a couple days ago. Let me go introduce you, and we'll have them get you squared away."

"Thanks, man, I appreciate it. For real."

Con lifted a brow. "Jesus. You find a woman and get all soft. Get out of here with that shit."

I let out a laugh. "Just wait, asshole. Some chick's gonna come along and blindside you one of these days."

He shuddered in mock horror, though shadows entered his eyes. His tone was hard when he spoke. "That won't happen."

I sobered, immediately regretting my words. He'd been through the emotional wringer when he was younger and had his heart ripped out by his childhood sweetheart. Ever since I'd known him, Con had stayed away from women as much as possible. He wasn't a saint by any means, but I had a feeling he was still deeply in love with his ex. He kept every emotion and thought under lock and key, sharing only necessary details. I wondered if anyone would ever learn the real story.

I clapped a hand on Con's shoulder. "Introduce me to the newbies. I fully expect to see them in those heinous-ass shirts you bought."

A feral grin lit his face. "I'm not sure who bitched more, you or them."

I followed him out of the office and into the bullpen. "That's because they're fucking terrible."

He chuckled and shrugged good-naturedly. "Just testing your loyalty."

I rolled my eyes as Con punched his code into the keypad and the door unlocked, emitting a low beep as it granted access to its inner sanctum. A dozen or so cubicles were set up in the middle of the room, divided by low gray walls to give a semblance of privacy. Two men occupied the front two cubes, and they looked up as we entered.

Con lifted a hand. "Guys, I want to introduce you to

Blake Lawson."

I stepped forward as both men rose to their feet and extended their hands almost simultaneously. I shook and allowed Con to make introductions.

"This is Vince Incarnato, Ink for short." Not quite as tall as myself, Vince was stocky with a muscular build, tattooed sleeves running down both arms. I wasn't sure if Ink was short for Incarnato or for the colorful images covering a good portion of the man's body, but the nickname was appropriate regardless. I nodded a greeting.

"And this," Con continued, gesturing to the second man, "is Jason Doyle, resident tech expert. Stole him from the bureau. He's the man you need."

Jason's gaze flicked toward me. "What can I do for you, sir?"

"Just Blake." He nodded in acknowledgment and I handed over the box. "I need you to put a tracking device into my girlfriend's necklace."

Saying the words aloud sounded creepy as hell, but Jason tipped his chin like the request wasn't at all out of the ordinary. He pulled the locket out and examined the interior compartment of the golden oval. "Are you putting pictures in here?"

"Yeah. I'm working on that right now, so whatever you're using will be concealed."

I glanced at my watch. My lunch break was almost over, but fortunately I was just a few blocks from the healthplex. The jeweler had called this morning to let me know the necklace was ready, and I'd rushed over to pick it up. I wanted to give it to her as soon as possible.

I'd coerced Detective Sanchez into releasing it, briefly explaining my plan after Victoria's house had been broken into. The man had been surprisingly cooperative once I assured him that he had no intention of interfering with the investigation. I merely wanted what was best for Victoria, and I'd help in any way I could.

Victoria was under the impression that Sanchez had kept

it for evidence, so she wouldn't be the wiser until I surprised her with it. The jeweler had soldered the bail on the locket, and it now hung from the new gold chain I'd purchased. My plan was to put pictures of both Leah and Victoria inside the locket. Now I just had to find them. Social media was just getting off the ground back in those days, so the quality of the photos online was pretty poor. The local newspaper had printed a picture of the beautiful blonde after her death, but that too was grainy and unclear.

I couldn't reach out directly to either Victoria or Leah's parents without jeopardizing the case, so I was left to my own devices. I'd come across their high school yearbook on the school's website and had put in a request to the school's principal, telling the woman that my security firm was looking into the cold case, but needed a copy of the photo, preferably digital, if they had one. I'd explained that I didn't want to contact the family and get their hopes up and left my contact information. I'd yet to hear anything back, but it'd only been a couple of days.

"Give me a day or two to get what I need." Jason flicked a look my way. "You know these aren't fool-proof, right? Even active, it will only alert us to the general vicinity."

"Anything is better than nothing. Will you keep it active all the time?"

"That's up to you." He shrugged. "I can run perpetual radar on it, or I can activate it if shit goes down. That'll be a lot cheaper."

I hated the thought of not being able to find her. "Can you hack the system and trace her phone, if necessary?"

The other man raised a brow. "Probably. That's a little more complex, though, and gives about the same results. Tracker will generally place you within a few hundred yards or so."

I scowled. "That's hardly accurate."

"No, it's not." He shook his head. "But unless you're working with the Feds and have access to their system, this is what we have to work with."

Damn. "Well, just put it in the necklace as a safeguard and we'll activate it if we need to." I turned back to Con. "I've gotta get back over there. Benny's holding down the fort, but Victoria should be finishing up soon and I want to make sure I'm there."

Con tipped his head toward the door. "Come on."

I gestured at the still-empty receptionist's desk. "When does Abby start?"

"Two weeks. I'm flying out for her graduation this weekend, then we'll drive back. I'm helping her move all her stuff down, so I'll be out for a few days. I'll need you to be my backup while I'm gone."

"No problem."

Con shoved his hands in his pockets. "You're sure you know what you're doing?"

I stiffened. "I'm going to do everything in my power to make sure she's safe, regardless of the cost."

He waved me off. "No, I mean... I understand. Just be careful."

Again, I wondered about his history and the woman who obviously still had the man tied up in knots. Choosing not to press, I just nodded. "I will."

Victoria was mine now, and I would do anything for her.

CHAPTER TWENTY-EIGHT

Victoria

"Hello, Victoria. Do you have a few minutes?"

As if it mattered now. I glanced to where Phyllis stood in the doorway, eyes narrowed at Johnathan in blatant disapproval. I offered a soft smile, letting her know it was okay.

"I can spare a moment or two."

I skimmed over Greg Andrews's social media page one last time. I'd spent a little time each day trying to dig into the man's life, seeing who he was friends with and what he liked. Though I'd learned a little about him while treating him, I was fascinated by some of his interests. I'd begun to follow some of his friends as well, trying to find any kind of connection to the recent murders or to myself. Unfortunately, I hadn't been at all successful.

If I didn't find anything relevant here soon, I was going to have to resort to desperate measures and invite the man back to counseling. I didn't particularly want to see him again, especially if he was responsible for the recent upheaval, but I'd do anything necessary to put the killer behind bars. I closed the window on the browser with a dismayed sigh and swiveled my chair toward Johnathan. "How have you been?"

He lifted a brow. "I think the better question is, how have you been?"

"Fine, I suppose." I'd told Johnathan about the break-in

a couple days ago, and he'd been calling or stopping by my office each day. "I've had new locks installed on all of the doors and made a few enhancements to my security system."

In all honesty, even though the new mattress had been delivered just yesterday, I wasn't looking forward to sleeping in my own bed again. I'd spent the past three nights at Blake's house, unable to fathom the idea of going home, knowing that the killer had been in there. I'd have to go back to my place soon. Just... not yet. Blake hadn't pushed me, either. He'd taken the necessary precautions to ensure my safety, telling me he'd be right beside me when I did decide to go home.

I'd kind of lied to Blake about never having a man over, though it was more a lie of omission. Although I'd never had a boyfriend, Johnathan had stopped by frequently before Blake and I had started dating. Thank God he hadn't shown up unexpectedly like he used to. It was bad enough that I had to worry about Blake seeing Johnathan show up here. I knew Blake was jealous of Johnathan, even though he had no reason to be. Although I had to admit, I'd feel the exact same way if Blake had female friends.

Licking my lips, I took a deep breath and decided to come clean. "I've decided to take your advice. About dating," I clarified.

An expression of pure elation passed over his face before he could school his features, and guilt slammed into me. He really was such a nice guy, and I hated to have to hurt him. He spoke up before I had the chance to elaborate. "Is that so?"

"Yes." I nodded slowly. "In fact, I've been talking with someone. Even been out on a couple dates."

His face fell. "Well, that's wonderful. How did you meet him?"

I fought the urge to fidget. "He actually works here, in the healthplex."

"Another doctor, Victoria, really?" His face screwed up. "You know how badly those relationships turn out. Do you really want to date someone in the same profession?"

Ironic, coming from him.

"No, it's not…" I took a deep breath. "After that poor woman was murdered a few weeks ago, you suggested we try to get some extra security around here. Remember?"

"Of course." Disbelief colored his features as realization dawned. "You're dating that… that cop downstairs?"

"Not a cop," I corrected. "Personal security agent."

A muscle in his jaw ticked. "Isn't that a bit of a conflict of interest?"

"Mr. Lawson was brought in as a precaution for the entire healthplex—not for me specifically. Blake has been wonderful enough to help me after hours."

"I'm sure he has," Johnathan muttered under his breath, and I shot him a glare.

"My house was broken into," I snapped. "It's nice to have someone there who actually cares about me and is willing to go out of his way to keep me safe."

It was a cheap dig, and I almost—almost—felt guilty when Johnathan's lips turned down in a frown.

"You seem to rely quite heavily on Mr. Lawson."

I stiffened. "Isn't that the point of a relationship? To give and take, to be able to trust your partner and accept their help?"

"Of course," he soothed. "I just meant that you've only known him for a very short time. I would hate to see you get hurt."

"I really like him." I hadn't admitted it aloud before, and I dropped my gaze to my lap.

Johnathan was quiet for a moment. "Are you happy?"

I nodded. "Yeah. He's a good guy. He makes me feel safe."

"After everything you've been through, you deserve to feel safe and cared for. Does he love you?"

"We've only known each other for a couple weeks. Who can tell?"

He lifted a shoulder. "Some people know right away."

I shifted under the scrutiny. Was that true? All of my training told me no, it wasn't possible. It took time to develop those kinds of feelings. "I don't know. We'll date for a while and see what happens."

"When does his job end here?"

"He has about a week and a half left on the contract, I think. I haven't heard anything about them extending it."

"I'll bet he'll be busy soon," he replied. "I heard one of his colleagues just took a security assignment for Gemma Malone."

My gaze snapped to him. "The singer?"

A wry grin quirked his mouth. "America's sweetheart."

Oh, God. A sudden surge of jealousy twisted my stomach into a knot. Gemma Malone was incredibly talented—and incredibly gorgeous. The thought of Blake surrounded by women like her—blonde, beautiful, successful...

"I'm really sorry, Johnathan," I managed to choke out. "My next patient will be here in just a few minutes and I have to get ready."

"Of course, my apologies." He stood and brushed a hand over his slacks. "Call me if you need anything."

After Johnathan left I sat in my chair, twirling a pen and staring out the window as thoughts swirled through my mind. What would Blake do once he was done here? Was there already an expiration date on our relationship?

CHAPTER TWENTY-NINE

Victoria

"You okay?"

Blake's voice cut through the silence as I pushed my food around my plate. I met his gaze and shot him a wan smile. "I'm fine. Just thinking that I should go home soon."

A wary light entered his eyes. "Well, you should be safe there now. I'll bet you're getting tired of living out of a suitcase."

His gentle teasing caused my heart to constrict. "A little bit. It's just... I can't let someone run me out of my own house. I can't let him win."

"I understand." He scooped up another bite of food. "Well, we can head over to your place after dinner if you want."

We. I sucked in a sharp breath at the word. "Blake? Can I ask you a question?"

"Sure. What's on your mind?"

"I was just wondering... What will you do after your job here is up?"

"You mean working at the healthplex?" He shrugged. "I'm not sure. I put in a request for an extension after your house was broken into, but it hasn't been approved yet. The landlord may deny it and turn the responsibility over to the PD since you've been targeted at home. But to answer your question, I honestly don't know. Why do you ask?"

"No reason." I pushed the rice around my plate before sighing and setting down my fork. "Will we still see each other?"

Surprise flashed in his eyes. "Of course. Is that what you're worried about?"

I nodded and swallowed down the lump that had formed in my throat. "What if your next job takes you far away?"

He tipped his head to one side, hazel eyes studying me intently. "We'll just have to take it one day at a time."

"But what if you're gone for months?" I pressed. I cringed at the insecurity and neediness in my voice but I couldn't help it.

"Sweetheart, everything will be fine. I promise."

He sounded so sure of himself, yet my doubts lingered. "But how can you know?"

"I just know." His voice was low and patient as he took my hand in his, gently stroking my palm with his thumb. "We'll still talk and spend time together, just like we do now. Maybe I won't get to see you every day, but... we'll work it out."

"I just... What if you find someone else? What if you get bored?" He opened his mouth to speak, but I cut him off. "Johnathan told me today that Gemma Malone hired your company—"

His eyes narrowed and he pulled his hand away. "Johnathan? Is that what brought this on?"

"Well, he and I were talking today and—"

"Of course you were." He abruptly pushed back from the table and grabbed up his plate. I winced as he set it in the sink with a little more force than necessary. "And what did Johnathan have to say?"

I hesitated, a little thrown by his reaction. "Just that your company is taking on more high-profile contracts—like the one with Gemma."

"Mhmm..." He crossed his arms over his chest and leaned back against the counter. "He's been around a lot lately the past few days."

To anyone else, it would have sounded like he was merely stating an observation. But I heard the faint thread of jealousy just beneath the surface. "He just wanted to... check on me."

"Right."

"He's just a friend." It sounded feeble to my own ears, and I fought the urge to look away as Blake stared at me.

"A friend who checks on you every day out of the goodness of his heart?" My cheeks burned at the implication, but he wasn't done. "How would you feel in my position? What if a woman came to visit me every single day, right in front of you?"

His words were like an arrow to my heart. It hurt just thinking about it, and tears burned the backs of my eyes. "I... I didn't think."

"Does he know we've had sex? That I was your first? I thought we were in a serious relationship—"

"We are!" The chair screeched as I shoved it back and jumped to my feet. "I swear, there's nothing between us. He's a friend—that's all."

Blake sighed. "Come here, sweetheart."

I threw myself at him, burying my head against his chest to conceal the tears creeping from the corners of my eyes. He kissed my temple before tipping my head up to meet his gaze. "You don't have anything to worry about. I want you—no one else."

"I just..." I blinked away the moisture clinging to my lashes. I didn't know how to voice my fears without sounding irrationally needy or insecure. I swallowed the emotion clogging my throat. "I'm sorry."

"I'm not going anywhere. But inviting a third person into a relationship is trouble," he admonished softly as he stroked one hand over my hair. "It's no wonder he thinks he has a chance if you continue to cry on his shoulder."

"I know, but he's still my friend. He helped me work through a lot of my old fears and..." I trailed off with a small sigh. "Kate told me the same thing—that I needed to be upfront with him—but I didn't want to hurt his feelings."

"I know he's your friend, sweetheart, and I respect that. There just have to be boundaries." He tightened his hold on me. "You see the good in everyone. It's one thing I love most about you, but it also worries the hell out of me."

My heart gave a funny little lurch. He loved that about me? I tamped down my pleasure as he continued.

"You're too goddamn trusting." He pulled back, hazel eyes searching mine. "I'd do anything for you—you know that, right?" I nodded. "I know this is new for you, but we need to work on your communication a little bit."

He smiled to take the sting out of his words. "You help so many people by talking them through their fears. I want you to be able to come to me when you're worried about something."

A wry smile twisted my mouth. "Always easier to fix someone else's problems, right?"

"It is," Blake agreed. "But you're not in this alone."

"Do you..." I licked my lips. "Do you see us, you know... dating for a while?"

"Yes." He framed my face and gave me a single hard kiss. "A long while."

My chest warmed at his words. "I want to make this work."

"Me, too." He studied me for a moment. "I appreciate everything Johnathan has done for you, but he needs to learn to respect our relationship."

He left the rest unsaid, but his tone was heavy with disapproval, and I shivered at the possessiveness. He wouldn't stand for having another man around. What would happen if Johnathan tried to interject again? Would Blake leave? Johnathan had been my friend for years, but what if he cared more about his own happiness than mine? What if he really was trying to coerce me into leaving Blake?

I nodded. "I'll talk to him."

His features softened. "Okay. Do you still want to go

home tonight?"

Without a word, I laced my fingers through his then led him down the hall to his master bedroom. Stopping next to the bed, I slid my hands up his chest. "I want to be with you tonight." I pulled him down for a kiss. "*Every* night, until you get tired of me."

He let out a low growl and slipped his hands around my hips, inching my shirt up and revealing the satiny flesh of my stomach. "That'll be a long damn time."

*

I rang the bell and fiddled nervously with the strap of my purse. From inside the house, I could hear the beginning of Beethoven's Symphony No. 5 and I rolled my eyes. No plain old chime here—of course Johnathan's doorbell would play strains of classical music.

The front door swung open to reveal the man behind the pretentious façade. Even on a Saturday, he was dressed in business slacks and a polo, and expensive leather loafers adorned his feet. For just a moment, I cataloged the differences between him and Blake. Johnathan was worried constantly about his image. He'd come from nothing, and he worked every day to make more money, be more successful, putting more time and distance between the boy he'd been and the man he'd become.

Blake was comfortable in his own skin. He didn't care what people thought, and he forged his own way through life. Johnathan bowed to everyone, adapting to fit whatever image someone wanted him to project. I doubted he really even knew who his real self was anymore. It was rather ironic, given his line of work.

"Victoria, what a lovely surprise." Johnathan stepped backward with a smile and held the door open in welcome.

My heart hammered against my ribcage as I crossed the threshold. "Thanks. How is everything?"

"Busy as ever." He closed the door, and I fell into step

as he strode toward the formal living area. Settling into a plush leather chair, he motioned for me to do the same. "I was actually just reviewing some files from this week. How are you holding up?"

I fidgeted in my seat. "Oh, I'm fine. Not really ready to face going back to my house yet, you know."

He threw a sympathetic look my way. "I understand. It's difficult to feel secure again when something like that happens. But you have an amazing support group, Victoria, people who care about you. You know I'd do anything for you."

I did, indeed, and that was precisely the reason for my visit today. Blake was right—Johnathan overstepped his bounds on a regular basis, always trying to tell me what was best. As a doctor, I knew that Johnathan was qualified to guide me. But he didn't know every aspect of my life. I wasn't going to risk a good thing with Blake because Johnathan wanted me all to himself. I knew things between us would never progress. I was going to have to let him down easy... Just as soon as I worked up the courage.

"Has Mr. Andrews made an appointment with you yet?" Johnathan shook his head and I sighed. "I really wish he would. I truly think he exhibits some signs of sociopathic behavior. The things he said about Rachel..." I shuddered. "I don't trust him."

Johnathan nodded gravely. "Have you told the police of your suspicions?"

"Yeah, and I know they're looking into it." I rubbed my temples. "I'm just ready for this to be over. I want justice for Monique and Kate. And Leah, if it really is the same person. I want to be able to go to and from work without having to look over my shoulder. I want to sleep in my own bed without worrying about every creak and groan in the house, thinking he's come back to finish me off."

Tears slipped down my cheeks before I could stop them. I felt Johnathan's arm come around my shoulders as he moved beside me, and I leaned in for a moment, soaking up the comfort he offered. Johnathan was a good friend, but it just wasn't the same feeling as when I was with Blake. I pulled out of his embrace and glanced up with a tremulous smile. "Thank you. I'm okay now, it's just been a little chaotic."

"I understand completely." He returned to his chair and crossed an ankle over his knee. "These last couple of weeks would push anyone to the edge."

I smiled and stared at the carpet, debating when to drop the bomb. Thankfully, he continued. "Hopefully the police have a good lead and they'll get it figured out quickly. Are they investigating Mr. Andrews, I hope?"

"I would assume so since he's the only one who makes sense, but I'm not sure."

Johnathan nodded. "It's definitely someone who wants your attention. He called you out specifically at the murder scene. But why?"

That was the million-dollar question, wasn't it? "This all seems to be a cry for attention, but I'm not sure why. If it is Greg, maybe it's an obsession. He's asked me out several times, but I've always turned him down because he was a patient."

Johnathan's eyes darkened for a moment. "Would you have gone out with him otherwise?"

I shook my head. "No, I even told him that the day I ran into him at the mall. I have no feelings for him. He seemed disappointed, but I don't know if he's the one responsible. I would like to say yes, but... I just don't know. He was my patient for months and I never really got that impression from him."

"You know as well as I do that people can harbor deeply rooted feelings of possession or resentment. Maybe he bided his time until he thought he could win you over."

"Perhaps. But then why hurt Kate?"

Johnathan puzzled that for a moment. "Maybe she was in the way somehow?"

"We were supposed to go out that night," I admitted.

"That's as good a reason as any. Separate the two of you,

eliminate Kate so he had you all to himself."

"I just... Something doesn't fit." I bit my lip. "It just doesn't feel right."

Johnathan offered a small smile. "Well, let the police do their jobs and investigate. I'm sure they'll turn something up. Maybe all of the evidence will point to Greg Andrews."

"Maybe." But like I'd told Johnathan, I seriously doubted it. There was something I was missing—something big. I could feel it.

"I know you've said no in the past, but I'm really hoping you'll reconsider this time." My heart dropped as Johnathan glanced away, an uneasy expression on his face. "You're more than welcome to stay here for as long as you need until they catch this guy. You'll be safe with me."

"Listen, Johnathan, I really appreciate everything you've done. You've been a great friend, but..." I took a deep breath. "I think we need to keep our relationship professional from now on."

Confusion creased his features. "Have I done something to upset you?"

My heart constricted at his dejected tone. In a lot of ways, Johnathan was like a puppy, sweet and eager for approval. Despite his loyalty, he was beginning to interfere in my personal life and I cared too much for Blake to lose him now.

"You've given me some really great advice over the years, and I probably never would've confronted my fears without you. It was your idea for me to get out and date again, and I'm incredibly thankful to have a good friend like you. But I'm seeing Blake now and I need to focus on my relationship with him."

"And he sees me as a threat?"

I nodded. "He does. He's worried about another man— you, specifically—trying to sway my opinion."

Johnathan threw a pitying glance my way. "Oh, Victoria, I'm so sorry."

"Maybe you'll meet a woman and we can double date." I

offered him a smile.

"I'd enjoy that. I just hope you know what you're getting into."

"I know you worry about me, but Blake is really amazing. He even gave me this." Johnathan's eyes widened as I pulled the locket out from where it lay concealed beneath my shirt. "Remember my friend who was killed back in high school? Leah? We had matching necklaces. Mine was broken, but he had it fixed up for me and put our pictures inside."

Blake had surprised me with the gift yesterday and the unexpected gesture had brought tears to my eyes. I'd been reluctant to hand it over to Detective Sanchez last weekend, afraid to part with the last remaining tie to Leah, even for a short period of time. After it'd been released from evidence, Blake had apparently taken it to a jeweler to be fixed. I had no idea how he'd come across our pictures, but it was as if they'd been taken yesterday. Leah and I smiled at each other from opposite sides of the locket, frozen in time. Last night I'd thanked him for the wonderful gift—twice.

I smiled at the thought as I tucked the necklace safely away next to my heart. I met Johnathan's unhappy expression, steeling myself for his words.

"Well, that's... interesting," he remarked.

"It was a lovely gesture," I said defensively. "He knew how much it meant to me."

"Exactly. And now he's taken something important from your past and made it all about him."

"That's not—"

"I've seen a lot of women in your shoes, Victoria. They change who they are for a man—a man who controls them and manipulates them to their advantage. This is how it starts, Victoria, you know that. First, you're alienated from your friends and family. He'll feed you empty promises, anything to get you to stay."

"Blake's not like that." I shook my head. "He's sweet and caring and..."

He leaned forward and took my hands in his own. "It's

a hero complex, Victoria. With everything that's happened recently, you've developed an attachment to the man. I understand—"

"That's not true."

His eyes flashed as I yanked my hands away. "How well do you really know him? What if he's preying on you because you're too inexperienced to know better?"

"You're only saying that because you're jealous," I shot back. "We're friends, Johnathan. At least, I thought we were. If you cared about me at all, you'd support me in this."

Johnathan sat back in the chair and steepled his fingers. Finally, he gave a little shake of his head. "I'm sorry. I can't."

"I need to go." Tears blurred my vision as I popped up from my seat. He would clearly never see my side of things.

Seething with a combination of anger and sadness, I stormed from the house and climbed into my car. I'd never been in love before, but I felt something for Blake. Whether it was lust or something more, I couldn't quite be sure. Viewed clinically, I knew the sex influenced my opinion—but I couldn't help it. When I was with Blake, I felt as if every nerve ending was on fire. And that look in his eyes when we made love...

I was terrified to admit that I might actually be falling for him. I'd protected my heart for so long, hiding from reminders of my past. But Blake was different. It was amazing how well he understood me. He knew of my history, yet he didn't pity me. Instead, he'd taken the bad memories and replaced them with something good. He'd shown me how to trust again, how to rely on someone other than myself.

Since our relationship had become physical, it'd added a new dimension, a new depth. But that in itself raised the question, was he there for more than just the sex? Now that he'd gotten what he wanted, would he leave? Or worse, would he do as Johnathan said and use that to control me? I didn't think he would stoop to using my emotions against me, but then again, I'd never felt this way about anyone before. It worried me. Maybe it was too much, too soon.

I shook my head to clear the thought away. No, Blake had said he cared about me, and he would never lie about that...

Right?

CHAPTER THIRTY

Blake

I scrubbed a hand over my face. I'd been staring at the blueprints so long my eyes were starting to cross. My gaze drifted once more over the large drawing I'd picked up from the developer before I pushed away from the desk and strode to the small window.

This far downtown there wasn't much to look at. I was afforded a view of another ancient, crumbling red brick building next door and the spires of an even older church a block over. I was missing something, and it was bothering the hell out of me. Maybe some fresh air and a change of scenery would do me good. I tended to think better as I moved anyway.

I grabbed two manila folders from the corner of my desk and left the office, flicking the lights off as I went, then made my way down the hall to the bullpen. I tapped in the five-digit code and the door beeped, granting me entrance.

Three heads swiveled my way then just as quickly resumed what they were doing. I approached Doyle's desk and propped a hip on the corner.

"I need a favor."

"What's up?"

"I need you to run a couple names for me. See what you can pull on both. I want full history." I turned to Jason and handed him the dossiers on both Greg Andrews and Dr.

Johnathan Martin.

"Anything in particular I need to look for?"

"That one"—I motioned to Andrews's file—"is a disgruntled ex-patient of Victoria's. See if there's any history of violence, and put some priority on it if you don't mind. When Victoria's friend was killed years ago, the guy introduced himself as Marc. See if there's any possibility that Andrews could've been in the vicinity at the time of the murder. He may have used an alias, or he may have changed his name since then. Whoever broke into Victoria's house left behind a hunting knife. Maybe you can do some checking to see if he's purchased anything recently. According to the police report, the blade appears to be the same one used in the Henderson murder a couple weeks ago, too. There's a good chance he may be tied into all this somehow.

"And him…" I flicked Martin's folder. "He's an arrogant pain in the ass who's in love with my girlfriend. I need a reason to knock his ass down a couple pegs."

Jason nodded his understanding. "Fair enough."

I couldn't quite dispel my unease, and there was a heavy feeling in the air, almost tangible in its intensity. Something bad was going to happen—I could feel it. I'd been at QSG most of the day chasing leads, but I was still no closer to finding an answer. Victoria had called earlier to let me know she was going to see a friend, then would meet me back at her house.

With my stint at the healthplex almost complete, I wanted her to feel comfortable at both my place and hers in case I needed to be away from her. She'd insisted she'd be fine staying home alone today, so I'd reluctantly kissed her goodbye and come in to catch up on some work. Something had been nagging at me all day, but I couldn't quite put my finger on what exactly was bothering me.

Victoria and I had discussed some of her concerns over the last few days, which seemed to have soothed some of her fears. I hesitated to come right out and tell her exactly how I felt—that she could be the one. My mom had called a few nights ago, and when I told her I was planning to bring my girlfriend home for a visit, the excitement in her voice had been palpable. There was only one reason I would bring a woman home. I wasn't quite sure Victoria was ready for so many Lawsons at once, but I had no doubt she'd pass any test they threw at her. She was naturally sweet and personable, and I knew my family would fall in love with her the second they met her.

As for me, well… I was almost there. I wanted to put all of this craziness behind us, toss the killer behind bars so we could move on with our lives in a more normal capacity. I could see myself beside her fifteen years down the road, a couple kids in tow, sipping coffee side-by-side each morning. Oh, I knew we'd have some ups and downs, but I was looking forward to every moment with her, good and bad.

Just the thought of being with her sent anticipation zinging through my veins. I glanced at Jason. "I'm taking off. Shoot me what you find, if you would."

"No problem." He didn't bother to look away from the computer screen as his fingers flew across the keyboard.

I waved to Vince and Con, who were reviewing something on the computer. I'd seen Xander around once or twice, but with everything going on with Victoria, I hadn't had much of a chance to really talk with him. From what I'd heard, the other man had his hands full with a woman of his own.

Con had been busy pulling strings and making connections, and inquiries and odd jobs were beginning to trickle in. Clay would be directing firearms qualifications for the local PD at the gun range downtown at the end of the month, and Vince had picked up the position working detail on the local singer Con had originally offered me. I hadn't asked how things were going, but from the perpetually agitated expression Vince wore, it probably wasn't good.

A string of burglaries had cropped up around the city and the PD had contacted Con to see if they could dig up some more information. Apparently the thieves were targeting wealthy homes or smaller business that lacked security, then holding an internet auction each week to net the highest bid for the stolen items. The problem was, the IP address was never the same, and the signal bounced off of several towers before finally landing at its final destination. The person—or group—knew what they were doing, and Jason so far hadn't been able to get a good hold on the hacker's method. But I knew he would—it was only a matter of time. The next auction was set up for Friday night and Jason would be at it again, doing his best to pinpoint the thieves' location.

I pushed open the door and squinted in the waning sunlight before slipping my sunglasses into place. I headed for my truck, then changed direction and strode to the corner market to grab a few things for dinner.

As I drove toward Victoria's place, I contemplated the layout of her subdivision. It was well-designed, as far as security went, with an eight-foot metal fence surrounding the entire property. While the black metal was more decorative than daunting, it at least provided a sense of security. It would deter most people from trying to climb it, especially since the subdivision itself was surrounded on two sides by a natural preservation.

I turned onto the main thoroughfare and stopped at the gate—another added boon. The gates here were reinforced, and cameras were posted on each side to survey traffic. Although the gatehouse was patrolled, it would be easy enough for someone to slip by, especially in the dark. But they would have to either scale the fence or bypass the gate—or tag along on foot behind a vehicle entering the premises.

I tapped in the code and watched as the gate swung inward. I pulled through and kept an eye on the rearview mirror, counting the seconds until it closed. Plenty of time to make it through if someone was close enough, but there wasn't much to use for cover. A few decorative trees and shrubs dotted the entrance, but nothing of substance. Someone sneaking through on foot would be fairly obvious.

I dug my phone out and tapped the recently dialed number, then waited for the call to connect.

"Dallas Police, Tenth Precinct."

"Hey, Angie, it's Blake Lawson." I'd spoken with the officer a couple of times over the last few days and already recognized her voice.

"What can I do for ya?" her syrupy voice drawled.

"Is Sanchez free?"

Angie was silent for a beat before responding. "He's interviewing someone right now. I can have him call when they're finished."

"Maybe you can help me." I turned into Victoria's driveway and cut the engine. "Are you able to tell me if the footage from the gatehouse at Victoria's subdivision has been reviewed?"

"I don't think so, but I can find out."

Anger churned in my gut and I tamped it down. They were doing the best they could with limited information and resources, and a B&E was probably pretty low on their priority list. "Let me know for sure, please. I've been thinking..."

I told Angie what was I was looking for and she hung up with a promise to call me later. I climbed from the truck and entered the house using the spare key Victoria had given me a few days ago when we'd assessed the damage and fixed up her place. I took a quick look around to make sure everything was in place. Even though I'd upgraded her security system and changed the code, it was better to err on the side of caution. Finding nothing out of the ordinary, I made my way to the kitchen and set the grocery bags on the counter.

I unwrapped the salmon I'd picked up and popped it inside to broil while I cut and steamed the broccoli. It wasn't gourmet, but I hoped she'd at least appreciate the gesture. I was coming to enjoy these nights with her more and more. Maybe I could renovate my house and flip it, stay with Victoria until we found something better suited for a family. Her house was nice, but it was small and I'd still prefer a little more privacy. Once we had kids, it'd be nice to have a big back yard for them to play in.

Yeah, I knew I was putting the cart before the horse, but I couldn't help it. I was ready to put down roots and start a family. I hadn't said anything to Victoria yet, skittish as she was, but I was already looking years down the road. I'd spent the last decade having fun; now it was time to settle down. And I couldn't imagine doing it with anyone but her.

CHAPTER THIRTY-ONE

Victoria

The savory smell wafting on the air hit me the second I stepped inside. I closed the door and flipped the lock before slipping out of my shoes. On silent feet, I padded down the hallway toward the kitchen. Blake stood at the stove, his back to me, and the sight sent a little jolt through me. What kind of man would take care of me the way he had, come into my house and make dinner like it was something we'd done for years instead of days if he was planning to leave me?

Blake turned and caught my gaze, a warm smile spreading over his face. "Hey, beautiful. Did you have a good time?"

Before I even realized I'd moved, I was across the kitchen and in his arms.

"Whoa, sweetheart. Is everything okay?"

I kissed his throat. "I need you."

He pulled back and stared at me for a moment before nodding once. Reaching behind him, he flipped off the burner and turned off the oven, then scooped me into his arms. He paused only briefly to check the lock on the front door, then carried me upstairs. He lowered me to my feet beside the bed and settled his hands low on my hips. "You sure?"

I nodded, unable to form words. I pulled the hem of his polo from his waistband and eagerly slid my hands underneath. His skin was hot, his muscles hard, and I ached to feel every inch of him pressed against me. I shoved the material of the shirt higher and he reached behind his head to draw it up and off, then tossed it to the floor.

I silently perused him, the need for words superfluous. The language between our bodies was all the communication we needed. I laid my palms on his chest, tracing the contours of the thick muscles over his pecs and down his ribs. He shuddered slightly under my touch as I moved to his waistband and slipped the belt free of its buckle before popping the button fly on his black TDUs. Blake stood motionless—watching me, allowing me to take control—and power rushed through me. I shoved the pants down his legs and he stood gloriously naked, a wall of solid muscle.

A smile tipped up the corners of my mouth as I placed a hand in the middle of his chest and pushed him backward onto the bed. He allowed himself to fall but pulled me with him, drawing me up the length of his body. His mouth found mine and I gave in to the passion of his kiss, letting it sweep me far away from reality. Blake's fingers delved into my hair and it tumbled around my shoulders, shrouding us like a silken curtain. I lifted my head, absorbing each tiny detail of Blake's face and committing it to memory. Passion rocketed through me as his hands slid down my back and settled on my bottom.

The heat spreading through me was suddenly overwhelming and I jerked to a sitting position, already tugging at my clothes. I fisted my hands in the hem of my shirt and drew it over my head. Blake's hands followed the fabric, gliding over the exposed skin of my stomach. His touch scorched me as he ventured upward and cupped my breasts in his large palms. His hands followed the band around to my back and unhooked the clasp of my bra, then drew the straps down my arms. I flung it to the side, not caring where it landed. My head fell back on a silent moan as the coarse pads of his thumbs brushed the sensitive peaks.

Banding one arm around my waist, he rolled me under him and deftly unsnapped my jeans. Hooking his fingers in the waistband, he drew them down my legs and dropped them to the floor. His eyes dropped to the tiny scrap of lace hugging my hips and a slow smile spread over his face. Dipping his head, he nipped at me, catching the fabric between his teeth and drawing it down my legs. With a soft whisper, my panties were added to the ever-growing pile of clothes beside the bed.

His gaze skated over my body before meeting my eyes again, and I grabbed his shoulders, pulling him back to me. His mouth fused to mine, the hair of his beard tickling my lips and cheeks, and I smiled against his lips. He broke the kiss to study me, his eyebrows drawing together, and I couldn't contain the grin that spread over my face. He fell to his back when I gave him a playful shove, and I perused his body for a moment before shyly straddling his waist.

I'd wanted to do this before but hadn't had the nerve. Though we'd made love several times over the last few nights, it had been tentative and sweet, Blake taking extra care to make sure he wasn't hurting me. Once I'd gotten over the initial pain and soreness, I was eager to explore. Lifting up on my knees, I positioned myself the head of his cock at my entrance and slowly sank down. Blake grimaced as I enveloped him and I froze, caught off guard by his reaction.

Blake opened his eyes and caught my stare. He fisted one hand in my hair, and his hips surged upward, urging me to continue. I braced myself against his chest and began to move, the delicious friction igniting a fire deep within me. A searing heat swept over my body, and I came on a silent scream, speckles of light dancing before my eyes as I hurtled over the edge. His cock swelled, and he came just moments later, holding me close to his chest and letting out a ragged groan as he emptied himself deep inside me.

I nestled my nose into the crook of his neck, breathing in his masculine scent. One hand swept over my back and I snuggled closer.

Blake kissed my forehead. "You okay, sweetheart?"

"Better than okay." My stomach rumbled and I let out a rueful laugh. "Sorry I messed up your dinner plans."

His arms tightened around my waist, and his chin brushed my temple as he shook his head. "I'll take this over dinner any day."

"I'll bet you would." I laughed and pushed to a sitting position. "But I've kind of worked up an appetite now."

I slid from the bed and tugged on my robe, tying the sash tightly around my waist. Sticky wetness coated the inside of my thighs, and my face flamed. I'd been on birth control for years to regulate my period, but this was the first time we'd made love without a condom. I knew Blake was clean—it was one of the many things we'd talked about. Ironically, we hadn't spoken of children. The thought of carrying a child— Blake's child—was both terrifying and exhilarating.

My gaze darted to Blake who lay reclined on the bed, hands tucked behind his head, a vague smile on his face as he stared at me.

My cheeks burned with embarrassment. "Stop looking at me like that."

"Like what?" His expression was the epitome of innocence, and I rolled my eyes.

"That. You examine me like some specimen under a microscope."

He lifted one shoulder. "I like looking at you." He rolled off the bed and moved to stand in front of me. "In fact, seeing you like this makes me hungry for a hell of a lot more than the salmon I picked up for dinner."

I sucked in a quick breath, swaying slightly toward him, and he chuckled. "C'mon, babe. Let's get some food first. We'll need the energy."

He tugged on his clothes and followed me downstairs to the kitchen. "Not sure how this is going to taste now," he warned. "I hope it won't be too bad reheated."

I glanced toward the table and saw the jar candle flickering softly, surrounded by my good China. A single rose lay on my plate. "Looks like you had this all planned out. Sorry I ruined it."

"Hey." He closed the oven and pulled me into his arms.

"No apologies. I just wanted to do something nice for you. You deserve it."

I melted into him as he kissed me long and slow. After today's argument with Johnathan, I needed the physical reassurance from Blake. There was no way he could be as bad as Johnathan said.

Blake released me with a wink. "I have to admit, though, I did have an ulterior motive."

"Oh? What's that?" A shiver of apprehension moved down my spine, and I crossed my arms over my middle.

"How would you feel about meeting my parents? I was thinking maybe we could go up there one weekend soon and you could meet them and my sisters."

He threw a grin over his shoulder, and I forced a smile. "That sounds... nice. But isn't it a bit soon?"

Hearing my hesitation, he turned and rested one hip against the counter. He studied me for a moment before speaking, his face unreadable. "It was just a thought."

I wasn't entirely sure how I felt about this turn of events. "I can see what I have going on."

He relaxed a fraction and smiled. "I know things have been a little hectic. Once this is all over, we can focus on you and me."

I nodded, not entirely convinced. This was the last week that he was scheduled to work security at the healthplex. What would happen when this was over?

"What do you think of the country?"

I blinked at him. "It's fine. Why?"

He studied me. "I think I'd ultimately like to find a home with a little bit of space, a big yard for kids to run around."

"Okay..."

Blake smiled at my obvious confusion. "It's just something I've been thinking, especially after someone broke in here. What if we moved in together?"

That was the last thing I expected. I probably should be glad he planned to stick around, since I'd been wondering just moments before what would happen between us after his contract at the healthplex was up. But this? It was all a little too much.

"I just…" I held up a hand. "Can we take a step back for a minute?"

He shook his head. "I'm sorry, I knew it was too soon. I shouldn't have said anything."

No, I'd needed to hear it. I just wasn't entirely sure it was what I wanted to hear. "We've only known each other for a few weeks. Why do you want to move in together?"

"For one," he ticked it off on his fingers, "I think you'll be safer. And two, I like being with you. I like spending my nights with you, having dinner together, waking up with you."

"Yeah, but… it's too soon."

Wasn't it? Johnathan's words from earlier resounded in my mind and I struggled to push them away. Blake wasn't like that.

"Do you think so?"

I shrugged. "I don't know. I just… Someone told me today to take things slow, make sure it was what I wanted."

"Johnathan."

There was no question in his tone, and I shifted uneasily, acutely aware of his intense scrutiny. "Well, I went over to his place and—"

"I thought you were going to stop encouraging him."

Disapproval drenched his words and irritation flared within me. "I actually stopped by to tell him that I wanted to focus on my relationship with you. I never pegged you for the possessive type."

"Only when some asshole is trying to seduce my girl-friend," he shot back.

I hesitated, the breath stolen from my lungs. "Is that what I am?"

He speared me with a look of disbelief. "I thought we'd established that."

"We never talked about it."

"I assumed you felt the same way." His eyes narrowed, his tone accusing.

"I…" It was exactly what I wanted, wasn't it? Thoughts whirled through my mind and I fought to focus. "That really isn't the point right now."

"Are you fucking kidding me? Of course it is!" He threw his arms wide. "Why the hell do you think I get so pissed about this whole thing? No guy wants to see his girlfriend with another man, Victoria. I know he's your friend, but we can't go on like this. All he's done since day one is try to coerce you away from me. That's not something a friend would do. If he cared about you at all, he would want you to be happy."

"He does want me to be happy. You're the one who's trying to isolate me from my friends."

"That's not true," he countered, pointing a finger my way. "Just him. I don't know what it is, but I don't like him."

"Please," I huffed. "You're just jealous and want me all to yourself. Why does it matter so much to you?"

"Because I love you, damn it!" Blake raked his fingers through his hair and turned away.

I froze, my heart constricting in my chest. Hearing him say he loved me filled me with a combination of elation and trepidation. I needed time to process everything and break it down rationally. "No, you don't. You can't."

He turned to me, a sad smile on his face. "I do." I automatically recoiled even as his voice gentled and he reached for me. "You were made for me. You feel it too, sweetheart, I know you do. We fit; we belong together. I love you and you love me."

"You don't love me, Blake. It's just the stress from the past few weeks, and…" I shook my head. "We wouldn't even be together if I hadn't gotten that phone call."

"Who cares how we met? All that matters is you and me. We're here now, together. I need you, Victoria."

I took a step backward and wrapped my arms around my waist. Maybe it *was* a hero complex—maybe the attachment we'd formed had been born from that alone. "I understand you think you need me, but you don't. It's not healthy to feel that way about someone. In a lot of traumatic experiences, people form a special bond. But it's easy to perceive that shared empathy as love. What's between us isn't—"

"I know how I feel." He cut me off, his tone firm and resolute. "Just because you refuse to acknowledge it doesn't mean it's not true. No amount of persuasion on your part will ever convince me that I'm not in love with you. My feelings won't change—not ever."

"I… I think you should go." I pulled my arms tighter against myself, afraid that I'd fly apart if I loosened my hold even the tiniest bit.

His eyes implored me to listen. "You let him plant that seed of doubt, Victoria, don't you see? This is exactly what he wants. He wants you to doubt me, to walk away from what we have. But you know me. And deep down you know I love you—will always love you. The truth is, you're afraid. You don't want to admit you love me, too. And that's what scares you the most."

"No." I shook my head. "I don't love you."

He pulled one hand free where it was tucked against my chest. I half-heartedly tried to pull back but surrendered, looking away to hide the mist gathering in my eyes. He placed a kiss on my palm before releasing me.

"When you finally start listening to your heart, you'll know the truth."

With a sad smile, Blake turned and walked out the door.

CHAPTER THIRTY-TWO

The man drummed his fingers on the expensive desk and stared out the window. He should feel happy. He should be content. Instead, he felt restless... incomplete.

He brushed his thumb lightly over his upper lip. It still felt strange sometimes to not feel the gap that had once split his mouth. Adult skin wasn't as resilient as children's, but the scar cream they'd given him after the surgery had worked wonders. Though the flesh had been healed for several years now, he'd continued to use it. Maybe it was all in his mind, but he was terrified of being associated with the boy he'd left thousands of miles and many years behind.

Once, he hadn't had two nickels to rub together. Now, he had a successful business and everything his heart desired. Everything but *her*. She should know by now how determined he could be once he set his mind to something. Of course, he'd never told her about his past; not the truth of it, anyway.

For as long as he could remember, rage had consumed him. His father had been an abusive drunk, taking his anger out first on his mother, then himself as he got older. His mother had abandoned him just after he'd turned twelve, turning to drugs to escape her dismal reality. He'd found her one afternoon when he returned home from school, her eyes cold and lifeless as she gazed at the ceiling from where she lay reclined on the couch.

He'd received the thrashing of his life that night as if he had wielded the needle himself, and the last scrap of humanity within him fell away. He lived with his father for the next five years until one night, he'd had enough. Father had come home drunk with fire in his eyes, and he knew one of them wouldn't see the light of morning. Self-defense, he'd claimed when the police questioned him about the knife he'd wielded against his raging father. With a track record a mile long and a bad reputation in town, the police had been eager to believe a seventeen-year-old boy struggling to survive under a tyrant's rule. Only he and his father knew the truth of that night—and now the secret would be carried to his grave.

For a brief period of time, custody had been awarded to his father's sister, an equally abrasive, worthless excuse of a human being. The tiny house had reeked of gin and cigarettes and he'd left the day he'd turned eighteen in search of a better life. She'd ridiculed him for going to college. She'd called him ugly and worthless, told him he'd never amount to anything; he was no better than his trailer park roots. He'd reluctantly gone back at her request several years later, one weekend during his senior year at West Virginia University. She'd been evicted from the house for not paying rent, and, out of familial obligation, he'd driven up to help her move. Little did he know that the trip would change his life. It was then that he'd experienced his first taste of raw, pure power. It was the same fateful weekend he'd met Victoria—although she'd gone by Bekah back then.

The morning following the murder, his aunt had accosted him as he came out of the tiny spare bedroom. Though he'd spent an hour or more cleaning himself and getting rid of his clothes once he'd gotten home, she'd somehow known he was responsible. The death of one local woman and the assault of another had been all over the morning news.

She'd looked him in the eyes and pointed a bony finger at him in accusation. "You killed that girl, didn't you?" When he failed to respond, she'd continued her tirade. "They know what you look like. They'll come for you."

She'd made to move past him, probably in the hopes of finding more damning evidence in his room. For a split second,

panic had assailed him. But then there was something...
more. Confusion had filled her cold, snake-like eyes as his
hand whipped out and fisted in her shirt. Fear immediately
replaced the confusion as he'd shoved her away from him,
watching with an odd sense of detachment as she'd tumbled
backward, her body landing in an awkward, lifeless heap at
the base of the stairs. For good measure, he'd kicked a moving
box down behind her and, as far as he knew, the authorities
still believed she'd broken her neck after she'd tripped while
carrying it down the stairs.

He'd gathered his things, wiped down every surface he
could have possibly come in contact with, then climbed in the
car and made the two-hour journey back to campus. His life
had taken a completely different turn that day. He'd thought
his father's murder had been a fluke—just a young boy trying
to protect himself and survive. But it was so much more than
that. It was the gateway that had set him on this path. While
he'd initially broken away to make a better life for himself,
he'd never imagined something so amazing lay in store.

For years he'd tried to recreate that feeling, the high of
his first. When he'd taken Leah's life that night, he felt like he
could move mountains. But none of the others had been the
same. Even Victoria's demise wasn't at all what he'd planned.
She was never supposed to fall over that bridge into the water,
and she certainly wasn't supposed to live.

And then he learned she'd become a psychologist, of all
things. He couldn't help seeking her out, putting himself in
her path. He'd concocted the most ridiculous reason to speak
with her, but she'd fallen for it hook, line, and sinker. And in
turn, he'd fallen for her. He'd come to her with an intricate
plan of revenge but had been blindsided by the reality of her.
She was nothing like Leah, nothing like the other women
he'd taken over the years. Victoria was the embodiment of
perfection. Clean and untouched, sweet and devoted, she
was perfection personified. He'd spent years perfecting his
plan and instead had found his perfect mate. The revelation
had hit him hard—he wanted to keep her by his side forever,

cherish her.

It was almost comical how uncomfortable she was with men, and he felt a momentary twinge of regret for the discomfort he'd caused her all those years ago. That feeling was eclipsed, however, by the possessiveness he felt for her. He had marked her as his own that day, and she would never belong to anyone else. Red flashed before his eyes as he thought of the man he'd seen her with. He couldn't allow that. Victoria was meant for him alone, and he would take her with him.

He clutched the paper in his hand, crumpling it in his fist, and let loose a low string of oaths. The short newspaper article declared that the police were following a new lead from the break-in at her house, and an eye witness was supposedly giving them a composite sketch. Had someone actually seen him? It was possible, he supposed, but he'd taken the utmost care in concealing himself in plain sight. He was there often enough to blend in, but he couldn't take the chance. He would have to move soon—it would only be a matter of time before he popped up on their radar. He had to get to her before then.

He regretted the way he'd left things the last time they were together. He hadn't meant to upset her, but desperation had overruled him and he'd lashed out. Now, he'd have to find a way to get to her and get back into her good graces. But how? Victoria was a complex creature, and he would have to find something that called to her, something she wouldn't be able to ignore. A slow smile spread over his face as a plan began to form in his mind.

CHAPTER THIRTY-THREE

Blake

"Well, you look like shit."

I flipped Con a one-finger salute and returned my focus to the papers scattered across the desk. Jason had pulled everything he could find on Greg Andrews but, so far, there didn't seem to be any motive to hurt Victoria, nor did the man have any ties to Ohio that we'd been able to find. I'd been scouring the pages for hours now, almost certain I was missing something, unsure exactly what it was.

"Things go sideways already?"

"Fuck off." At his intent stare, I growled and leaned back in my chair. "Goddamn it. Yes, we had a fight."

"And?"

"What the hell do you mean, 'and'?"

Con shrugged. "What are you doing about it?"

Nothing. I was doing absolutely nothing. Worse, I was pretty sure things were beyond repair. She had completely ignored every call and text for the past two days. When I tried to apologize the other morning at the healthplex, she'd run in the opposite direction—but not before I'd seen the tears in her eyes. The thought gutted me.

In retrospect, I probably should've kept my mouth shut, at least until she'd had a little more time to come to terms with everything. Yeah, we'd only known each other for a few weeks, but I knew deep down I didn't want anyone else. I wanted Victoria by my side—forever. I was willing to wait that long, too, but I couldn't fix things if she continued to ignore me. And she wouldn't be upset if she didn't care, right?

I let out a heavy sigh. "I don't know. Maybe she just needs some time."

Con shook his head. "That's the last thing she needs. Trust me. The longer you give her to stew over it, the harder it'll be to overcome. Go see her, make her talk to you. You'll never accomplish anything by sitting here doing nothing."

I stared at him. "You get that from a greeting card?"

He returned my sentiment from earlier and flipped me off.

"I think you missed your calling." I grinned. "You should have been a motivational speaker."

Con pushed off the doorjamb. "Turn off the lights when you leave, asshole."

"Hey." He paused, back still to me. "I appreciate it."

He nodded once, then disappeared. As I watched him go, I thought back on the snippets of conversation we'd shared over the years. I wouldn't trust advice from just anyone and I couldn't help but wonder if the guidance he offered was from personal experience. Whatever had happened between Con and his high school sweetheart was a mystery, but it had obviously affected him deeply. I was curious about what had happened, but I had enough of his own shit to worry about. Hell, I couldn't even fix my own relationship. I dropped my head back against the chair and stared at the ceiling.

Damn that asshole Johnathan for manipulating her into believing the worst. I wanted to rip him limb from limb, claim her as my own and force him to accept it. But Victoria had to make that decision. I'd been vindicated, at least, when the other man had shown up at the healthplex a couple of days ago and presumably been turned away by Victoria. Johnathan had swaggered into the building with a confident smirk only to return minutes later, shooting daggers my way as he left. I hoped Victoria had given the man the set down he deserved and more.

It pained me to know that Johnathan was being so selfish. He clearly wanted her for himself, though she refused to see it that way. He knew Victoria and I were happy but he was too jealous to do what was best for her. I felt bad for the guy. Kind of. I couldn't imagine being just friends with a woman like Victoria. Any man would be lucky to have her, and it would be torture to have her in my life but not be able to touch her intimately. I prayed to God she would come to her senses, and soon, because not being able to hold her, love her, laugh with her, was driving me crazy.

Con was right—I did need to talk to her.

I shoved out of my chair, flipping off the lights as I went, and caught up to Con in the lobby. "Hey. Wanna grab a drink?"

"Sure."

My attention was drawn toward the reception area, now cluttered with a handful of knick-knacks and pictures. I hadn't even noticed it on the way in.

"I forgot all about Abby. Looks like she's settling in okay."

Con rolled his eyes. "I'll never understand why women feel the need to clutter every inch of space with stupid shit."

"It's not so bad." I didn't admit it out loud, but I kind of liked the lived-in feel. Abby had obviously chosen to surround herself with stuff that made her happy. While Abby was bubbly and outgoing, Con was stark and stoic, and the décor in his office—or lack thereof—reflected his personality. I thought of Victoria's office and how welcoming it felt. I'd have to drop a word in Abby's ear about getting some pictures to spruce up the walls. And maybe some kind of plant.

I turned my attention back to Con. "Baby sister bring a boyfriend home with her?"

"Hell no." He growled. "I'll kill anyone who gets close to her."

"She's what, twenty-two? It's bound to happen. Remember what we were like at that age?"

Con shot a glare my way. "Twenty-three. And don't

fucking remind me."

Con pulled a keyring from his back pocket and locked the door behind us as we stepped into the humid night. I took a deep breath and closed my eyes. I'd give anything to be in bed next to Victoria right now instead of heading to a bar. The thought alone was distasteful. How I'd endured years of the bar scene, many nights with a different woman, I had no idea. Granted, I'd had a lot of fun, but it had never meant anything. Not until I met Victoria.

We fell into step together but remained silent as we walked toward the corner bar. Aptly named, The Shield was a popular hangout for local law enforcement, and QSG had been welcomed in with open arms. It helped that we'd made it very clear to the locals that we wouldn't step on any toes—we'd assist with investigations if needed and offer training operations but otherwise keep to ourselves. Con had spoken with the Chief of Police a few weeks ago in regards to sharing information about Victoria's case, and the man was on board. They would take first shot at it, but if resources ran low, QSG was more than welcome to help. I nodded to a couple patrolmen I'd met after Monique Henderson's murder and took a seat two tables over. Con slid into a chair across from me and signaled the waitress.

One of the patrolmen stood up and ambled toward us, and I lifted my chin at him. "Phelps. How's it goin'?"

He gestured to the table. "Not bad. Mind if I have a seat?"

"Not at all." I used my foot to push the chair out in invitation.

He sank into the wooden seat and glanced at Con. "I know you'll both want to know, so I'll send the information your way tomorrow."

"What's that?" I raised a brow at the man, who shook his head.

"We interviewed Greg Andrews, but he has a solid alibi for the time of the murder, as well as the night that Dr. Winfield was attacked in her office."

Shit. He'd been the only good lead with any motive.

Jason had found that Andrews's sister lived just three streets over from Victoria, which allowed him access to the subdivision. This bit of news brought us right back to square one. Andrews had been associated, if only briefly, with both Kate and Victoria. But now I was beginning to wonder if the two instances were even related.

So, who had it out for Victoria? Another patient, maybe? We needed to dig deeper into her past, see who might have ties to her hometown. We'd need to pull her list of patients, both former and current, and run checks on each of them. Victoria would throw a fit about that. She was incredibly stringent about doctor-patient confidentiality, even at the risk of putting herself in danger.

I glanced at Phelps. "I think we need to look at the people she interacts with on a regular basis. What about her patients? Can you get a warrant to run background checks on them, see if anything stands out?"

He grimaced. "I don't know if the judge will sign off, but we can try."

"Why now?"

Con asked the question that had plagued me since I'd found out about her past. What the hell had triggered his obsession? And what was his end game? I'd originally suspected that the person—I was assuming it was a guy—had begun to follow her again with the intent to finish her off. If he'd wanted Victoria gone, he could've easily killed her instead of Monique.

The thought made me see red. Victoria hadn't recognized the man who'd abducted her ten years ago, but a lot could change in a decade. Whoever it was knew her on a personal level, was close enough to her that he'd gained access to her house with little difficulty.

It killed me that I couldn't be with her. She was safe enough at home with her new security system, and the locals were patrolling the subdivision frequently. Over the past few days I'd driven past a couple—more like a dozen—times just to check for myself that she was safe. I fucking hated being away from her, but I also wanted to respect her wishes and give her some space.

"We need to figure out if she's acquired any new patients, or if any existing or ex-patients had a thing for her. Whoever it is, is obviously infatuated with her."

"The phone call was a cry for attention." Con nodded and stroked his chin as he latched on to my train of thought. "The vandalism may have been the same thing. Guy broke in to make her feel vulnerable so she'd turn to him. He must not have known she and Blake were dating."

"What about an ex-lover?" Phelps asked with a hopeful expression.

I shook my head. "Uh... no. She hasn't dated anyone since college." At their dubious looks, I elaborated. "Trust me. You're barking up the wrong tree there."

I traded a glance with Con, who spoke up. "So he's been in her house at least once that we know of, right? And no one out of place showed up on the cameras the night of the B&E?"

Phelps shook his head. "Everyone coming and going that night was on the approved list."

"Maybe it's someone who lives in the allotment," I mused. "Can we get a list of the current residents?"

"I can forward it to you, but so far everyone has checked out."

That was all well and good, but it didn't mean the person wasn't there and meaning to do Victoria harm. It would make sense that it would be someone who belonged there, who fit in. He would go unnoticed by the other homeowners because he lived there. The sooner they got that list, the sooner Jason could start digging into it.

"Can we get a copy of the footage from that night, too? I'd like to double check all the cars that showed up on the camera from the gatehouse, ingoing and outgoing." Maybe we'd get lucky and something would jump out at us.

"You got it. I'll send it over first thing in the morning." Phelps hesitated. "Not gonna lie. Without a solid lead..."

He shrugged, and I understood the implication. They

couldn't continue to waste time and resources on a simple breaking and entering. It sucked, but they had more important things to focus on.

I nodded at the patrolman. "I gotcha."

Phelps tipped his empty bottle in appreciation. "I'm outta here. See you guys later."

Con glanced across the table as the officer said his farewells and headed toward the door. "We're missing something."

I was silent for a moment. "I know, I just can't tell what it is."

"Maybe Jason can pull something from the footage that they can't." He eyed me. "You seem pretty certain that it's not an ex."

I stared back. "I am."

Con raised a brow. "You're that certain?"

"Yep."

"Did you check into them?"

"Didn't have to."

Con growled. "What the hell does that mean?"

"It's a short list."

"Still, there could be—"

"There's not."

"Look, I know you like this girl," he pressed, "but is it possible that she could be omitting the truth? Maybe she's been with more guys than she wants to admit and—"

"She hasn't."

Con sliced one hand through the air. "How the hell do you know? You've only been with her for a couple weeks."

"When I say it's a short list, I mean it's got one person on it. Me."

"But how..." Understanding dawned and Con leaned back in his seat. "Shit. Seriously?"

"Yup." I shrugged. "After she was attacked in high school, she said she wasn't ready."

Con grimaced. "Damn."

My thoughts exactly. It was a bittersweet sentiment. I

wished there was another angle to pursue, but I was damn glad I didn't have to deal with some crazy ex-boyfriend. Thinking of her with another man made me want to rip something apart with my bare hands. I wondered what she was doing right this second. Damn, I really needed to talk to her and clear the air.

"Let's start with the homeowners and the camera footage, and I'll talk with Chief tomorrow to see if we have any chance of getting Victoria's patient list released. She should already have run background checks on each of them, so we can see if any have ties to Ohio that would have put them there at the time of the attack when she was young."

"Sounds like a plan." Con rolled the empty beer bottle between his hands, looking pensive. "Is she safe?"

I sighed. "As much as she can be with the new security system. I just hate that she's there all alone."

"Don't wait too long," Con reminded me. "Get everything out in the open before it's too late."

I opened my mouth to tell him to fuck off, then snapped it shut. I knew he was right. I only had two days left on this contract. When it was all over, I was going to find a way to make Victoria listen to me, no matter what it took.

CHAPTER THIRTY-FOUR

Victoria

I regarded the two women seated across from me. "I completely blew it out of proportion, didn't I?"

"Yes."

"No."

Kate and Phyllis spoke at the same time, then traded a glance.

"I was trying to be nice." Phyllis huffed before turning her attention back to me. "You did what you felt was right at the time, dear."

My heart fell. "I screwed up."

"Yes."

"No."

Again, the two women spoke in unison and contradicted one another. Kate shot Phyllis a quelling look before turning her gaze my way.

"I think you may have overreacted a bit." Kate held up a hand, halting my protest. "Don't get me wrong—it might be a little too soon to be talking about moving in together, but tell me this: were you happy with Blake?"

"Yes, but—"

"Just hear me out," Kate cut me off. "You were happy with him. Happier than I've ever seen you. Right?"

She directed the last part of her question to Phyllis, who

reluctantly nodded. "It's true."

Kate turned back to me. "So what changed your mind?"

"Well... Johnathan brought up a couple good points." I lifted my gaze in time to see both women roll their eyes. "What?"

My gaze jumped back and forth between the two, and I sighed. "Go ahead, just tell me."

Kate settled back in her chair, arms crossed, allowing Phyllis to take the lead. "Johnathan has been a good friend to you, Victoria, I know he has. But he's a little, well... condescending."

"Maybe," I admitted, "but he is a doctor, and he's very good at what he does. He assessed the situation pretty accurately," I felt compelled to point out.

"Did he really?" Kate pressed. "Or did he tell you what he wants you to believe?"

"I don't—"

"Do you see a future with Blake?"

"Maybe, but—"

"Yes or no?"

I huffed and crossed my arms over my chest. I shot a look at Phyllis, hoping for support, but she studiously avoided me. Apparently I was getting no help from that corner. I flicked an irritated glare at Kate. "Fine, yes."

"Johnathan's jealous," she clarified. "He doesn't want to be your friend—he wants to be your lover."

Kate had a point, even if I didn't like it.

"I think you let Johnathan sway your opinion more than you should have. If there's anything I've learned from my marriage, it's that your first instinct is always right. I think you should take some time to figure out what your heart wants—not what someone else tells you that you should feel."

My heart felt as if it was breaking all over again, and it was all my fault. Blake had sat here with me just weeks ago, talking about Rachel and comforting me though he'd barely known me at the time. It was more heartfelt than anything Johnathan had ever done. Blake truly cared for me; I knew that. Shame settled heavily in my stomach and hot tears burned the backs of my eyes.

"Look, Vic, I've seen the way he looks at you. That man"— Kate pointed in the general vicinity of the lobby—"would do anything for you. Hell, he didn't even know me, and he saved my life. Would Johnathan ever do something like that? Would he sacrifice himself for you? Johnathan has been your friend for a long time, but... sometimes the idea of a person is better than the reality."

I turned away, unable to meet her gaze as the moisture in my eyes spilled over. I vaguely heard the door open and close as Phyllis quietly exited the room. Seconds later a weight settled onto the couch cushion next to me, and Kate pulled me into a hug.

"I... I think I love him." Another tear slipped free, and I swiped it away.

"I know you do." Kate leaned back against the couch. "And he loves you. Everything will work out, you'll see."

"What if he won't take me back?"

"Of course he will."

I searched Kate's gaze. "But—"

She shook her head. "He loves you. And I promise he's just waiting for you to come to your senses."

Was she right? I'd hurt him by pushing him away. I hadn't trusted him, hadn't trusted myself, and he deserved better than that. I should have talked about it instead of shutting down—but maybe we could still make this work.

I wiped the remainder of my tears away and looked at Kate. "Thank you."

She studied me for a second. "You okay?"

"I think so, yeah. I'll try to talk to him before I leave tonight."

"Good."

"I'm sorry to drag you into this. You've got enough going on already."

Kate waved away my apology. "I'll always be here for you if you need me. Besides, Steve doesn't warrant any more tears than I've already given him."

I studied her for the first time since she'd shown up and dragged me back here for an intervention with Phyllis. Kate's eyes were rimmed with red as if she'd been on a week-long crying jag. Stitches cut across her forehead, and her flesh was bruised a deep purple around the wound. Her normally put-together appearance was disheveled almost to the point of sloppiness, and I knew the impending divorce was weighing more heavily on her than she'd ever admit.

"How are you holding up? For real?"

Kate's lips pressed together in a firm line before relaxing and letting out a soft exhalation. "You know what? I'm actually okay. I know I look like a mess"—Kate grinned and I couldn't help but return it—"but I've realized something over the last couple months. I'm not really mad at Steve. I'm not even mad at myself anymore. We shouldn't have gotten married, but I learned an important lesson. I need to do something for me. So much of my time has been spent catering to others. I'm selling my portion of the practice."

"But... Are you sure?" Kate loved it here. "I thought—"

She shook her head. "It was my decision. I want to do something that really matters, something that makes a difference. I'm applying to work for the VA."

"I think that's a fantastic idea. Tell me all about your plans."

We spent the next hour catching up, talking about the past, about the future, and I realized how much I'd missed these moments.

"I really haven't gotten to see much of you since..." I waved one hand in the air, not wanting to dampen the mood by mentioning Kate's attack from two weeks prior. "It's been so crazy recently."

"I know." She nodded. "I promise once all this is over, we'll get back to our normal routine."

"Deal." I glanced out the window at the setting sun. "We better get out of here. I want to talk to Blake on the way out."

"Good." Kate straightened and hitched her purse over

her shoulder. "Keep me posted, okay?"

"I will."

With one last hug, Kate let herself out and I closed up, making sure everything was locked up tight. I made my way to the lobby, but Blake was nowhere to be found. With a sigh, I trudged to my car and slid inside, then dug my phone out of my purse.

Should I text him or wait? Taking a deep breath, I quickly tapped out a message and hit the send button before I could rethink my decision. I tossed my phone back into my bag and headed for home, heart practically beating out of my chest. I'd finally found the man I loved—I just hoped I wasn't too late.

CHAPTER THIRTY-FIVE

Victoria

My phone rang, startling me from a restless sleep. Hope filled my chest as Blake's name flashed across the screen and I lifted it to my ear.

"Blake?" When he hadn't responded to my text I'd finally fallen into bed—I glanced at the clock—not quite an hour ago, and cried myself to sleep.

"Victoria." His voice was strained to the point of politeness, but I could hear the heavy undercurrent in his tone. It also wasn't lost on me that he hadn't used his nickname for me, and the knowledge stung. Silence filled the line for several seconds before he cleared his throat and began to speak. "Listen, I'm sorry to tell you this way, but there's been a break-in at the healthplex."

I sucked in a breath. "What happened?"

"We're not sure yet. Benny called to let me know the alarm went off about five minutes ago. The police have been notified, so they'll clear the building to make sure everything's good. I just wanted to give you a heads up."

"I'll meet you there." I threw the covers aside and slid from the bed, already tugging on a pair of sweats that lay discarded on the floor.

"No need. I'm already on my way, and I'd feel better if you stayed at home where I know you're safe."

"Blake…"

"Let me take care of it. Please."

His words stopped me mid-motion and I sank to the edge of my bed. "Will you call to let me know everything's okay?"

"Of course. I'll call as soon as I'm done."

"Thank you." I hesitated, gripping the phone so tightly my knuckles ached. "And, Blake?"

His voice was tentative. "Yeah?"

It took a moment to gather my courage, and my words came out on a whisper. "I miss you."

There was a sharp inhale on the other end of the line. "I miss you too, babe."

"Can we talk sometime? Maybe tomorrow after work if you're free?"

"I have all the time in the world for you, Doc." His voice was deep and full of promise. "Hey, I'm at the healthplex now, so I'll call you in a few."

"Be safe."

"I will."

I reluctantly hung up and stared at the phone in my hand, a riot of emotions swirling in my stomach. I wanted to laugh, to cry, wanted to throw my arms wide and dance for joy. He cared about me. Still clutching the phone, I collapsed onto the bed and stared at the ceiling. I needed to address things with Johnathan once and for all. He'd stopped by the healthplex to see me, but I'd turned him away. My heart hurt at the thought of losing a good friend and confidant, but today's discussion with Kate and Phyllis had opened my eyes.

Maybe Johnathan really was more concerned about his own interests than mine. He was a good guy, successful and handsome, but I would never feel about him the way I did with Blake, who went out of his way to make sure I was safe, always placing my needs before his own. More than once he'd dropped everything without hesitation. He was strong and sturdy, trustworthy and dependable, and I—

I jerked to a sitting position. *I loved him.* And Blake loved me, too. He'd told me days ago, but I'd refused to believe it.

It didn't seem possible that I'd come to care so deeply for him over just a few weeks' time, but I knew what was in my heart. For the first time, I wasn't scared. Instead, anticipation surged through my veins. There would be ups and downs, good times and bad—but we could make this work. As soon as he called back I would go to him, lay my heart on the line and tell him how much he meant to me.

Unable to wait a moment longer, I scrambled from the bed. I pulled a sweater over the camisole I'd slept in and yanked off my sweatpants, replacing them instead with jeans. Shoving my phone into my back pocket, I jogged down the stairs. Bubbling with emotion, I tapped the switch to awaken the coffee maker then scooped grinds into the basket. The potent aroma filled the air as the percolator jolted to life and spewed the hot brew into the cup.

My phone rang again, and I tapped the button to answer without looking at the screen.

"Dr. Carr speaking."

"Victoria, thank goodness I was able to reach you."

My heart sank as Johnathan's voice floated through the phone and his words registered. "What's wrong?"

"A man just called me—gave me a woman's name and an address. I think it was Greg Andrews."

Oh, God. "Have you called the police? Did—?"

"We need to go. You don't want him to hurt someone else, do you?"

Fear constricted my heart, and I sucked in a breath. I couldn't allow that to happen again. How would I live with myself?

"Okay, okay. I'm on my way out the door. Where is it?" I dumped the coffee down the drain and started for the front door.

"I'm already on my way to your house. I'll be there in just a minute. Get ready and I'll tell you everything on the way."

Adrenaline pumping through my veins, I slipped my feet into the ballet flats sitting on the rug by the front door and tossed my phone into my purse before slinging it over my shoulder. Rain pelted the windows, wind rattling the panes, and I quickly disengaged then reset the alarm before striding out of the house. A small silver Toyota sped around the curve on my street just as I closed the door, and it slowed to a stop at the bottom of my driveway. The window rolled down, and Johnathan waved to me from the driver's side.

I hurried toward him and slid into the passenger seat. I glanced around the interior of the sedan as I fastened the seat belt. "I didn't recognize you in this. When did you get a new car?"

"I've had it for a while, I just don't drive it much." Johnathan threw a quick glance my way before making a U-turn and speeding toward the allotment's exit. "You got ready fast."

"I was already dressed. I actually got a call from Blake just before you showed up." I shook off the water clinging to my skin and pulled my phone out to check for any updates. "Apparently the alarm went off at the healthplex and he stopped by to check it out."

"Is everything okay?"

"I'm not sure, I haven't heard back yet."

Johnathan nodded absently and turned right out of the complex, heading toward the outskirts of town. I watched the trees fly past the window in a blur as the streetlights became fewer and farther between.

"Do you know where we're going?"

"Of course."

I recoiled at his curt reply. He'd never lashed out at me before, never raised his voice. But underneath that carefully cultured tone I detected a slight deviation—was that a faint change in dialect or accent I heard?

"Okay." I nodded, unable to suppress the uneasy prickles spreading over my skin. I flipped the phone over in my hand and cast another surreptitious look at the screen. Still nothing. What was taking so long?

As if conjured by my thoughts, my phone rang and my heart jumped into my throat. I swiped my thumb over the screen and lifted it to my ear. "Hey, is everything okay?"

"It's fine, but—"

"Thank God." I breathed a sigh of relief.

"I'm coming over right now. We need to talk."

"I know. I think Greg Andrews might be after another woman. He—"

"It's not Greg Andrews—it's Johnathan."

I blinked, trying to process his words. "But…"

"Sweetheart, I need you to listen to me. Don't say anything, just listen, okay?"

"I—"

"Please." The pleading in his voice made my blood freeze in my veins. "Doc, it's him. It's been Johnathan this whole time."

No. That wasn't possible. It couldn't be. I was dimly aware of Blake speaking and I forced myself to focus.

"…the breaking and entering, the assault at your office. We found him on the cameras. Everything lines up."

My heart seized and every muscle went rigid, hyper-aware of Johnathan's eyes on me as I spoke. "What about…?"

I could sense his hesitation and he finally let out a resigned sigh. "Leah was his first." Tears pricked my eyes and I fought to control my breathing as I blinked them away. "I'm sorry, baby."

"Well, thank you for looking into that."

If he'd killed Leah, he would certainly kill me too. Fear and sadness and anger warred within me, twisting my stomach into knots.

"Do you know where he's taking you?"

I threw a quick glance out the window at the darkened road. "I'm not sure."

"Have you left your house yet?"

"Yes."

"Is he heading toward town?"

"Um…" I pretended to deliberate. "No, I don't believe so."

"Where the hell is he going?"

From the quiet tone of his voice, I could tell the words were more for himself than me, but I felt compelled to answer, my own response soft and unsure. "I don't know."

Blake swore under his breath. "Here's what I want you to do: pretend to hang up but keep the call connected. Put it between the seats or somewhere he can't reach it. Okay?"

"Thank you again for the update." I hoped he understood my affirmation, and I was rewarded when he responded a moment later, his voice thick with emotion.

"I'll find you, sweetheart. I promise."

Tears pricked my eyes, emotion clogging my throat. What if this was the last time I ever heard his voice? "Blake, I—"

"No." His voice was fierce and there was a moment of silence as he drew a ragged breath. "You tell me when I find you. Just hang in there for me."

"Goodbye, Blake."

My heart fractured and tears spilled over as I dropped the phone into the space between my seat and the door. Regret filled me for the time I'd wasted and I swiped at the tears coursing down my cheeks. It wasn't fair; I couldn't bear to lose the love of my life just when I'd found him.

"Are you okay?"

Johnathan's voice intruded on my thoughts. I wanted to lash out at him, scream, cry, tell him the game was up, but I could do none of those things. Not if I wanted to get out of this alive.

"Fine."

"You still care about him."

It was a statement rather than a question and, for a moment, I was unsure how to respond. Should I lie to him and tell him things were over for good? No, he was too good at what he did; he'd be able to see right through that. Opting for a semi-truth, I nodded.

"I like him a lot. But... some of the things you said made sense. I just don't know if we could have a future together."

And wasn't that the understatement of the century? I

sat inches from a man who, for years, had pretended to be my friend. He'd deceived me. Used me. And now... God, who knew what he was going to do now?

I was certain of a couple of things, though. The first thing was, no one awaited us at the end of this journey. The further we drove into the darkness, the more the butterflies in my stomach kicked up, filling my belly with dread. The second realization was that, if I survived this, I would never leave Blake's side again.

Johnathan drummed his fingers on the steering wheel, and his lips pursed pensively before turning down in a frown. "You're nothing like her, you know."

His Midwestern accent was back, and it hit me full force, transporting me back to that awful night. Somehow I managed to choke out the word, though I already knew the answer. "Who?"

"Leah."

Hearing her name roll off his tongue was like a stab to the heart. I'd known he was responsible, yet hearing those words from his own mouth somehow made it more real. Hearing him admit it, that he was capable of something so awful... My heart ached.

"Why did you do it?"

Johnathan shook his head. "You wouldn't understand. No one does. I saw her and I just knew. I felt this sense of... finality, like destiny calling me. Besides, it's not like she was the angel everyone wanted to believe."

He threw a look my way before continuing. "After her death, they painted a picture of her being this good little Christian girl. But we knew better, didn't we? She flaunted herself, treated others as if she expected them to bow to her, and I hated her on sight. It was like something deep inside me let loose, clawing its way to the surface, desperately needing to lash out. It was so overwhelming and I just couldn't hold it back anymore."

Bile rose in my throat and I forced it down with a hard swallow. "But why me? What did I ever do to you?"

"You never did anything." He sighed and lifted a shoulder in a very un-Johnathan-like shrug. "By that point, I was high on adrenaline—I couldn't turn it off. And you were a loose end. I knew you'd survived, of course, but I left the next day and headed back to college in West Virginia. I'd been gone for years by that point, and no one remembered me. I knew they'd never find me.

"But I couldn't let you go. It took me years to finally find you. Except..." He smiled ruefully. "It wasn't at all the way I imagined it would be."

"You look... different." His face haunted my dreams, but over time his features had dissolved away, leaving only the macabre mouth twisted into a sneer.

He stiffened in the driver's seat. "I'd already had the surgery scheduled. I mostly kept to myself, so no one thought twice about it."

Of course no one noticed. As far as anyone knew, he'd been miles away with no connection to the small town. His voice cut through my thoughts.

"Do you remember how we met?"

The question threw me for a loop and I hesitated for a moment before turning to look at him. "Yes. It was the conference in Austin, I believe."

"That's right." His head bobbed in acknowledgment. "I knew where you lived, what you did for a living. I'd planned for years to find you and finish what I'd started all those years ago. But then we started talking, and I got to know you, got you to open up about your past. And all I could think about while you told me your story was how much you'd changed yet stayed the same. You'd matured into this beautiful, intelligent woman, but inside you were still the same scared little girl you were ten years ago.

"Then I realized something—you'd been saving yourself... for me. Don't you see, Victoria? We're meant to be together. From now on, we'll never be apart."

Ice sluiced through my veins and fear clutched at my throat, making it almost impossible to swallow. I fought down the urge to cry, to scream. I wanted—needed—Blake. He told me he'd come for me… but what if it wasn't enough? I pushed the thought away and steeled my spine. I needed to get my emotions under control and think.

I leaned my head against the cool glass, watching trees rush past in a dark blur as we drove deeper into the unknown.

CHAPTER THIRTY-SIX

Blake

Four sets of eyes swiveled my way as I shoved open the door to the bullpen. "We have a problem."

I was just leaving the healthplex after investigating the false alarm when Jason had called with the information we'd been looking for. Since Greg Andrews's alibi had checked out, Jason and I had spent the past day and a half reviewing the recordings from the camera in Victoria's allotment. A nondescript silver sedan had appeared at relevant times and the license plate had come back on Johnathan Marcus Martin. A far cry from the flashy red Porsche he typically drove, I was furious that the man had managed to slip by us the first time we'd reviewed the footage. Jason had checked the Toyota against DMV records and discovered it was linked to Dr. Johnathan Martin.

After digging deeper into the man's past, he'd discovered an unsettling history. Martin came from a broken home in West Virginia, and his father had died under suspicious circumstances, as had the aunt who'd gained custody of the young man for several months before he'd turned eighteen and moved out. When the police had investigated the father's death, the seventeen-year-old had pled self-defense, claiming he'd stabbed the older man when he'd attacked Johnathan in a drunken rage.

The boy had been sent to live with his aunt, his father's sister, who, according to friends of hers, had been happy to send the boy on his way. Several years later, the very weekend of Leah's death, the woman had died of a broken neck from an apparent fall down the stairs.

I was furious for not looking more deeply into the man sooner. It all made perfect sense now—he'd introduced himself to Victoria and Leah using his middle name, then escaped back to college one state over with no one the wiser. Even Monique's murder was linked to the man—Johnathan routinely made rounds at the hospital where she worked.

I thought of Victoria's terrified voice, and I prayed it wouldn't be the last time I had the chance to speak with her.

I palmed the phone still in my hand and thrust it toward Jason. The mute function kept our side of conversation silent so Martin wouldn't overhear. "He's got Victoria. I think this is his end game."

Jason turned back to his computer as Con and the newest addition, Clay Thompson, looked on. "Any idea where they're headed?"

"No, she just said that they turned right out of her allotment and headed away from town. What's out that way?" Fury threatened to erupt and I ruthlessly tamped it down, fighting to stay calm.

"What's her address?" I rattled it off and Jason's fingers flew over the keyboard, pulling up a map of the surrounding area. "What should we be looking for?"

"Someplace secluded, quiet. He'll need privacy." I pointed to the screen. "Is this a river cutting through right here?"

Jason enlarged the screen and nodded. I ran my fingers through my hair. "Jesus. That's it. He's recreating the past. Find me a crossing point with a bridge—either on the road or the railroad tracks. I'm going after her."

"Hold up, I'm coming with you."

Con snatched up three sets of comm devices and fell into step behind me, Thompson on his six. I barely spared them a glance as I jogged from the building and out into the night. Raindrops fell from the dark sky, stinging my skin as I cut across the pavement and hopped into my truck. The other two doors slammed behind the men in tandem as they shut themselves inside.

I tossed my phone to Con. "Make sure the call is still connected. Can you hear anything?"

He held the phone to his ear and listened for a moment. "I can't make anything out, but they're still there." A low thrum of indiscernible conversation filled the cabin as he turned it to speakerphone and set the phone on the console.

The headlights cut a swath through the shroud of darkness swallowing the landscape and rain pelted the earth as we traveled farther into the empty countryside. Heavy tension hung in the air as I gripped the steering wheel tightly, the tempo of my heart increasing with each mile. Rain hammered the windshield and the wipers made a rhythmic swishing sound as they cleared the droplets, but I heard none of it. My thoughts were firmly focused on Victoria.

I couldn't lose her now. She was everything I never knew I was missing until that fateful day I'd walked into the healthplex. My heart constricted at the thought of her all alone. I never should have left her, damn it. I should have stayed and fought it out, made her understand how much I loved her. I'd waited too long, and now it might be too late. Despair threatened to consume me and I swallowed down the thick lump that had formed in my throat. I had to find her and bring her home safely. There was no other option.

I didn't realize the chatter inside the cab of the truck had died away until the sound of my name interrupted my thoughts.

"What?" I turned an agitated glare on Con.

He appraised me with a steady look before responding. "You got a plan or we going in hot?"

"I'm gonna kill him." At the moment, I wasn't entirely sure if the phrase was just an expression or the truth.

"Good plan," Con replied drily. He passed me an earpiece

and I slipped it into place. "If we could minimize casualties, that'd be great."

I ignored his snarky humor. "If it's anything like last time..." White-hot fury rippled through me. The man had raped and killed Victoria's best friend, and now she was alone with him in the middle of nowhere. "He's willing to go to any length to finish this. We need to make sure that doesn't happen."

"They've stopped moving." I could hear the tension in Jason's voice as it crackled through the headset. "About a mile up Oak Creek Road. Authorities are on their way."

"You'll want to take a left up here, past the train tracks." I lifted my eyes to the rearview mirror and met Clay's gaze.

"You been briefed on this?"

"Yes, sir." He leaned forward between the seats. "The next left will be Oak Creek Road. They shouldn't hear us over the rain. We can head about a half mile up the road and move the rest of the way on foot."

"We need to get her out of here unharmed." Con directed his next words at Clay. "I think we should split up."

The man grunted in affirmation. "Drop me at the tracks. I'll cut through the woods and come in from the east."

The railroad tracks came into view and I slowed the truck to a stop, allowing Clay to jump out. As soon as the door slammed shut with a soft *thunk*, I hit the gas, wheels spinning on the slick pavement. Fittingly, the road crossed over Oak Creek, one of the many small tributaries that met up with a larger river several miles away. It was just far enough away to give the illusion of privacy but not so far that it would compromise Martin's mission.

Con grabbed for the handle over the door as I whipped the truck onto the old dirt and gravel road. I let off the accelerator and killed the headlights, relying on the moon overhead to guide us. Deciding it was as good a place as any, I yanked the truck to the side of the road. We filed out and jogged toward the bridge, careful to not make any noise, though I seriously doubted Johnathan could hear anything over the steady drum of the rain pounding the earth.

Through the haze of raindrops, the arches of the bridge came into view and I slowed my pace. Pulling the pistol from the holster on my waistband, I loaded a round into the chamber with a quick tug to the slide and Con mirrored my actions. "You ready?"

He gave a sharp nod and we continued quickly toward the bridge. Voices rose on the night air and a red haze filled my vision as I took in the scene. Johnathan held Victoria captive in the middle of the old bridge, and even in the dim light of the half-obscured moon, I could clearly read the fear in her eyes.

Con clasped a hand on my shoulder just in time and I froze in place, closing my eyes for a moment. I needed to keep it together for her. There was too much at stake now; we couldn't afford even one wrong move.

Clay's voice crackled to life in my earpiece. "Almost there."

I wiped the raindrops from my eyes, my heart thudding painfully in my chest as I watched Johnathan force Victoria backward, closer and closer to the rail until her bottom bumped into the rickety wood, gray with age. Her feet scrabbled for purchase on the slippery surface of the old road and she threw a terrified glance behind her at the tumultuous waters below.

The tenuous hold I had on my control snapped and I charged forward. "Let her go, Martin!"

At the sound of my voice, Johnathan whipped around, eyes wild in the moonlight. A torrent of rain pelted down, matting his hair, accentuating his crazed look. Threatened and trapped, he yanked Victoria in front of him for protection. "You're too late, Lawson."

Every cell of my body went ice cold and my heart stuttered to a stop as the man lifted a pistol and held it to Victoria's temple.

CHAPTER THIRTY-SEVEN

Victoria

I stumbled as Johnathan yanked me in front of him, snarling with rage. Hands bound, I was completely at his mercy. As soon as we'd arrived at the old bridge, I'd known what was coming.

I shouldn't have tried to run—it was the thrill of the chase that excited him. As soon he'd stopped the car, I'd made a break for it, dashing toward the woods on the other side. I'd desperately hoped I could get lost within the foliage and escape, but Johnathan was faster than he looked. My hands and knees still ached from scraping the rocky terrain after he'd tackled me, and the abrasion on my cheek stung where he'd smashed my face into the cold, hard ground.

Helplessly, I'd watched as he'd secured the end of my restraints around the arch of the bridge, then his own. "Don't worry, darling," he'd told me. "I promise it will be quick."

Now he planned to take me with him in an apparent murder-suicide, and the rope around my neck tightened as he switched positions, shifting me closer.

"Come on, Johnathan. You don't want to hurt her, I know you don't."

I could barely hear Blake's words over the pounding rain, and I met his eyes for the briefest of moments. His gaze begged me to trust him and I swallowed my fear.

The muzzle of the gun dug into my temple and Johnathan's fingers tunneled into my hair, digging into my scalp as he angled himself behind me. I clenched my eyes against the intense pain.

"She's always been mine. Mine!"

"You've been a good friend to her, Johnathan," Con spoke up. "You don't want it to end like this. Just let her go."

I felt Johnathan shake his head, his chin brushing the shell of my ear. "It's not that simple. I need this. I need her."

"Put the gun down, Martin." The plea in Blake's voice was unmistakable. "You love her. Don't do this."

"I do love her." Pain rippled across my scalp as Johnathan clamped down tighter, his grip increasing with each word. Tears clouded my vision, mingling with the raindrops as they dripped down my face.

"And you took her away from me!"

"I would never do that." Blake held up his hands placatingly. "She's your friend, Johnathan. She needs you, just like you need her."

The grip on my hair eased just a fraction and I released a sigh of relief.

"She was never yours, Lawson, and never will be. She was mine first and I'll take her with me before I let you have her."

Johnathan took another step backward, and I felt the coarse rope slide against my neck. I met Blake's eyes again, pouring all the love I felt for him into my gaze.

The rope tugged again and I sucked in a breath as I felt the ground disappear beneath my feet.

CHAPTER THIRTY-EIGHT

Blake

Fire and defiance flashed in her eyes, and I saw the move coming before I could open my mouth to stop her. Hands lashed together in front of her, she threw all of her weight into Johnathan and her elbow landed hard in his ribs. A shot rang out as the man let out a sharp cry at the unexpected blow. Victoria screamed and I jerked back, vaguely aware of the searing pain shooting through my shoulder and down my left arm. I brought a hand to my shoulder and winced when my fingers came away wet and dark. *Shit.*

In the blink of an eye, all hell broke loose. A blur of movement appeared at the far side of the bridge, yanking Johnathan's attention away. The man lifted his gun and aimed at Clay as he came in low and fast, prepared to knock Johnathan to the ground. Two shots rang out almost in tandem over the drum of the heavy rain.

Johnathan stumbled backward, eyes wide with surprise as Con's shot made contact. Blood pulsed from the wound in his neck and his face contorted in pain. His body went slack as he slumped over the rail, ready to tumble into the raging river. Victoria let out a startled cry as her own restraints entwined with Johnathan's and she was jerked backward, his weight pulling her down.

In a swooping motion, Clay wrapped his arms around her

waist to keep her from going over. Con and I were a second behind and Con grabbed the rope holding Johnathan's body suspended over the river. I yanked a knife from my pocket and sliced through the thin nylon.

"Wait!"

The slippery rain-drenched material slid through Con's fingers as it released, and Johnathan's body plunged into the rushing waters below.

Together, Clay and I lifted a soaked, trembling Victoria over the rail and onto solid ground. As soon as her feet hit the pavement, she launched herself at me. I let out a hiss at the impact, my shoulder protesting the motion as I wrapped my arms tightly around her. Despite the fiery pain shooting across my nerve endings, I refused to loosen my hold.

I tunneled one hand into her hair, loose and hanging limp around her face, water dripping from the curly ends. "Christ, I was so scared. I thought I was going to lose you."

She lifted her head from where it rested against my sodden shirt and met my gaze. "Blake, I..." Her eyes rounded with surprise as they dropped to my shoulder. "You're bleeding!"

"I'll be fine, sweetheart." I pulled her flush against me.

"I'm sorry." She burrowed her head against my chest, her voice cracking on the words. "I'm so sorry. I should have listened to you."

"Shh," I murmured against her hair. "Everything is fine now. Everything's okay."

She threw a look toward the swollen creek below, the churning water battering the bank. "Is he...?"

"Gone, baby. I'm sorry."

"I still can't believe it." She shivered and I tightened my arms around her waist as if to shield her from the pain of the memory. "I never thought..."

I felt a hand on my shoulder and turned toward Con.

"Let's get out of the rain."

I hadn't even realized Clay had retrieved the truck until the headlights swept over us. I ushered Victoria into the back of the cab and climbed up beside her, pulling her into my arms as soon as the door closed behind us.

Clay reached over and cranked the heat. "Locals are on their way. We'll be outta here soon."

"Not much to see at this point," came Con's low drawl.

Victoria shuddered at the implication and I slid my free hand under her legs and scooped her into my lap. She turned her face into my neck, seeking comfort, reminding me again of how close I'd come to losing her. I looped my arms around her like a steel band and pressed a kiss to her temple.

"I'm so glad you're safe."

"Me, too." She turned those beautiful gray eyes on me, so full of love and trust. Concern filled them as they dropped to my shoulder. "Are you sure you're okay? I'm not hurting you, am I?"

"Not a bit," I lied. There was no way I was letting her go. I studied her. "How are you?"

"Fine." The understatement in her tone was evident and painful to my ears.

I lifted one hand and examined her wrist, stroking a finger over the abraded, bruised flesh. My gaze rose to her neck. An angry red line bisected the flesh of her throat where the rope had pulled tightly across the delicate skin. Fury rippled through me at the sight and I wished Johnathan was still alive so I could kill the man all over again, rip him apart with my bare hands. The urge to put my fist through the window was almost overwhelming, but I forced my attention to the woman in my lap. She was here with me, and she was safe. It was all that mattered.

"We'll get this fixed up for you as soon as we get to the hospital. Maybe we'll get a group discount."

She ignored my joke, a question in her eyes. I opened my mouth then immediately closed it again. That conversation was better had in private.

The sudden flashing of blue lights bouncing off the trees alerted us to the arrival of the locals. We took turns giving statements, though it was obvious to everyone from the state of Victoria's battered body what had happened. The rain had slowed and, come daylight, they would start searching for Johnathan's body, waiting for it to wash up on shore.

Fortunately, the man was a terrible shot, and the bullet had barely skimmed my shoulder. The flesh wound still hurt like a bitch, and the ER doc cleaned it and dressed it with gauze. Almost six hours later, we were finally on our way home. Johnathan's car had been impounded, and one of the officers retrieved Victoria's phone and purse for her. Around four in the morning, I pulled up in front of QSG, and Con and Clay filed out with twin nods and pointed looks.

As soon as the men were inside the building, I hooked an arm over the back of the seat and turned toward Victoria. "So...?"

She stared at me for several long seconds, the anticipation almost killing me. "We should talk."

Those were *not* the three words I'd been hoping to hear. Cold settled deep in my bones and my heart fell to the pit of my stomach. I'd been so stupid. I thought once Johnathan was out of the picture that we could be happy. Her reticence pierced me like a blade. I would give her anything, do anything she asked, yet she acted as if it all meant nothing. I'd saved her life, for Christ's sake. But it wasn't enough for her. She didn't trust me, didn't love me enough to make it work. Maybe it would never be enough.

Completely numb, I turned back to the road and put the truck in gear. The trip to Victoria's house was uncomfortably silent. Gray pre-dawn light had just begun to break over the horizon as I pulled to a stop in her driveway. I stared straight ahead, molars clenched as I waited for her to get out. The sooner she was out of my life, the sooner I could pick up the pieces and try to move on.

"Blake?"

Expression finally under control, I turned to her. It was so hard not to reach across the truck and haul her into my arms, beg her to give me a chance. Instead, I lifted my chin and fixed her with a cold stare.

272 | MORGAN JAMES

She bit her lip before speaking. "Would you like to come inside for a few minutes?"

Hurt lanced through me. "I'm really exhausted, Victoria. It's been a long night."

"Just..." She trailed off, tears glazing her eyes, and she shook her head. "Never mind."

My pulse accelerated as I watched her hand close around the door handle, head drooping dejectedly. Fuck. What if I was making a huge mistake? I'd let her walk away once before—I wouldn't let it happen again. I loved her, damn it, and I was going to fight for her.

I slid a hand around her elbow, halting her before she could escape. "All right. Let's go."

She hesitated then nodded. I slid from the truck and jogged around to let her out. Rain continued to drizzle from the sky, though noticeably lighter than before. Still, I used my body to shelter her as much as possible as we made our way to the porch. While Victoria disarmed the security system I leaned against the door, adopting a casual pose despite the surge of emotion running rampant in my gut.

Victoria finally met my gaze and I wished, not for the first time, that I could read those fathomless gray depths. Worry spread through me. I was willing to do whatever it took to make things work between us. But what if she wasn't? Could I walk away from her and pretend everything was all right? Victoria had touched my soul and she was a part of me, now and forever. My life would never be the same without her.

CHAPTER THIRTY-NINE

Victoria

Here we stood, so close yet so far away. I bit my lip. What if he wouldn't take me back? I'd wanted so badly to tell him earlier how much I loved him and beg his forgiveness. Now that the danger was over, would he still feel the same? I swallowed hard.

"Thank you."

He lifted a brow, and my fingers itched to slap the insolent look from his face. He clearly wasn't going to make this easy for me. I shifted from foot to foot, arms wrapped around my middle.

"I... I was wrong. I should've listened to you."

His face softened. "I never would've guessed he was responsible. I just thought—"

"I know." I held up a hand. "But you were right about Johnathan, about the type of person he is... *was*."

I shuddered remembering his plunge into the river. Even had he not been fatally shot, it would have been almost impossible to survive a fall like that. I shrugged off the guilt and stood straighter, staring Blake in the eye. "Will you..." I cleared her throat, shoving down the emotion welling up within me. "Could you ever forgive me?"

"Oh, Doc."

The nickname sounded so sweet to my ears, and I threw

myself at him as his arms opened in invitation. "I'm sorry, Blake." The tears I'd held at bay let loose and I buried my head against his neck. "I'm so sorry."

"I know, sweetheart, I know." Strong arms banded tightly around my waist, holding me close.

I stared up at him. "Please tell me I haven't ruined things between us."

"Of course not." Blake shook his head. "I told you I'd wait forever, and I meant it."

"I don't deserve you."

"No, you don't." The words were like a dagger to my heart, and I felt my knees go weak. I bit my lip and ducked my head, blinking away the tears scalding my eyes. One large palm slid under my chin and lifted my gaze to his. Hazel eyes stared into mine, burning a path to my soul.

"You deserve better, but you're stuck with me now." He winked, and relief washed over me.

"I love you."

His arms tightened around me almost to the point of pain. "I love you so damned much. I'm never letting you go."

I shook my head. "Never."

His mouth covered mine, savage and brutal. One hand left my side to flip the deadbolt on the door before he swung me into his arms. Despite his injury, he carried me as if I weighed nothing. I relished the feeling, and I sank deeper into the kiss, pouring every ounce of love into it.

I whimpered as his lips left mine and he settled me on the bed. He took a step backward and my heart lurched in my chest as I watched him pull his damp shirt over his head then toss it to the floor. I struggled with my jeans for a minute before he stilled me with a hand.

His hungry gaze swept over me and I lay back, allowing him the control he craved. He slipped his fingers inside the waistband and tugged my jeans over my hips and down my legs. He continued until I was bare before him and with one swift motion, he shoved his bottoms to the floor and stepped out of the pool of material.

He placed a knee on the bed between my thighs, caging me between his muscular arms. I stared up at him, watching him watch me with those intense hawk-like hazel eyes. I wanted to stare into his eyes every day for the rest of my life. This was what I'd waited my whole life for. I'd been waiting for him.

I lifted a hand to his cheek and he closed his eyes, turning his head to kiss my palm. "I love you."

He showed me without words just how much he loved me, too, until we lay tangled together and drifted off into a comfortable, exhausted sleep.

✳

I stood at the kitchen window, looking out at the horizon over the backyard. The rain had stopped just after noon and the sun shining through the puffy white clouds brought a rainbow across the sky. Absorbed in the beauty of the scene, I didn't hear Blake approach until his strong arms wrapped around my waist and pulled me to him. I released a sigh of deep contentment and allowed my head to fall back against his good shoulder.

"Do you remember the verse in the bible about Noah's Ark?"

"Sure." He paused. "Two of every animal and they were stuck on the boat for weeks until they found dry land."

I smiled. "Something like that. Do you remember the rainbow?"

His head shook against my shoulder. "Can't say I do."

"God sent a rainbow to appear after the flood; it was his promise to the world that he would never allow rain to flood the earth ever again."

"Mmm. I see."

I could tell he didn't. "I just... I saw the rainbow and it reminded me that good things still happen—that there are still good people in the world." I turned in his arms and peered up at him. "Even if something bad happens, there's always hope to continue on. Blake... You're my something good. My salvation."

"I think that rainbow's a good omen, then, don't you?" His head canted to one side as he studied me. "I would do anything for you, Doc. I'll always be there for you. No matter how bad the storm, I'll always be there at the end waiting for you."

"I love you so much." Hot tears sprang to my eyes. "I'm sorry it took so long to realize it."

"I'm just glad you're safe. When I got that call from Jason last night..." His voice trailed off and I slid my arms around his waist, anchoring myself to him. I felt his lips on my hair as he spoke. "God, baby, I thought I'd never see you again."

"I know, but now we're both home where we belong."

"Speaking of home." He pulled back and stared down at me, eyes full of regret. "I'm sorry about our fight that night. I never should have—"

I lifted onto my toes and pressed my lips to his, stealing the words that had driven us apart. One kiss turned into two, and several long moments later I broke away, taking a deep breath to slow my racing heart.

"I realized something over the past few days. I tried so hard to fight my feelings for you—my mind kept telling me it was impossible, that it was too soon to love you. But my heart knew better. It doesn't matter where we are, as long as I'm with you."

Hope lit his eyes and his arms tightened, binding me to him as I was enfolded into his embrace.

"I'm right where I'm supposed to be." My cheek rested over his heart, beating in time with mine. "Home."

Also by Morgan James

QUENTIN SECURITY SERIES

The Devil You Know – Blake and Victoria
Devil in the Details – Xander and Lydia
Devil in Disguise – Gavin and Kate
Heart of a Devil – Vince and Jana
Tempting the Devil – Clay and Abby
Devilish intent – Con and Grace
*Each book is a standalone within the series

FROZEN IN TIME TRILOGY

Unrequited Love
Undeniable Love
Unbreakable Love
Frozen in Time: The Complete Trilogy

DECEPTION DUET

Pretty Little Lies – Eric and Jules, Book One
Beautiful Deception – Eric and Jules, Book Two
*Each book can be read as a standalone, but are best read in order

SINFUL DUET

Sinful Illusions – Fox and Eva, Book One
Sinful Sacrament – Fox and Eva, Book Two
*Books should be read in order

BAD BILLIONAIRES

(Novella Series)
Depraved
Ravished
Consumed
*Each book is a standalone within the series

STANDALONES

Death Do Us Part
Escape

About the Author

Morgan James is a *USA Today* bestselling author of contemporary and romantic suspense novels. She spent most of her childhood with her nose buried in a book, and she loves all things romantic, dark, and dirty.

Made in the USA
Las Vegas, NV
02 May 2022